Meet Cutter Force Initiative

COLONEL R. A. "RAGS" CUTTER: A career military man, Cutter left the GU Army when he ran afoul of Army politics. At large, Cutter realized that there was a need for his kind of expertise and created a fighting force for specialized, smaller-scale actions.

JO SIMS: A former PsyOps lieutenant in the GU Navy, Sims is drop-dead gorgeous and as adept with small arms as she is with her mind.

TOMAS "DOC" WINK: An ER doctor before he joined the Cutters, Wink is an adrenaline junkie who doesn't feel alive unless he is on the razor's edge defying death.

ROY "GRAMPS" DEMONDE: Previously the PR director for a major corporation, Gramps lost his family in the revolution and is always looking for a way to stick it to the GU.

FORMENTARA: A *mahu* and cybernetics whiz, Formentara is adept at installing and maintaining all kinds of bioengineered implants.

MEGAN "GUNNY" SAYEED: Gunny is a master weaponsmith and expert shooter. If it throws any kind of missile or a particle beam, Gunny can use it, upside down and over her shoulder.

*KLUTH*FEM "KAY": Kay is a Vastalimi who can kill using only her bare hands, feet, or fangs.

D0377461

Praise for
THE RAMAL EXTRACTION

"A cutting-edge, militaristic sci-fi novel . . . There's also plenty of action and adventure and blood and guts."
—*Fresh Fiction*

Praise for the novels of Steve Perry

"A crackling good story. I enjoyed it immensely!"
—Chris Claremont

"Heroic . . . Perry builds his protagonist into a mythical figure without losing his human dimension. It's refreshing."
—*Newsday*

"Perry provides plenty of action [and] expertise about weapons and combat." —*Booklist*

"Noteworthy." —*Fantasy and Science Fiction*

"Another sci-fi winner . . . Cleanly written . . . The story accelerates smoothly at an adventurous clip, bristling with martial arts feats and as many pop-out weapons as a Swiss Army knife." —*The Oregonian*

"Plenty of blood, guts, and wild fight scenes." —*VOYA*

"Excellent reading." —*Science Fiction Review*

"Action and adventure flow cleanly from Perry's pen."
—*Pulp and Celluloid*

Books by Steve Perry

The Cutter's Wars Series

THE RAMAL EXTRACTION
THE VASTALIMI GAMBIT
THE TEJANO CONFLICT

The Matador Series

THE MAN WHO NEVER MISSED
MATADORA
THE MACHIAVELLI INTERFACE
THE 97TH STEP
THE ALBINO KNIFE
BLACK STEEL
BROTHER DEATH
THE MUSASHI FLEX

SPINDOC
THE FOREVER DRUG
THE TRINITY VECTOR
THE DIGITAL EFFECT
THE OMEGA CAGE
(with Michael Reaves)

MEN IN BLACK
STAR WARS: SHADOWS OF THE EMPIRE
STAR WARS: MEDSTAR I: BATTLE SURGEONS
(with Michael Reaves)
STAR WARS: MEDSTAR II: JEDI HEALER
(with Michael Reaves)

With Tom Clancy and Steve Pieczenik

NET FORCE
NET FORCE: HIDDEN AGENDAS
NET FORCE: NIGHT MOVES
NET FORCE: BREAKING POINT
NET FORCE: POINT OF IMPACT
NET FORCE: CYBERNATION

With Tom Clancy, Steve Pieczenik, and Larry Segriff

NET FORCE: STATE OF WAR
NET FORCE: CHANGING OF THE GUARD
NET FORCE: SPRINGBOARD

THE TEJANO CONFLICT

CUTTER'S WARS

STEVE PERRY

ACE BOOKS, NEW YORK

THE BERKLEY PUBLISHING GROUP
Published by the Penguin Group
Penguin Group (USA) LLC
375 Hudson Street, New York, New York 10014

USA • Canada • UK • Ireland • Australia • New Zealand • India • South Africa • China

penguin.com

A Penguin Random House Company

THE TEJANO CONFLICT

An Ace Book / published by arrangement with the author

Copyright © 2014 by Steve Perry.
Penguin supports copyright. Copyright fuels creativity, encourages diverse voices,
promotes free speech, and creates a vibrant culture. Thank you for buying an authorized
edition of this book and for complying with copyright laws by not reproducing, scanning,
or distributing any part of it in any form without permission. You are supporting writers
and allowing Penguin to continue to publish books for every reader.

Ace Books are published by The Berkley Publishing Group.
ACE and the "A" design are trademarks of Penguin Group (USA) LLC.

For information, address: The Berkley Publishing Group,
a division of Penguin Group (USA) LLC,
375 Hudson Street, New York, New York 10014.

ISBN: 978-0-425-27349-4

PUBLISHING HISTORY
Ace mass-market edition / January 2015

PRINTED IN THE UNITED STATES OF AMERICA

10 9 8 7 6 5 4 3 2 1

Cover art by Kris Keller.
Cover design by Lesley Worrell.
Interior text design by Laura K. Corless.

This is a work of fiction. Names, characters, places, and incidents either are the product
of the author's imagination or are used fictitiously, and any resemblance to actual persons,
living or dead, business establishments, events, or locales is entirely coincidental.

If you purchased this book without a cover, you should be aware that this book is
stolen property. It was reported as "unsold and destroyed" to the publisher, and neither
the author nor the publisher has received any payment for this "stripped book."

This one is for Dianne, as ever;
and for Ginjer Buchanan,
the patient, long-suffering, and excellent editor
who has taken care of me for a lot more years
than either of us wants to think about . . .

ACKNOWLEDGMENTS

Thanks this round go to: Dal, whose help was most valuable; Doug Atkins, for the snake-and-stick line; Dan Moran, in general; Alan Carruth and Woodley White, luthiers par excellence, for inspirations in wood and string.

PROLOGUE

Hotel Orleans—New York Metroplex

Cutter arrived at the door, which swung open as he got to it.

He stepped inside. It was a first-class meeting room, part of a suite, expensive and plush. Good signs. Meant the clients who hired Zoree Wood's military unit, The Line, had money and didn't mind spending it. Be interesting to see how much of it would come CFI's way . . .

Other than the woman who met him at the door and himself, it seemed they were alone.

"Hey. How has the galaxy been treating you, Rags?"

"Can't complain," he said. "Yourself?"

Wood smiled. "Come on in, have a seat. I cashiered out a colonel, and now I'm a general. Pay is way better, and I get to call more shots than I did in the GU Army, no uplevels second-guessing over my shoulder. What's not to like?

"Have a glass of this?"

She held up a bottle of very good bourbon.

He grinned at that. "Know my weakness, do you?"

"Word gets around."

He sat on the couch, as comfortable as it looked, and it looked comfortable. He returned her smile. She was still fit, still handsome. Not in uniform, though she might as well have been, everything about her clothes and bearing said "soldier."

She poured him a drink.

Wood's preferences ran to women, there had never been anything other than work between them, but the respect had been mutual. He'd been a captain and she a lieutenant when they'd done the Jusian Campaign. Clean and mean, that one; it had given him a boost toward colonel, and put her further along the path to her captain's bars. A good memory. Long ago and far away.

He said, "How are the wife and kids, you still married?"

"Kids are grown, off making grandchildren, and I am still with Gemma. She's her same ornery self. She wants me to retire, for us to buy a star-fruit orchard, raise puppies, and watch grandchildren. Couple more years, we'll be able to afford it."

He smiled.

She said, "Looks like you've done all right for yourself, considering. Sorry it went down the way that it did."

"Scroom," he said. "Onward and upward."

"So, are you in?"

"I am. Gramps is exchanging photons and dickering with your contract people as we speak."

"Demonde? He's still around?"

"Yep."

"Only the good die young."

"Explains why we are still here."

They smiled.

"Okay," she said, "down to the nitty-gritty?"

"When you are ready—I've irised the NDA."

She nodded. "What we have here is your basic license-limit industrial. The Line represents Tejas Enterprises, a conglom whose reach spans everything from photonic computing to earthmoving gear to agro and fish farms.

"Our opposition is called United Mexican Corp, they have fingers in most of the same pies. The Resource Allocation Act parses a lot of stuff neatly, but there aren't as many resources as there used to be on the homeworld, and that makes the cost of doing business spendy. Negotiations between TE and UMex for sharing the water rights have broken down.

"The H_2O in question is predinosauric and down deep, and theoretically owned by a convoluted mix of corporations and governments, a rat's nest of rights and subrights. Local and planetary govs have waved eminent domain and condemnations all over the place, but the inks lease their lawyers by the shipload, and it is a tangle that might take decades to sort out."

He nodded. "Our goal?"

"Forty thousand acres of land, with wells going halfway to the core, apparently, producing all of the groundwater in the region that isn't completely tied up legally."

"How is this even possible in these times? And wouldn't it be easy just to channel desalted from the nearby gulf?"

"Good questions. Apparently during the various changes of government and corporate mineral and water rights being tossed around over the last century, there came a loophole regarding this particular lot. Some arcane and highly technical hairsplitting and what resulted was a big chunk of property that belongs to either everybody or nobody, depending on which authority you ask. And what it appears is, there is a ticking clock. On such and such a date, whoever is in possession of some substantial portion of the aquifer located at such and such a longitude and latitude, vis-à-vis the operational flow—and I'd have to ask the lawyers to get into the details—has some kind of a priori claim. At least long enough to run things until it all eventually gets sorted out.

"If nobody is there, it goes back to the government.

"It's apparently cheaper to pump the water that's there up than build a new plant and pipeline. The current ones are running at capacity and the water allocated. There are all kinds of environmental-impact studies that have to be done to run a new conduit across private properties. Condemnations, rare birds, endangered field mice, all that takes a lot of expert study and legal wrangling. Plus what it would cost to put up a desalination plant and rig dins or hire people to run it. Last time somebody built a new osmosis plant and channeled the freshwater more than a hundred kilometers inland anywhere locally, it took ten years to get it done."

"All about the money," he said.

"Always is, isn't it? Anyway, a lot of stuff can happen before the legal mud finally settles."

"That sounds downright goofy."

She smiled again. "Does, doesn't it? Ours is not to reason why . . ."

He nodded. "Got it. Strategy and tactical situations?"

"The area is being held by a small security force run by a bunch of locals. TE and UMex have convinced the powers that be that a dukes-no-nukes dustup is the quickest way to settle things, citing the Zeller Accord. Commencement officially starts in fourteen days. So the locals bail. We can field recon now though no hot engagements are allowed for two weeks. After that? We have seven days to shoot and win it, so three weeks total. Somebody needs to range, sneak-and-peak, and this is your kind of thing. Do this right, we hit the ground running and clean it up PDQ."

"Numbers and hardware?"

"Licensed for two thousand troops each side, personal augmentation, no limits; small arms, light APCs, up to 30mm on the cannon end. AP grenades, G2A, G2G, A2G, A2A, nothing bigger than Class-V rockets, little stuff. It'll be stoppered-velocity everything; they don't want strays leaving the range and killing civilians in their homes halfway across the region. No railguns, no lasers, no big boomers. No deep, ugly craters in the local landscape.

"No orbital boomware or zappers, spysat feeds only. Troops are however we want to divide 'em—infantry, armor, air. Pretty tight limits."

"Still a lot bigger than anything on Earth in a long time."

"Yes. And a nice feather in our caps when we win it."

"Okay. When do you want us operational?"

"Yesterday. I'll have my XO squirt the maps and intel your way as soon as the contracts click. They are almost a day ahead of us on this; so they'll have their own rangers on the ground before you get down there if they have anything on the ball."

"Got it."

"Welcome aboard, Rags. Always good to see a competent face at my door."

"Happy to have somebody think so."

ONE

It was hot here in this particular region of Earth. And humid. Kay's fur was damp with perspiration. Still, she'd been in warmer places; she could stand the heat. The things about which you could do nothing? You simply endured them.

The smells were odd, but she was sorting those out. She had never been to Earth before. There was a lot of civilization here, but also pockets of nature. An interesting mix, but it didn't feel anything like Vast. No other world felt anything like Vast.

She watched the two combatants circle.

*Mish*fem stepped to her left, wary, and rightly so.

Jo Captain maintained her distance, also edging to her left.

Em was slightly faster, but Jo knew more about fighting Vastalimi than Em did fighting humans, and Jo was more than passing adept at positioning. To overcome this, Em would have to move closer; however, to move closer was to court Jo's attack. Even though Em was faster, the difference was not so great when reaction time was factored in. In theory, a nearly even match.

A few years back, Kay would not have believed it possible that a human could spar with one of The People and have any chance of winning at all, even one as augmented as Jo Captain. Now? Jo could manage a win against Kay half the time, and against Em, still three of four. Many on Vast would react with scorn to hear such a thing spoken. *A human? Are you mad?* A natural mistake, but one that could be fatal, should the situation arise.

Em wanted to leap and claw, that was her nature—just as it was Kay's nature—but they both had learned that flight time from where they were to where Jo was could only be hastened so much. Seldom enough to compensate for Jo's superior position. To fly was to find yourself unable to change your trajectory against an opponent who knew how to exploit that.

Millions of years of evolution taking prey by leap-and-claw, however, were not that easy to overcome.

Humans didn't mind defending and countering, so the first attack needed to be telling or they—well, at least in Jo Captain's case—could block or parry and land a critical response. Bare-handed and sheathed in a bloodless cub match like this, it didn't mean anything save wounded pride, but had she a blade? Jo could inflict a fatal wound even against a Vastalimi's superior claws. There would likely be mutual slaying, and while such was not technically a loss, it would be a high price to pay for a technical point . . .

Kay and Jo had learned much from each other; Em had more than a little left to learn. None of the humans against whom she had fought had Jo's skill and physical abilities combined. Kay wasn't sure there were any humans that good.

Em feinted, a quick false step.

Jo did not react, save to smile. "Am I a cub?"

"Never know until you try."

"Your sire is a rhinoceros," Jo said

Em frowned. "What—?"

Jo had already charged, and as Em shifted, dropped, and extended her lead hand to cover, Jo fell to the ground on her side, sliding below Em's defense. She hooked her right ankle behind Em's lead ankle and thrust with her left foot in a kick at Em's thigh—

—Em twisted away a hair, but that's what Jo wanted, and her instep took Em behind the knee, bending it and throwing the fem off her stance—

—Jo came up, fast, onto one foot in a balance that seemed impossible, and dropped with an elbow that caught Em on the shoulder blade, taking her to the ground—

—Em dived, rolled, and came up in a half turn, but she was a quarter beat behind, and Jo was there to deliver the spear hand into Em's solar plexus. Painful with a bare hand, but a telling strike had her fingers been a knife.

Em's belly muscles were like thick leather, and while she obviously felt it, there wasn't any real damage, but had it been claws or a blade, the match was done—

Em knew: "*Jebati* me! *Tzit, tzit,* tzit!"

Kay whickered. She had said much the same more than a few times when dancing with Jo Captain. Humans sometimes did something so unexpected it stalled one for just long enough to make their point. No normal Vastalimi would have thrown that attack.

Probably a normal human wouldn't have, either.

Em said, "How can you possibly leap onto one foot and hold that balance?"

"Formentara," Jo said. "I sport a proprioception aug she created."

"Most humans would not have this thing, would they?"

"Nope. But you won't know if one does until you get there."

"Point made. And the comment about a . . . rhinosaur?"

"A nonsensical distraction. While you were thinking about it, it bought me an eighth of a second."

"It did. Again?"

"I'd like to, but I have to go see Rags about the mission."

Em nodded. "I am in your debt."

"Everything I learned about dancing with Vastalimi I got from Kay. Thank her for it."

Em looked at Kay.

Kay said, "She is too modest."

"I have noticed."

"Gotta run, fems."

After she was gone, Em turned to Kay. "It does seem as if we have found ourselves an exemplary group of humans."

"I believe it to be so. Perhaps you might favor me with a match?"

"I would. Although you seem to have picked up enough from Jo Captain so that you are equally unpredictable."

"It pleases me to hear you say so. Predictability can get one killed."

– – – – – –

Gunny was practicing her draw when Jo arrived at the staging area. For a human with only the most basic of augs, she was passing quick, and outside Rags himself, nobody in the unit could outshoot Gunny with a small arm of any kind. And Rags only because of some kind of freak talent he had.

Gun in holster. *Blur.* Gun on target. A considerably less quick return to the holster. No hurry with that, the shooting was gonna be all over with and if you were still standing, you could take all day to reholster your weapon.

Jo said, "Getting slow in your old age."

"Don't Ah know it. That shoulder has never gotten back to a hundred percent."

"It was a joke, Gunny."

"Might as well save your breath," Gramps said as he

appeared in the doorway. "A fire brick's got more sense of humor than she does."

Gunny looked at Gramps. "Ah dunno about that, old man. Every time Ah see your ancient face, it makes me want to laugh."

"Jealousy doesn't become you, Chocolatte."

Now Gunny did laugh.

"I stand corrected about the sense of humor," Gramps said. He smiled.

Jo shook her head. One of these days, the two of them would find themselves alone and maybe have to deal with how they really felt about each other. She'd love to be a fly on the wall when that happened.

"Rags just got back. Might as well come on in and let's hear what he's got to say. You too, Gunny, if you can tear yourself away from your obsessive practice in death dealing."

— — — — — —

Jo already knew the gist, having gotten it from Rags when it was first brought up just after their visit to Vast, but she didn't know the on-the-ground specifics. Rags had gone and talked to his old friend General Wood, who now commanded a well-respected private army called The Line. Rags had liked what he heard.

They had flown south, and here they were.

She raised an eyebrow when he was done, but Gramps spoke first:

"Water rights?" He looked left, did a slow scan to the right, squinting as he did.

"What *are* you lookin' for?" Gunny asked. "You forget who and where you are?"

"What am I looking for? Cowboys, Amerinds, bison, camels, like that," Gramps said. "Because we must have stumbled into a time slip. *Water* rights? On Earth?"

"It's complicated," Rags said. "And it doesn't matter as

far as we are concerned. We have to scope and report, and since they are paying us to the finale, occupy some ground once the shooting starts."

"I remember the offer, but how many are they actually paying for?" That from Jo.

"Short company: three rifle platoons, one ranger, one light air- and groundcraft, one support, including electronics. Hundred and ten troops. Relatively-low-velocity ammo. Total force maximum is two kay each side. There will be medical support and supply available if we need it."

"Four thousand. That's a good-sized dustup," Gunny said.

"Biggest allowed on Earth in sixteen years," Rags said. "We need to field our fastest and sharpest for recon, and we needed to do it yesterday. We have fourteen days beginning now when we are theoretically not being shot at."

They nodded. *Theoretically.* The official stance was supposed to mean no engagements resulting in the exchange of fire until the official start date, but everybody knew that recon resulted in clashes—a silenced sniper rifle or a knife in the back? It happened, and Monitors sometimes missed it—or deliberately looked the other way. When big money was on the line, any advantage you could get without being caught was worth a lot. A few hundred thousand noodle to bribe a Monitor to turn his or her back while you did something not quite covered under the rules? Cheap insurance.

Industrial mercs were like samurai—you were supposed to be vigilant all the time. If you weren't ready for an enemy's action once you stepped onto the field, it was your own fault—you knew what he was and what he wanted, and it was all snakes and scorpions.

"We've got all the geosat and overfly maps and images in the tactical files, but there are some gaps; we need to tread the dirt and smell the flowers, you know the drill."

They knew.

"Let's get it out to the others, set up an S&T plan, and get this going. Jo?"

"I'll tap people for the initial rangings," she said.

It had been a while since they'd been in a real war; mostly they had been doing extractions, retrievals, escort duty. It would be nice to not have to worry about who did what to whom, when, where, and why, and get back to the simple business of recon and combat.

TWO

Wink honed the edge of his sheath knife against a leather strap, finishing the task. The knife was a stubby-bladed spear-point, thick across the spine, with a fat, cylindrical handle, Damascus steel, and an oval guard made of the same material.

He was a doctor and a surgeon; he favored shorter knives because he knew where to stick them and how to achieve the best results, going and coming. He looked up to see Jo approaching. He touched the edge with one thumb. It was as sharp as it was going to get. He tucked the knife away into the belt sheath behind his right hip.

"Hey, Jo."

"Wink. I'm putting together my ground team for the initials. How is Singh doing?"

Singh, late of Ananda, had been with them a relatively short time, but he was a bright kid and dedicated. He had gotten too close to a concussive grenade while training and lost an eardrum. The new one had taken a while to regen, but it was back to normal. The auditory hair cells should also be up to par, but Wink hadn't tested them yet.

"Should be good to go. You taking him along?"

"Yeah, I think so. He's still a little green, but he picks up stuff quick, and he won't learn sitting on the sidelines. Gunny'll keep an eye on him."

"So it's sneak'n'peak?"

"For two weeks, then we go online with the rest of the army. One week hot, we're done."

"Been a while since we did a war," he said. "You know, I'm caught up here, the machines and my assistants can handle things. You might ought to have a decent medic out there with you."

"A decent medic? You know any?"

"Ow. That's cold, fem."

She smiled. "Rags would kick me seven ways to Sunday if I let you go play in this situation, Doctor Death-wish."

"I only want to dance, not die."

"You are an adrenaline junkie."

"*You* have no room to talk."

"But *I* am not the medic who needs to be in one piece to help keep the rest of us in good health. You stay in camp unless the colonel okays it."

"I'll have a word with him."

"You probably already have—you know how Gramps likes to spy on everything. If I had to guess, I'd bet that your answer will be a fat 'No.' And Rags won't be going out to play, either."

"You are a harsh mistress, Josephine Sims."

"I try."

After she was gone, he smiled. They had a history, albeit brief; a short, athletic sexual liaison after their adventures on Ramal, and he much enjoyed the memory of it. They were all friends here, sometimes with benefits, but probably there was no future in that direction for the two of them. They both loved putting themselves at risk too much, testing to see how close to the edge they could come and survive. It wouldn't do to make any deep connections with anybody while they did such things; it wouldn't be fair to a partner, even one who knew of it and why.

Jo knew. And there was Kay, who also knew. The Vastalimi had an offhand disregard for dying that came pretty close to a shrug. And Kay was . . . one of the most interesting sexual partners he'd ever had, too.

The idea of a three-way polyamory sometimes arose in his thoughts . . .

Too early in the day to be going down those lanes, Dr. Horny . . .

He voxaxed his com: "Singh?"

After a beat, the response. "Sah?"

"You need to drop round the office and let me check your hearing again."

"Sah."

He thought about telling the kid why but decided to let Jo do it. She'd enjoy the smile on his face when she told him . . .

- - - - -

For the first run, it was just Jo and Kay. They were the most experienced, the quickest, save for Em, and the best two-person team in CFI. They knew each other's moves, they knew their own, and it was unlikely that the opposition would have anybody to match them.

They met with Wink, Gunny, Gramps, and Formentara for the final rundown.

Gramps led off: "Here, take this."

"What is this?" Gunny said.

"Why, it's a *map*, child," Gramps said. "A two-dimensional representation of the forest wherein we are about to commence our recon op."

Gunny gave him a fuck-you look. "Ah know it's a *map*, you doddering fossil! And Ah also know this is *Earth*, and they have so many geosats circling you can footprint any spot on the planet from twenty thousand kilometers up sharp enough to read a flatscreen Bible over somebody's shoulder! So why are we looking at this . . . *parchment* sheet instead of a holoproj real-time goog? Future shock too much for you?"

"No, because your ordinary visible-spectrum satcam stops at the tree crowns, and what we want to see won't show up on IR or pradar. Part of what we need to do is update this map—remind me to teach you the difference between 'paper' and 'parchment,' by the way."

"What do you mean, it won't show up on IR or pradar? Both of those should paint the ground like those tree crowns are made of air."

"Ah, but there's the rub." He grinned.

Jo, standing next to Kay, added her smile to the mix. Always entertaining, the Gunny and Gramps show.

Gunny turned to look at Jo. "What is this . . . unwrapped *mummy* blathering on about?"

Jo started to speak, but Gramps picked it back up. "It's the *trees*, Chocolatte. Which, if you had read your background packet, you would know are native to the area but genetically modified *Cupressus arizonica.*"

"So what?"

"Commonly known as 'Arizona cypress,' the natural version is a medium-sized evergreen tree that grows to between ten and twenty-five meters in height. These have been genetically modified so that they achieve a height of forty meters, with a broader crown."

"Uh-huh. It's a fucking tree. Making it taller and fatter stops pradar and IR *how*? Are you gonna get to it or keep dancing?"

Jo said, "Don't let him give you a hard time, Gunny, we didn't know it either until the guy from Tejas told us. It's one of the reasons they hired us."

Gramps said, "Attend: Back in the day, there were a lot of revolutionary factions on Earth, peaking during the late twenty-first century. There were ecoterrorist groups, tax revolts, multinational corporate infighting. Some of them came and went in a hurry; some of them lasted a lot longer."

Gunny said, "Ah knew that. Primary ed stuff. Again, so what? Why the history lecture? You do it just to fuck with me, don't you?"

He ignored that: "You recall hearing about a group called Children of the Alamo?"

Gunny shook her head. "No. Ah do know about the Alamo."

Formentara said, "The what-amo?"

"A prespaceflight war," Gunny said. "A small force of soldiers and civilians, somewhere around two hundred and fifty, were holed up in a makeshift adobe fort, an old religious mission, called 'Alamo.' The defenders gave a good account of themselves, but they were outnumbered five to one; eventually, they were overcome and slaughtered.

"The battle became a rallying cry of the Alamo's defenders, whose armies went on to defeat their opponents: 'Remember the Alamo!' "

"That's the war," Jo said. "The defeated group was forced to cede a lot of territory to the victors, which became part of a new country. There were some who never got over the loss, apparently. One faction determined to reverse their fortunes, to win back the lost real estate."

"Did they?" Wink asked.

"No, but not for lack of trying for multiple generations over several hundred years. They hold grudges a long time here on the homeworld."

Kay shook her head.

Jo continued: "To shorten Gramps's long story, the CotA group eventually became insurgent, tried to foment a revolution. It failed, but along the way, they did some things, one of which was to create and grow several forests of the local cypress tree throughout the region. The plants could be made to take up minerals and metals from the fertilized soil that would then concentrate in the wood and needles in specific proportions."

Gunny got it. "No shit? Organic shielding?"

"Grow-your-own Faraday cage and chaff all in one.

"It had been done before, on a smaller scale," Gramps said. Before Gunny could say anything else, he said, "I looked it up. Anyway, they were in it for the long haul, and once the trees were big enough, the revolutionaries conducted much of their business underneath the canopies. Simple, but effective."

"Nobody noticed they couldn't see through the trees from above?"

"Not for a long time, there was no reason to. IR was mostly used for weather, and little forests don't create much of that. Long-range pradar was expensive and used mostly for military applications, and dinky forests in the middle of nowhere weren't considered a problem."

"Hidin' where nobody would look. Or could if they tried."

"So it was," Gramps said. "Eventually, the would-be revolutionaries fell apart, ran down, and went away, but the trees they planted were hardy, and they are mostly still there. Which brings us to us . . ."

Gunny nodded. "Got it."

"So Kay and I will make the first pass and record what we see. Gunny will be backup, Gramps on the com, Formentara will assemble the vids," Jo said.

"What about me?" That from Wink. "I talked to Rags."

"Yeah, you did, and don't lie, I know what he said. You and he can have some beer and argue about smashball stats. Or count your tongue depressors."

"Come on—"

"Don't start. We don't need you there, and we might need you here."

"Crap."

"Life is hard, Doc," Jo said.

THREE

There was an old saying, "Trust, but verify," that amused Gramps whenever he thought of it. It was populist babble that sounded meaningful but was a contradiction on the face of it: If you trusted somebody, there was no need to verify what they said.

One of the first truths he had learned when he had begun doing backgrounding for CFI was that a lot of people lied. Some merely shaded the truth in their favor a bit, a little spin, a little polish to shine a thing brighter; some went straight to damned lies, and would space a long way to avoid any more of a connection with reality than was absolutely necessary to sell a story. People would put twice as much effort into a lie as telling the truth, and as often as not, for no reason he could see.

Truth was the default and easy. Lies were hard to track; you had to keep them straight.

Sometimes a man put his hand out, and said, "I'm your friend," and it was so. Sometimes the shake was to grip your own hand tightly so he could keep it occupied while he pulled a hidden knife and stabbed you.

It behooved you to know which was the more likely possibility, and part of his job was to try to determine that. In this case, it wasn't really CFI's responsibility, they were just hired eyes and guns, but after Ananda, there had come a decision: never again.

Not always easy, sussing out the reality from the fantasy. They had been caught flatfooted on Ananda, had never seen what was really going on until they were almost done. In that case, it hadn't hurt them much, save maybe for pride, but it reminded Gramps that the next time might not be benign.

That didn't mean you walked around in a constant state of high-alert paranoia, but it did mean that if you were caught sleeping when you should be awake, it was *your* fault.

So the rule was, "Trust *after* you verify," and even then, keep an eye peeled. Trust could be so ephemeral . . .

Corporations these days tended to be like mazes, especially the multiplanetary ones. Given the complexities of law from world to world, it was often easier to pay for forgiveness than to ask permission. What they did for fun on Glade would be cause for imprisonment and serious rehab on a dozen planets in three systems. What was legal on Earth might get you executed on Morandan. So it went.

Corporations fielded platoons of lawyers and spindocs and PR folk and they became star-chamber cultures, keeping their business secret and handing out their own punishments for crimes against the company. The largest corporations spanned systems, and their operant phrase could be boiled down to one concept when it came to keeping in step with local laws: *What* they *don't know won't hurt* us . . .

Tejas Enterprises and UMex were not happy exceptions. There was the surface scan, which showed shiny fronts and polite smiles, and a centimeter under that, a tungsten-steel wall upon which the curious would smack their heads and be stopped cold.

Say there, friend, what does this little phrase you have on your financial report mean?

NOYFB, pal.

None of my fucking business? But, really, if you have fleas and I'm about to get into bed with you? That, uh, kinda makes it my concern, you know?

Unless the curious happened to be adept at finding ways to get past it and into the belly of the beast, finding out who had what could be difficult.

Gramps didn't have the chops, nobody at CFI did. Formentara was brilliant enough so zhe could have figured it out, but it was a waste of hir skill since there were others who had the talent and who could be rented. Over the last few years, CFI had developed a go-to group of simadams and their freaky-clever AIs, and they were have-guns-will-travel paladins. A call, a deposit into an account, and the lookers would probe whoever or whatever Gramps sicced 'em on, and eventually get information that would benefit CFI to know.

The problem was not that they couldn't find it, it was that sometimes it seemed so obvious to Gramps and Rags and Jo what was going on that they didn't check.

Well. They had learned that lesson. Look-before-leaping had become CFI's mode of late, and while that was expensive, it was hard to put a price on keeping your ass alive and in one unbloody piece . . .

The com was clean, the transmission encoded out the wazoo, and the person who might or might not be a woman, and who ran one of the sharpest and fastest C-AIs in the galaxy smiled across however much time and space there was between them.

"Ah, my friend. How nice to see you again."

What she was seeing—if indeed she was actually a fem

at all—was also a computer construct of him that looked like somebody half his age and of a different genetic makeup. Certainly, she could rascal that and get his true image if "she" wanted, given her expertise. And while the encryption on the pipe they were using was as good as anybody could afford, they avoided names, just in case.

"My own sentiment," he said. "I have bought some new artwork," he said, continuing the verbal fugue they used. "I was wondering if you might take a look at it and evaluate it?"

Even if somebody broke into the pipe and managed to unravel the encryption, what they heard wouldn't do them much good.

"I would be happy to. Drop a copy into my mail chute, and I'll have a look."

"You are too kind."

"Not at all. Well, I must run, things to do, people to see. So good to talk to you again."

"The pleasure was all mine," he said.

The names of the corporations would be sent steganographically, buried in a complex image of computer-generated art, and even if somebody knew it was there, good luck on finding and decoding that. The key was iffy even for a high-function AI running quantum—the person to whom he had just spoken had told him that and certainly should know. And even if a spy somehow managed to suss that out? So what? It wasn't illegal to send a corporate name hidden in a picture anyhow.

Gramps felt better after the call. With the tame Connections AI on the case, it would only be a matter of time before they had what was there to be had. Might even have it done before the war proper started though sometimes the fine sifting took a while.

Well. It was in play, and it would take however long it took.

– – – – – –

Jo and Kay didn't wear the shiftsuits that would have made them mostly invisible and impervious to a lot of small-arms fire. The suits were good, but they slowed you down, and both preferred freedom of movement when they had the choice.

Despite the state-of-the-art climate control they ran, the suits were too hot in the summer and too cold in the winter, too. Field equipment was never perfect, no matter how much it cost. The top-of-the-line com would work just fine until it didn't; the big-scale purifier that would turn raw sewage into potable water might leave a little turd flavoring in your tea. The loudest sound on a battlefield was *click!* when you were expecting *bang!* It was a never-ending wonder: What was going to go wrong next?

Rags had made a *pro forma* protest over Jo's decision to skip the shiftsuits, but he knew it as well and Jo and Kay did: The perfect scout was one nobody ever knew had been there. They couldn't shoot what they didn't know about, and Jo and Kay were faster and better than most anybody they were likely to find in the woods. In and out quick was their plan.

The area they needed to scout was a large patch of the genetically modified trees that shielded the ground from pradar and IR sats, bordering the contested wells on the eastern and northern sides, near some place called Choke Canyon, some 130 klicks south of the biggest city in the region, San Antonio. The forest was only about ninety years old, a ragged kidney-bean shape that was eight kilometers long by four wide, narrowing slightly in the middle. There were rivers there, and a reservoir farther south.

They took a flitter to the northern edge, parked it, programmed their coms to the shielded opchan, and headed in.

There was a two-man Monitor team near the road. Jo sent their ID on a short-range pulse, and the Monitors—unarmed but connected to Central—checked the sigs against their list, then waved them through.

Jo said, "I don't suppose you've seen any of the opposition come by here recently?"

The Monitors smiled. They were neutrals, and they didn't give anybody anything.

Given her choice, Jo would have waited until night. Both she and Kay could see in the dark, and even if the rangers from the other side had spookeyes, that made their chances of being spotted less. But speed was of the essence in more than one way. They had to assume the opposition's rangers were already on the ground and scouting, and letting them get too far ahead was not good strategy.

They wore POV cams that would let them record what they saw, and that would be integrated into the maps Gramps was compiling.

"Weapons check," Jo said. She unslung her carbine, looked at the diode and counter. Green and six-zero."

"Green and full," Kay said. She restrapped the weapon over her back, snugged it tight.

"Cam diagnostics," Jo said.

Kay nodded. "Green."

"Com check. Anybody home?"

"Online," Kay said.

"Nobody here but us chickens," Gramps said, from back at the base.

Kay looked at Jo. "Chickens? A kind of bird?"

"Old joke."

Gunny piped in: "All his jokes are old."

"Speak to a passing parade, Egg. Funny if you haven't heard it."

"We are moving into the target area."

"I'd get some popcorn, but there won't be much of a show, given those trees," Gramps said. "Break a leg."

Jo and Kay separated and moved into the woods.

- - - - - -

The first hour was mostly quiet. There were animals and birds, deer, turkey, squirrels, but no sign of people as they scouted, mapping trails and landmarks. Not really much of a surprise—noncombatants had been warned away, there were signs posted on the trees, and transponder sigs marked the area as off-limits—so Jo didn't expect they'd run into a family of campers or nature lovers taking a hike. That was a good way to get shot, and that's what the sigs and signs said: Go away or risk dying.

Mostly, their coms worked inside the forest though there were patches where they cut out. Beaming a sig through the canopy? Didn't happen.

Another thirty minutes, and Kay, half a klick to Jo's west, said, "I have human scent, male. To my north-northwest. Not close enough to see."

Jo marked the general location of the source. Her own olfactories were enhanced as much as they could be but still weren't as good as that of a Vastalimi; plus, she wasn't downwind from the source's position.

"Affirm that. Marked. Might be a Monitor."

Nobody knew where the Monitors would be, or how many there were, and you had to be careful when they were on-site. Killing a Monitor was good for a monstrous fine, maybe even a forfeit, depending on circumstances. As was disguising yourself as a Monitor. You didn't fuck with them when they were deployed. Not all wars used them, but the big ones usually did, and probably even the small ones here on Earth would. Part of doing business.

Kay would try to spot the source of the scent without being seen, to ID and narrow down the location, but that was less important than avoiding contact. They hadn't come to shoot, only to look.

After a few more minutes, Kay subvocalized into her com: "Here he is. Appears to be a human in a yowiesuit, crouched, not moving."

"Not a Monitor. Sounds more like a sniper than a ranger. Unless he spots you and starts shooting, best leave him be."

"Affirm that," Kay said.

They were almost two klicks into the forest from the edge, and there were opposition rangers, so they'd have to move carefully if they were going to finish the recon.

They'd have to come back later for the section where the enemy had a squatter, chances were the scout wouldn't stay there, and they could log that area once it was clear. If he wasn't gone when they were ready to withdraw, they'd come back another day.

An initial crisscross recon didn't have to be perfect, but the more you knew, the better. Might be something important where the enemy scout was, and it would be short-sighted to assume otherwise.

After six hours, they were done for the day. Studies had shown that rangering skill on the ground increased for the first few hours, peaked at five or six, then began to decline. There was no sense in pushing it; they had covered a lot of territory, had recordings of it, and knew considerably more than they had before.

Formentara would add what they'd collected to the maps. Zhe would also talk to the locals Gramps had found who knew the area. Paying them was cheap, and often, locals would know things even a thorough CCR would miss.

They nodded at the Monitors outside the forest as they headed back toward their vehicle.

"Nice work," Gramps's voice came over the com implant. "Got some information: Looks like our opposition is Dycon Limited."

Jo said, "Ah." They were reputed to be one of the better SoF companies around, though CFI hadn't been on the other side of the battlefield from them.

"In fact, we got a call from them not an hour ago. They want to meet with us, have a chat."

"Really."

"Yep. Rags thinks you and Kay should go."

"And why is that?"

"You two are our best observers, you'll pick up stuff the rest of us will miss. And Gunny, if you are eavesdropping, don't even bother with the blind-deaf jokes at my expense."

"Ah'm sure Ah have no idea what you are talkin' about. Which would make two of us."

"And why CFI in particular?"

"I dunno, ask him when you get there."

Jo said, "We are going off-line. See you in an hour or so. Discom."

After they shut down their opchans, Kay said, "Can Gramps and Gunny truly not see how they feel about each other?"

"If they do, they don't want to admit it."

"How interesting," Kay said. "The human capacity for denial sometimes seems to be quite large."

"Ain't that the truth."

FOUR

The caller was in San Antonio, and after Jo and Kay got cleaned up, they arranged to meet him that evening. Gunny and Singh were backup, in a following vehicle, just in case the opposition was trying to be cute.

The trip was uneventful, if slow. The traffic-control auto-drive notwithstanding, there was only so much the TCA computers could do once the carts and lorries and assorted scooters climbed past a critical density on the road. Plus, there were always drivers who got around the rush-hour controls and elected to do it manually. Despite strict licensing requirements that demanded public-vehicle operators be skilled and knowledgeable, there were always idiots who somehow slipped though . . .

Jo herself preferred manual, she didn't like to give up the control, but of course, she was an expert operator, and her augmented reflexes gave her an advantage. In a situation where the traffic was bumper-to-bumper, there was no point in doing it yourself—less stressful to let the TCA pilot.

She tooled the wheeled cart into the hotel's underground parking. The air had that city smell, hot concrete, dust and mold, leaked cart lube.

Welcome back to civilization . . .

— — — — — —

Gunny parked the cart, and she and Singh alighted, to follow Jo and Kay into the hotel.

The place was designed to look as if it had been built in the . . . seventeenth—eighteenth?—century. There was a baroque look to it; there were faux oil paintings of men cradling shotguns and servants holding up small, dead animals; more images of women in long dresses and bearing baskets, surrounded by children who seemed miniature adults. Some of the paintings were life-sized, all had ornate, gold frames, and though well lighted, had a dark tone to them. The hotel's walls were patterned in muted colors, flowers here, geometric designs there. The floors were beset with Oriental carpets. There were overstuffed couches and chairs perched on carved wooden legs, made of leather or what appeared to be crushed velvet in deep shades of red or green.

The staff wore period costumes: odd-looking trousers that ended just below the knees and long stockings, squared-toed shoes and brass buckles, with frock coats and frilly shirts for the men; long dresses with some kind of hoops under them for the women. All of the clothes were in bright colors, reds, greens, blues, with buttons made to look like shiny brass or bone.

Must have spent a small fortune on this ornate crap.

She thought it looked silly, and said as much to Singh.

"But very posh," Singh said.

"What exactly does that word mean?"

"It is a term used on my homeworld, originally from Terra. As I understand it, in the days when oceangoing ships were powered by wind, predating electric engines and air cooling, the voyages on such vessels from the colonizer country of Breetan were long and slow, and the trips were often in tropical waters."

"Okay, so?"

"The heat was greatest on the side of the ship that mostly faced the sun. Traveling to India, that would be the starboard side, and returning from there, the port side."

"Ah'm still with you, but you been talking too much to Gramps, you are starting to sound like him."

Singh laughed. "Sorry, sah. For reasons of comfort, passengers apparently preferred to travel on the shadier side of the ships, so if given the choice, they elected for port-out-starboard-home, which gives the acronym p-o-s-h. It has come to mean luxurious, upper-class."

"Is that true?"

"Who can say? It might be, and it makes a good story."

"You really need to stay away from Gramps, the man is going to infect you with his babble."

They followed Jo and Kay to the elevator, paying attention to the patrons of the hotel, several of whom were obviously startled by Kay's appearance.

Gunny had tuned that out long ago, and you tended to forget something you became acclimated to after a while. There were still people who had never seen an offworld alien up close though you'd think in a big city, that would be unlikely.

Of course, Vastalimi were rare away from Vast, and they had a reputation for danger that was, if anything, understated.

"Nobody steps into Kay's path," Singh observed.

"Ah see that."

"I confess when I first met her, I was myself somewhat nervous. She appears formidable just standing there."

"She does that. Because she is."

"Do we follow them up?"

"We catch the next elevator, find a spot where we can watch the room they go into."

Jo marked Gunny and Singh as they entered the hotel lobby behind her.

If the period piece they had stepped into bothered Kay, Jo saw no indication of it.

Fascinating what people will spend their money on.

Kay got a few stares as they crossed the lobby to the lift.

Along the way, they heard the whispers nobody knew they could hear:

"Look, Mama, a Vastalimi!"

"I never saw one in person before!"

"Man, that's an ugly-ass critter! Look at that face!"

Kay ignored the whispers.

They achieved the elevator. Although such things would not have been found in a hotel of the period represented, it being pre–Industrial Revolution, it had been made to match the decor: There were wrought-iron gates that slid back to allow entrance to the elevator cage, a space large enough to hold a score of people. The inside was carpeted, some floral design, with plush red velvet, pleated into a tuck and roll on three of the walls. There was a mirrored ceiling.

A man in colorful livery stood to one side, by a mechanical device, brass and dials, that looked like it belonged on an ancient ship's wheelhouse. He smiled at them. "Floor?"

"Fiftieth," Jo said.

The man cranked a lever on the control, and the elevator started to rise. With nothing but ornate bars blocking the entrance, one could see out of, or into, the cage as it passed each floor, and it was moving slowly enough to give good views either way.

A few floors up, a mother and a little girl of maybe three got onto the lift. The child lurched closer before her mother could stop her. She put out a tiny hand to touch Kay's leg fur.

"Soft!" the little girl said.

Kay smiled at her, an expression that made the mother's eyes go wide.

"Come here, Darla!"

"She won't bite," Jo said, but the mother pressed herself against the elevator's far wall and got off at the next stop.

Kay waved at the child, who smiled and waved back. "Bye!"

There were a pair of guards in civilian clothes outside the room, but they opened the portal without speaking or asking for weapons. Just as well; Kay's weapons were biological, and Jo wouldn't have given up her flat-pack pistol if they'd asked for it, even though she did have a one-shot electrical zapper built in.

Inside, the rep who had called was waiting. He smiled at them.

"Fems, come in, come in! I am Dhama, delighted to meet you!"

There was an almost inaudible hum in the background, something electrical, and the air was overfiltered and lacking any real scent.

Single-name Dhama had the look: tall, well made, handsome. Black hair, a few streaks of gray at the temples, a four-day stubble of beard. He had a firm jaw, perfect teeth, green eyes. Old enough to look as if he knew what to do, young enough to look as if he could do it. He wore a perfectly tailored uniform, understated in gray silk, a holographic Dycon patch over the right breast pocket, his name shimmering over the left pocket. He sported handmade boots of some kind of patterned, mottled leather Jo didn't recognize. The Willis 4.4mm pistol holstered on his right side had grips of what looked like ivory and rode in a holster that matched the boots.

If he was as good as his clothes, he would be formidable.

According to her radiopathic pickups, her olfactories and otics, he had several augs running, nothing esoteric she could tell.

Right out of an entcom vid casting director's top choices for a soldier-of-fortune officer; couldn't miss him.

Jo was not one to put a lot of stock in looks, however, and while Kay could tell the difference between humans visually, she wouldn't be impressed by anything so superficial, either.

"Fems, this way."

He turned to lead them down the hall.

Kay subvocalized quietly: "He does not move well."

Jo responded in the same way: "No. Though he looks as if he should."

"Bukvan," Kay said.

Jo didn't know the term, but before she could ask, Kay continued:

"A preener. We have them on Vast. They make themselves appear better than they are."

"You just described most of the human race."

"I am aware of this."

Jo chuckled.

They arrived at the conference room, a large space with a small oval table and three chairs, no other furniture. Dhama gestured. "Please, sit."

Kay and Jo sat on opposite sides, to be able to watch each other's back. Not that such was likely to be necessary, given their hearing if somebody tried to sneak through the walls, but better safe than sorry.

Dhama sat at the head of the table, accompanied by a creak of his holster leather. He leaned back in the chair, affecting a relaxed pose. He smiled but didn't speak.

We are beings of the galaxy here, ho-hum.

Jo returned the smile and the silence. He had asked for the meeting, let him offer the reason.

After a few seconds, he said, "Well, I'm sure you are wondering why I wanted to speak with you."

Jo and Kay said nothing, waiting.

His smile faltered just a hair. "We at Dycon Limited seek to represent the best interests of our employers. There are ways, and then there are . . . ways . . ." He gave her another of his shiny smiles.

Jo waited. She knew where this was going; she had done it herself a few times. Wars were expensive. Sometimes a client would make out better by channeling the money into bribes or payoffs to achieve the same results as a battle. For the cost of a few missiles, a key opposition figure might be socially engineered to look the other way at the right moment, or maybe forget to enter a coordinate into a targeting computer. Even Monitors might be influenced though that was tricky. As a result, the bribed could walk away richer, and one's client would save a lot of money and grief.

"I don't think we can help you there," Jo said.

"You haven't heard what I have to say."

She shrugged. "Doesn't really matter."

"We are prepared to be extremely generous to our friends."

"Not how we do things at CFI."

"Never?"

"Not so far."

"How would three million New Dollars sound?"

"Like a lot of money," Jo said.

He smiled. "It is."

A bribe offered without actually offering anything.

"Thank you, but, no."

"Four million."

"You have deep pockets."

"And full ones. My clients want this to go their way."

"We'll pass."

"Six."

Skipped right over five. Jo stood. "Thanks for the meeting, we appreciate it."

He looked entirely nonplussed. He frowned. "Seven."

Probably as much as either side would spend on ammo and then some. "Save your breath. Like I said, that's not how we do business."

He stood. The holster and belt creaked again. *Some kind of reptile skin, maybe? Lizard? Serpent?*

His puzzlement shaded into a controlled, but apparent, anger. "You are making a mistake."

"Possibly."

He stepped closer. She could smell his hormones roiling. *Yep, definitely pissed off.*

Jo stood her ground. She wasn't worried. He might be augmented so he was stronger, but he wouldn't be better than Formentara's tweaks, and he was within reach. He blinked crooked, she would deck him.

Kay came up like hot smoke on a cold winter's day.

Dhama glanced across the table at her motion.

She gave him a wicked smile though he probably didn't recognize it as such.

The sight of the Vastalimi and augmented human warrior focused on him must have finally arrived. Caution kicked in. He edged back a hair.

Which was the smartest thing he had done so far.

"Fems . . ."

"We don't fault you for seeking to help your clients, M. Dhama, that's what you are supposed to do, but you have asked, and we have answered, and we are done here."

She could smell his sweat, which now had a sharper odor than before.

When Jo and Kay entered the elevator, Gunny and Singh joined them. Nobody spoke as the lift descended. It might look like something from a long-past century, but Jo knew the building was modern, and she could feel the surveillance cams looking at them.

They trooped across the lobby, accompanied by raised eyebrows and furtive looks from the staff and patrons of the hotel.

They split up for their separate carts in the parking area.

Back in the roller, Kay said, "He thought we would accept his offer. It seemed to surprise him that we did not."

"That's a bunch of money, many people would have gone for it. It's kind of fun to think about what a small fortune can do, a nice fantasy, but that's all it is."

"It would not be honorable to deal with such a person," Kay said.

"Nope."

Kay was silent.

Jo said, "What?"

"I am reminded now and again of something Em said recently: that we chose the right group of humans to associate ourselves with."

"Yeah, I suppose we could have done worse on the Vastalimi front, too."

Kay whickered.

– – – – – –

The warmth of the semitropical afternoon lay over the camp like a damp blanket. The ferrofoam stink from the buildings was something you tended to tune out after a while, but you noticed it after you were gone and came back. It would fade away eventually, but they wouldn't be here long enough for that to happen.

As Cutter got to the HQ, Gramps stood in the doorway, looking grim.

"What?" Cutter asked.

"Commanding general of the local GU Army sector wants to see you."

"Not a real surprise. Why the face?"

"It's Junior Allen."

"Oh, fuck," Cutter said.

"My feeling exactly."

Sixteen of the thirty largely-human-settled planets and twenty-eight major wheelworlds scattered across a thousand light-years of space still remained at least partially outside the GU's control.

Morandan, in the Meyer System, was one of these.

Morandan was where the revolution had gotten to its ugliest. It was the world where eight thousand civilians had been slaughtered due to incompetence and arrogance and the offhand banality of careless evil.

They really hated the GU on Morandan. It was one of the most dangerous postings you could get, as a soldier or an ambassador. Assassinations were ongoing and frequent.

Here was one of the main reasons for that hatred.

The man sat behind a desk made of rare and terribly expensive endangered Brazilian Rosewood; he wore a shit-eating grin. He was the man responsible for the deaths of those eight thousand civilians on Morandan—as well as the end of Cutter's career in the GU military.

Major General John D. Allen II.

Cutter had taken the fall because Allen was smart enough to rig that much. CMA was in the man's soul; he always covered his ass first, before he did anything else.

Cutter's DGF unit had been there, and it was take the bullet or let them take it, and Allen had known how that would go. Cutter protected his troops at whatever personal cost, and while Allen wasn't particularly smart, he was sly. He knew.

If you reveal a handle to some people, they will grab and use it.

It was complicated. Politics had to be served. The military powers that were had their hands tied. Cutter had enough friends among them so that he wasn't court-martialed, he was allowed to retire. Those who knew the truth couldn't go directly at Allen for the atrocity, but he hadn't escaped entirely. He never got the third star; he was overranked for running a minor post on a world where he would have no chance to do any real damage, and, no doubt, being monitored, to be sure he didn't get into trouble.

And yet, Allen was still in the Army, still able to draw active-duty pay, still looked like a cat full of cream and canary with his two stars.

Cutter knew that real-time justice was out of the mix. He hoped that karma might still operate.

Not that he ever expected to see the man again, but he had considered this moment theoretically now and again for years. He had thought about killing him. Hand-to-hand, with the satisfying feel of fist on flesh, a beatdown ending in a boot to the throat, maybe a broken neck.

He had considered a long-range shot, a klick or two away, single sniper's round to the head or heart. It had been long enough so he wouldn't be at the top of the suspect list though he would have to avoid being seen. If authorities knew he was on the same planet as Allen, they would want to speak to him.

He had thought about it. Mostly, after the fantasies, he had let it go. It was done, history, no point in bumping into the furniture while looking back over your shoulder. Mostly he had let it go, but not entirely. The man who had gotten away with mass murder by blackmailing Cutter into taking the heat was right here in front of him, and even a saint would have trouble smiling and forgiving.

Cutter wasn't anybody's candidate for saint.

A lot of choices presented themselves: Allen's father had been a four-star general, a rank his son would never achieve. It was a small barb, but the man's ego was such that it would sting.

"Hello, Junior."

The smile vanished, and rage danced briefly over Junior Allen's face.

Cutter's own smile arose.

"Just so you know: If you spit crooked, you're going away," Junior said. "You will have more eyes on your operation than a swarm of horseflies on scat. Anything, anything at all, give me a reason."

"Not a problem, Junior. I know you're behind me this time. I'll watch my back."

"Get the fuck out of my office."

"Nothing would please me more."

As he walked away, Cutter felt only a little better. Dinging the man's ego was nothing compared to what he had done. Nothing Cutter could possibly do would compare. It was still hard to think about, after all the years since.

Hard, but unavoidable.

— — — — — —

Cutter's Detached wasn't within two klicks when the shooting started though the official records were altered to show they were on-site. That they had pulled the first triggers. He had heard the noise, but it was distant, and by the time he'd sorted out the reports and sped to the site, it was far too late.

He looked at the vids, and they were gruesome.

Amazing how many people you can kill with full-auto carbine fire and fragmentation grenades when you open up on a plaza full of demonstrators.

Average-density-event-space put the crowd at ninety thousand, mostly human, men, women, children. Some were armed, but a scattering of hidden sidearms didn't matter, wouldn't have mattered if there had been ten times the hardware in the plaza. Anybody who tried to shoot back would have bounced non-AP bullets off military-grade armor.

It was an out-and-out slaughter.

— — — — — —

—sound was a mix of gunfire mostly overridden by screams of terror as the crowd mind realized it was trapped. The main opening between the buildings at the entrance to Strout Plaza was essentially a funnel, and no more than thirty people wide. The designers had never envisioned the possibility of what happened. Those in front couldn't move fast enough for those being shot at the rear. The stampede turned into a crush, tight enough so people were carried along. To fall was to die underfoot, and dozens perished that way—

—the shooters never appeared on cam. How anybody could not see that as unbelievable seemed impossible. There was the constant chatter of full auto, punctuated by the odd grenade. It was like shooting animals trapped in a pen—

—Cutter was a soldier, he had seen soldiers die, he had killed more than a few himself, but this was stomach-churning to watch. He had to watch it, he couldn't not, but still. How had those troops kept it up? What was it in them that made them keep firing, keep replacing spent magazines, when there was no threat? Had it been spontaneous? Had somebody given an order? Shoot until you run dry?

Until they are all dead?

Man's inhumanity to man was made manifest.

Eventually, it stopped. It lasted nine minutes and forty-three seconds.

In the course of nine minutes and forty-three seconds of sustained action, eight thousand people were killed. Most died by bullets or grenade, some by being trampled. Some died of density suffocation. Some from organ injury, people pushed together so violently that they were crushed. Some suffered heart attacks, some probably perished from outright terror.

Twelve thousand more sustained wounds, some of which involved amputations, shattered bones, torn flesh.

To watch was to weep.

– – – – – –

Martial law clamped hard and fast. News media were shut down, cameras and recorders confiscated, spindocs came up with stories. There was no way to hide what had been done, too many people had been there, and too many cams escaped the roundup.

How it was spun:

It was the mob's fault, they attacked the military, but the Army admittedly had overreacted a bit, and those responsible had been disciplined. Because there was a war on, details were necessarily kept secret . . . and in the end, Cutter's was the only senior officer's head to roll. His not so much because the uplevels knew he wasn't really the guy, but, well, that's how it goes. Somebody had to take the hit. No hard feelings.

Right. No hard feelings after all the years of loyal service . . .

Well, done was done, and he had managed to build CFI into something of which he was proud. But it still rankled that he had gotten blindsided that way. He'd known how Junior operated; he should have prepared himself better . . .

– – – – – –

Back at the base, Jo was waiting.

"How'd it go with the Dycon guy?"

"He offered a bribe."

"How much?"

"Seven million?"

"Each? Or together?"

"I didn't ask."

"Really? You should have taken it. I would have."

They both smiled.

Jo's grin faded: "Gramps told me about Junior."

"Yep. Into each life a little shit must fall. We'll have to do this by the numbers, he's gunning for us. Document everything, and if we need to overstep, make sure nobody is watching."

"I hear you."

"You going back to the woods tomorrow?"

"Kay and Em. I'm doing delivery inventory on the weapon shipment."

"Okay. Keep me in the loop."

FIVE

There was no sense of foreboding, nothing to mark the moment as different than any other. Kay caught Em's spasm peripherally and the sound of the projectile as it broke the sound barrier followed half a second later, echoing over as she turned and saw Em, six meters away, still falling, the back of her head blown out . . .

The wound was obviously fatal, and the boneless manner of her comrade's collapse told the story: *Dead as she falls* . . .

Kay dropped flat and the *crack!* of the bullet meant for her followed the round as it zipped past, a meter and some above her.

There was only one direction from which it could have reasonably come, and she rolled, staying prone, until she put one of the larger tree boles between herself and the sniper.

Half a second between the time the missile blew past and the sound of it achieving the speed of sound. Allowing for a short travel from the weapon's barrel to get up to that velocity, maybe a hundred and sixty-five meters, *that* way . . .

She came up, and sprinted to her left for five meters, turned, zigged, then zagged, stutter-stepped, changed direction; she made no attempt to stay behind cover, working for maximum speed—

The sniper fired again, but the bullet passed well behind her—

She jinked. Stopped cold for two heartbeats, then cut to her right for two more steps before pivoting to her left—

The sniper fired again. The missile flew in front of her. He had tried to lead her, anticipate her path, but he was two meters off—

Another shot, this one hit a tree to her left rear, a meter back—

She kept dodging, side-stepping, dropping, rolling, leaping. She slowed down, sped up, covering ground fast but never more than a second or two in one direction—

She couldn't see him, but she had angled downwind and she had him now by scent, and knew where he had to be. He was well-camouflaged visually, a combination of electronics and a yowiesuit stuffed with local vegetation, but he couldn't hide from her now.

The sniper rifle was accurate at long range, but not designed to track a fast-moving target that changed direction quickly.

He should have dropped the rifle and reached for his sidearm as soon as he realized that she was coming at him.

He finally did, when she was close enough to see the movement despite the camo.

She should have used her pistol, too, but she didn't want to do that.

"Fuck!" he screamed, as she sprang, claws extended.

It was his final word before she tore out his throat.

- - - - - -

At their HQ, Kay stood across from Cutter, making her report. Regarding *Mish*fem, it was short:

"She hunts on the Other Side."

There was a moment of silence. "I'm sorry," Cutter Colonel said.

"We are predators, but in the end, we are all also prey. We all die. We arise each day knowing it could be our last. *Mish*fem died well, doing what she chose to do. It was quick. It was clean.

"She was here, and of a moment, she was gone. Such is the way of war. There are worse ways to die."

That was true. Not much anybody could say to that; they all knew.

The gloves were off, though. Nobody was supposed to be shooting in this period, and while they all knew that was always a possibility, until the first round zipped by, you were never sure it would come.

Cutter understood why this had happened. A chance to take out a couple of Vastalimi? That would be hard to resist. That killing one only cost a single sniper? It was a trade most commanders would make in a heartbeat. A Vastalimi soldier was worth a platoon of regular troops, maybe more. Em had not been as adept as Kay, but even so.

This didn't mean that CFI was going on a ranger hunt, looking to take out anybody they saw, but it did mean that enemy scouts who shot at you were fair game. And the opposition couldn't complain since they'd initiated the action.

There were rules in war, more so in the modern versions, but the rules weren't absolute; they got bent, twisted, broken. The nature of the game. In the heat of battle, when looking through your sights at somebody who might kill you tomorrow, sometimes shit happened.

Junior was watching, so they'd have to be careful, though. Self-defense was allowed, but it would need to be documented did the need to prove it arise. Kay hadn't been wearing a cam when the sniper killed Em. He believed her, but he needed to ask:

"How long before they find the body, do you think?"

Kay said, "I removed his locator. And the remains are in a place where a simple search will not uncover them. Certainly not all of them at once."

— — — — — —

Jo and Kay walked in the hot afternoon. Kay said, "Something else you should know."

Jo looked at her.

"The opposition has one of The People working with them."

"Really?"

"A male. I caught his scent. Faint, and after *Mish*fem's death, I did not explore it further, but I find it hard to believe that he was there by coincidence."

"I wouldn't think so either."

"It bears more investigation."

"I agree." Jo waited a second before she said, "Maybe I should—"

"No need," Kay said, cutting her off. "I will do it."

Jo nodded. The Vastalimi were stoic about many things, death notwithstanding. People came and went, that was the way of it, and there was no need to be overly disturbed; nothing could be done to change the general pattern, only the individual ones. Everybody got onto the hoverbus, and eventually, everybody got off; the questions were, how long was the ride, and how did you leave?

"Are there rituals to observe for Em?"

"No. She *was*, now she is *not*. She was a good companion, she moved well enough. What was left is but a husk; her essence has departed. If you believe in the Other Side, she is there; if not, then she is wherever she is. *Sudbina*."

She looked at Jo.

Jo nodded. *Yes. Fate.*

SIX

Despite Kay's offhand attitude, Em's death cast a shadow over the camp. The body was cremated, the ashes scattered, and business went on. When you worked in a profession whose tools included guns and bombs, death was always on the menu; only a matter of time until the order you placed arrived . . .

Jo worried about Kay's mental state. Em had been with them only a short while, there weren't any long-standing bonds, but still; save for the recent discovery that there was a male Vastalimi working with the opposition, Kay and Em had been the only two of their kind on this part of the planet as far as anyone here knew. Surely that had to resonate somehow.

Jo broached it carefully. "Is there anything you need?"

"Need? No. I wouldn't mind having a chance to hunt, but that is not a need, only a desire. And there is no prey worth chasing in this area, save for humans."

"Probably not a good idea to bag any of those, except

maybe for the opposition. And I suspect the colonel would frown upon that, given the extra scrutiny we are under."

"Agreed."

Jo was still thinking about Kay's mind-set when she went to see Formentara for a tune-up.

All of her augs were functioning properly, as far as Jo could tell, nothing bothering her, but Formentara required frequent checks. Much easier to prevent a problem than to repair one, zhe said, and given the number of augmented systems Jo was running, problems could crop up. Anybody of lesser talent and skill than Formentara would be hard-pressed to keep Jo's system in balance. Most people with anywhere close to as many augs as Jo had were looking at short lives. Generally, each major aug would cut ten years or so from one's life span unless precisely tuned and balanced, and until she'd met Formentara, Jo had expected to die young. A price she had been willing to pay . . .

"On the table," Formentara said.

Jo obeyed, lying there naked as Formentara waved hir magic hands over the reader fields to observe and adjust. The room was warm enough so Jo didn't need to worry about her temperature.

"Anything bothering you?" zhe asked.

"Not really."

"Yeah, something is—your hormones are off. What?"

"Well, Em's death."

"That was a bitch."

"I'm more worried about how it affected Kay. She says she's fine, but I'm not sure that's so."

"Too bad she won't let me work on her."

"She's faster and stronger than a human, even augmented ones."

"Yeah, but I could turn her into a super-Vastalimi. She'd be a blur."

"Not in the cards."

"A parochial prejudice, that attitude toward simple augmentation."

"What can I tell you? They are aliens."

"What are you going to do?"

"Not much I can. She'd like a chance to go hunting, but there's nothing around that would offer her any kind of challenge. This is Earth, which as you point out endlessly, is the cradle of human civilization. Not many critters running loose that would give one of The People much of a workout."

"Hmm."

" 'Hmm'? What does that mean?"

"How busy are you in the field? How much time could you give Kay to play?"

Jo thought about it. The main part of the ranger work was done even though there would be forays to tweak the intel already gathered. They didn't really need Kay until things heated up. "Four or five days, maybe. Why?"

"Just because there's nothing to give a predator of Kay's ability any challenge around here doesn't mean there isn't anything on the planet that might. I know some people. Let me talk to them."

"Okay."

"Meanwhile, shut off your beta-blockers and give me an epinephrine spike, half-strength."

Jo obeyed.

"Good. Three-quarters . . . good. Two seconds at full . . . fine . . . reboot to carrier levels . . ."

Jo went through the tests. Everything seemed to be in optimum condition. After she was done here, she was going to go and find Kay, see if she could come up with something to keep her busy and not thinking too much.

– – – – – –

Wink came around the corner and found Jo lying on her belly, staring intently at something on the ground.

"What *are* you doing?"

"Tracking. Be careful, don't step on the grass."

"What? Why? Who are you tracking?"

"Kay."

"Uh-huh . . . ?"

"She's been teaching me how to cut sign. It's an important skill for a hunter."

He looked at the ground, which, like most of it around here, was a mix of dirt and dust, with frequent patches of scraggly grass and a few ratty-looking shrubs.

There was nothing he could see that offered any clue to Kay's whereabouts.

"Sign?"

"Any physical evidence left behind by somebody or something's passage."

"I don't see anything."

"Can't from that angle. Come down here."

"On my belly in the dirt?"

"Suddenly you are Doctor Fastidious?"

He grinned. He squatted, then stretched out.

"See that little tuft of grass?"

"Yeah. It looks like a little tuft of grass."

"Look closer."

"I don't have your optical augmentation, I can't look any closer."

"Yes, you can. I'm not using any of my augs. That's part of the game. No opthalmic, no olfactory, no enhanced otics, just basic biological issue."

He stared at the grass. "I still don't see anything. It's *grass*. No, wait, there's a bug of some kind. That Kay, in disguise?"

She ignored the last. "Now, look over there, next to it, at that patch."

He looked. "Okay. And . . . ?"

"That patch is undisturbed. See how the stalks stand, the angles?"

"Okay."

"Now, look at this one again."

He did. "Some of the grass here is bent down."

"That's it."

"That's what?"

"Somebody stepped on it."

"Whoopee. How does this help you find Kay?"

She came up to her feet in a smooth, easy motion. Wink also stood, albeit not quite as smooth and relaxed. He looked down at his tunic and trousers. He shook his head.

"Damp or wet ground takes tracks. Look behind you, at where you and I walked."

"Yep, I can see that, we're sublime, we've left footprints in the sands of time."

"But Kay came this way, and she didn't leave obvious footprints. You see any?"

"I do not. How did she do that? She float?"

"Sort of. She hopped from one bit of vegetation to the next. Plus the odd rock here and there."

"Ah."

"If I examine the grass within a Vastalimi's jumping range around this one, I should be able to find two places where Kay came down. One getting here, another leading away. The closer the distance, the harder it will be to see."

He thought about that for a moment. "Because she can step lightly from this to that, but if she has to jump farther, the impression will be deeper. Or if she lands on a stone that doesn't leave any sign."

"See, already you are learning. Since I know I'm tracking a Vastalimi and not a human, I know she can jump farther. I can look at the closest grass first, and if I find something, recalculate where her next step or leap might be. If I don't find anything close, I range longer."

"Makes sense. Doesn't even sound that hard, once you explain it this way."

"Yeah, except that Kay knows I'm tracking her."

"So . . . what?"

"She might backtrack."

"Um . . . ?"

"She knows what I'm doing because she taught me how to do it. I'm looking for a flattened bit of vegetation, maybe a partial print slopping over onto the bare ground. Maybe a squashed insect."

"Yeah . . . and . . . ?"

"Think about it."

He did. Didn't come up with anything. He gave her an offhand shrug. "I'm just a doctor. I can follow a blood trail."

"Okay, so we have this sign we just saw. And back to my left, there's another sign. Past that, a couple of meters away, another one. That's how she got here."

"I got that part."

"What if Kay came that way, then went back onto the same spots? She'd use them twice."

He considered that. "Ah. So if you can't find any other sign past this one except the one that led you here, you work on that assumption."

"Yep. And if that's right, somewhere back along the way, I should find *two* disturbed bits of vegetation, where she backtracked to leave a false trail, then went off in another direction. Plus landing on the identical area twice should, in theory, make it a little deeper and messier than doing so only once."

"Right. So, not as easy as it seems."

"Nope. And slow. Hard to cover a lot of ground when you are spending a fair amount of time lying down and trying to see which way she went; it makes for painstaking work."

"If you could use your enhanced vision, you could do it faster."

"Sure. And if I com her and ask her where she is, I can do it really fast. If I were trying to track somebody for real instead of this game, I'd dial up the magnification, and it would be relatively easy. I could maybe use IR to see warmer patches, except that in this weather, it doesn't work so well. But the idea is to get good at doing it the hard way; after that, you can cheat."

"Well, have fun out here broiling in the sunshine. I'm going to go change clothes and have myself a cold beer."

"You don't want the thrill of victory when we find her?"

"You can tell me about it, I'll share your joy."

— — — — — —

It took Jo nearly two hours to follow the winding trail Kay left, stops and starts and backtracks, but eventually, she came to where Kay sat on a tree stump, waiting.

"Very good, Jo Captain."

"How long would it have taken you to follow that trail?"

Kay shrugged. "Thirty minutes."

"Great."

"Everyone starts off an ovum," she said. "Formentara has called me."

"Yeah?"

"Zhe has found a place where I can seek prey."

"That's good."

"It is. If I have a few days."

"Nothing going on here you need to stick around for, go."

"Thank you, Jo. It will be a good thing to do."

— — — — — —

Overall, Earth was not a good place for a Vastalimi to hunt. Prey animals had been domesticated here for thousands of years, and there was no joy to be found in catching a lumbering bovine and killing it. Most humans no longer ate meat, fowl, even fish; they consumed ersatz versions of these made from plants, designed to look and smell and taste like the real thing. Of course, with their poor senses, humans were easy to fool.

The cattle and sheep and llamas and assorted mammals that were once on the menu now produced milk or cheese or eggs or whatever, and under strict rules. Eating such creatures or their produce was expensive and even frowned upon.

Predators who ate mostly plants. It was hard to comprehend.

Walking up to a creature bred for docility and opening its throat with a claw as it stared stupidly at you, too inbred to be afraid?

Pah. Maybe even less satisfying than eating plants made to taste like the real thing. One expected a plant to be still . . .

There were game preserves, of course, places where tourists could go and see creatures that would be extinct otherwise. Big felines, wild canines, ursas, and the like. They frowned on having those creatures poached.

There were apparently secret hunting clubs, wherein armed humans could go and shoot "wild" animals, using computer-controlled rifles that needed no guidance to speak of; dial in the target parameters, point it in a general direction, squeeze the trigger, the gun would do the rest.

Pah.

Not many places on this world where one of The People could get her claws righteously bloody without running afoul of the local laws.

There were, however, exceptions. And through the grace of Formentara, Kay had access to one of those exceptions . . .

The area was called Alaska, and much of it was still forested. The local region, Denali, surrounded a snow-capped mountain of some size, and most of it was a park, sans development, and rugged.

Animals were allowed to run loose here, kept in the park with electronic fences, and some of them were predators, including brown bears, the largest of which were nearly seven hundred kilos in weight and three meters tall when rearing upright on two legs. Most of the adult animals were tagged and easy to locate, via Planetary Position Satellites

Visitors to the park carried transducers that repelled the tagged predators, so it was generally safer for humans.

Generally. However, now and again, there were births that escaped the game wardens. And some of these unregistered births resulted in adult animals that did not sport electronic devices. Which, to a tourist expecting a beast twice his height and nine times his weight to turn and pad off, could be a nasty surprise when it decided he was prey.

Apparently, at least one such creature was running loose, surprising tourists; thus far, it had killed and eaten parts of three visitors to the park, and apparently once a bear developed a taste for human flesh, nothing else would be as satisfactory.

Kay didn't think human was that tasty herself.

– – – – – –

Kay looked at the warden. The human fem was trying not to stare but was obviously intrigued by her contact with a Vastalimi.

"So, that's the situation," the warden said. "It's a bear, grown, and we're guessing six hundred kilos, from the tracks. We typed his DNA from scat and shed hair, and know his parents. The mother sow had what we thought was a single-cub birth five years ago; apparently there were two. We seldom saw her and never laid a cam on him, and it's a big forest, so he was able to thrive unseen. Rare, a perfect storm, but it happens.

"We haven't had one kill any humans for more than twelve years, this was quite a shock."

Kay nodded. Humans were much more concerned with their own kind dying than most other intelligent species.

"Anyway, the protocol is to find and dispatch such rogues. For a while, we tried catching and relocating them; we tried drugs; in the end, nothing seemed to settle them down. Zookeepers were at risk, like that. So now, we eliminate them.

"This is such a rare event," she continued. "And since the animal has to die, the, uh, powers that be decided that there should be some benefit to the park, so the right to hunt and take such bears is auctioned off to the highest bidder. The winning bid, as I'm sure you know, is generally . . . quite high."

The woman looked at Kay, and the unasked questions lay between them:

How did a Vastalimi come to be here? How are you able to afford this?

Kay let them lie. Formentara had told her there was a hunting fee, and zhe had paid it, as a gift. Formentara had not mentioned an amount.

Humans were also overly concerned about money. Kay didn't worry about that. She had enough for her needs, and her needs were mostly provided by CFI, so past that? What was the point?

"Um. Anyway, this is map sig where we most recently spotted his spoor. We haven't gotten a visual on our parksat, but the area is heavily wooded, and we don't use pradar or IR much, too expensive for our budget."

Kay nodded.

"If you find him and kill him, use this locator, and we'll come and collect the corpse."

She held out a thumb-sized lozenge.

Kay took it.

"What, uh, kind of weapon system will you be using? We recommend at least 10mm Hoarse Whisper loads in rifles; ten-gauge smoothbore with plus-P rifled slugs; or .50 GR in handcannon, but that only if you are expert with a sidearm."

Kay smiled. She raised one hand and snapped the claws out with an audible *snick!*

"I'll be using these," she said.

Kay had gotten fairly good at reading human expressions during her years among them. This one was a mix of shock and amazement.

"You're kidding!" the woman said, confirming that.

"No. The bear is larger and stronger, but I am much faster and with far superior intelligence. I have seen vids of these creatures, read what is known about the way they fight and take prey. I am prepared for what it can do, while it has no experience of my kind. The advantage is mine, by far."

"One misstep, and it will swat you dead."

"I will strive to avoid taking that particular step."

The warden shook her head. "You signed the waiver."

"I did. My responsibility, not yours."

– – – – – –

Jo, on her way to see Rags, ran into Formentara, on hir way to some kind of conference at a major university in a place called Woomera.

The heat of the days here was muggy, the humidity high, making for a fast sweat that didn't want to evaporate from skin or clothes.

Jo said, "Kay has left on her bear hunt."

Formentara nodded. "Good."

"Thank you for that."

Zhe shrugged. "She needs to hunt. Not much of that going on on Earth anymore, but there is some."

"You paid for it."

"So? I have money."

Jo knew that. Formentara had created several commercially successful augs and had royalties from those; nobody knew for sure how wealthy zhe was, but zhe certainly wasn't poor even though there was nothing about hir that spoke to having wealth.

"I poked around. I understand that the previous bear-hunting license issued in such a situation cost more than nine hundred thousand ND."

Formentara's smile was small and almost reflexive. "I wouldn't know about that one."

"If I had to guess, I'd say that the cost of Kay's hunt would be more than that, given the rarity, plus inflation and all in the years since."

Zhe shrugged again.

"Christus, you paid a *million noodle* for Kay to risk getting killed by one of the largest predators still allowed on Earth?"

"Million and a half," zhe said, "since you obviously want to know. You worried that she'll get killed?"

Jo considered it for a few seconds. "Not really, no."

"Then what the hell? It's only money, and it'll make her happy."

Jo laughed. "You are something else."

"Don't I know it," zhe said. "My job is to take care of my team." Zhe paused. "I have to run. My shuttle leaves in an hour. The locals have need of my specialized knowledge. I might even learn something in return."

Zhe looked happy at the prospect.

Jo smiled and nodded. "Have fun."

"I always do."

Formentara headed for hir transport.

There would be a six-person covert ops team going with hir, and others fore and aft. Once a war was in play, it was a good idea to protect your assets. Technically, nobody was supposed to bother people away from the site of a battle, but then again, technically, Em wasn't supposed to be dead, either. Better safe than not, and Formentara rated the protection. It was possible zhe might not know how thick it was, but knowing hir, zhe probably did know. Not much got past Formentara if zhe wanted to bother tracking it.

Anybody who blinked at hir funny on hir trip was going to be made unhappy about that in a hurry.

Jo hoped Kay would enjoy her hunt.

SEVEN

In Cutter's office, with glasses of premium bourbon over ice wafting a delicious odor into the cool air, Gramps said, "What are we going to do about Junior?"

Cutter shook his head, sipped at his drink. *Ah.*

He allowed himself one glass a day, and the stuff was passing expensive though that wasn't the reason he drank but one. "We could kill him, but that probably won't help at this point."

"Heartwarming thought, though." Gramps sipped his own liquor and smiled at the taste.

Cutter nodded.

"He'll be looking for a way to stick it to us," Gramps said, "and if he can't find one, he'll make one up. Not a matter of 'if,' but 'when.'"

"Yep. My capital in the GU Army is mostly pocket change these days. I don't have enough clout there to get somebody to pull his leash tight."

Gramps said, "Hmm. Maybe that's not the only way to go."

Cutter looked at him.

"Let me reach out to some people," he said. "The military isn't the only power in the galaxy with a long reach. Maybe we can find something to help."

Cutter nodded again. "Okay. Meanwhile, how is this op shaping up?"

"So far, so good. Aside from losing Em, nobody has taken any hostile action on our recons. We have built up a pretty good model of the area, I'm talking to Zoree Wood's intelligence folks, hardware deliveries are on schedule. Jo is at the port collecting troops and supplies. Kay is out in the Alaskan wilderness hunting a rogue bear. Gunny is at the range, practicing with her shiny new pistol to beat you."

Cutter grinned. He had an innate talent when it came to CQ combat involving arms, something he cultivated but couldn't claim credit for: He was a born shooter. Gunny, who trained more than anybody he knew, was the best pure shooter in the unit, maybe on any single planet at a given time, but he consistently beat her in competitions. He couldn't claim credit for it, but he enjoyed it anyhow . . .

"That's not a bad idea. Maybe I'll go to the range and program the attackers with Junior's face."

"Don't. If you do have to shoot him later, I'll have to erase those records; it's a lot of trouble."

– – – – – –

At the range, Gunny recharged the new toy's triple-stack magazine with thirty-six rounds of practice loads. The pistol was a 4.4mm Mead Caseless semiauto, ultrahigh-velocity. It had a ten-centimeter barrel, and it was a tack-driver with combat-match ammo. It would keep them in a five-centimeter circle at fifty meters all day long, if you didn't sneeze when you pulled the trigger. She had tuned the capacitors to competition grade, polished the action so it was as slippery as No-Frik lube, installed aftermarket springs and a D-steel button-rifled barrel. She'd put five hundred rounds through it without a misfire, and it was as good a handgun as you could find anywhere. It should be, it had cost her enough.

So far, she had cut almost a quarter second off her best shoot times, and that might be enough so she could finally take Rags . . .

Think of the devil.

"Gunny. I see you found a way to spend your money. I must be paying you too much."

"Like hell. I had to save up for months to get this."

She handed him the Mead.

He ejected the magazine, then the chambered round, inspected the weapon.

"Nice. Carbon-fiber grips, but not custom-fitted?"

"Ah might have to shoot with my weak hand. Or lend it to somebody in a hurry."

He nodded. He handed it back to her.

She reloaded the piece. "You come to play?"

He patted his own holstered sidearm, a Willis 4.4 double-stack thirty-rounder. Until recently, that's the same model Gunny had carried. "Got practice rounds loaded. You want me to give you a head start?"

"Fuck you."

He grinned. "Set 'em up."

Gunny waved her hand back and forth over the reader, and the range's computer lit the scenario. Four attackers each, and judged on time and placement of the rounds. If you got the same score for hits, then it went to the clock to determine the winner.

In a straight, slow-timed target match, Gunny would beat Rags all day every day. But when things heated up, something in his wiring gave him an advantage. It was like he could read the future; he anticipated random movement and shot where the target was going to be. Gunny had never seen anybody else who could do that the way he did.

Sometimes it wasn't by much that he got her. A quarter

second here, eighth there. If the new piece could help her shave that much off her time? Maybe she could beat him. Or at least play him to a draw.

As goals went, it wasn't so much, but it was at the top of Gunny's list.

"Ready?"

"Anytime."

They both had holstered their weapons. Gunny took a deep breath. "Go!" she told the computer.

Four men with carbines popped into electronic reality in front of her five meters away. She pulled her pistol, a smooth, fast move, practiced tens of thousands of times, and started shooting, one round each, *pop-pop-pop-pop!*

Her four attackers fell, each of them head-shot. That felt clean; it was a good run—

The computer's counter lit up downrange. Same score on the hits, but—

The son of a bitch beat her: 0.127ths of a second. A fast blink.

Fuck!

She holstered the pistol and waved her hand over the reader.

– – – – –

The People hunted by sight and scent, and though Kay couldn't see the bear, she could smell him. It was distinctive, the odor, potent, and tracking him would not be a problem if what looked like threatening rain held off. Rain cleared the air, held the scent close to the ground, made it harder to locate. Her nostrils worked fine, but The People were sight-hunters more than sniffers.

That would just make it more of a challenge, which was the point, was it not?

Kay stepped into the forest and opened up her senses to the new hunting ground.

The sights, sounds, smells, the tactile feel of the dried needles and leaves under her feet, the temperature of the air on her fur, they all blended together, and she became one with the place. Yes, she had been born on a world light-years from here, but she had hunted on other planets, and while they were all different, they were all also the same.

The chirps of the birds, chattering of small mammals in the trees and in burrows, insects buzzing, the wind creaking the wood and stirring the leaves, the sound of her own heartbeat, filled her ears.

The many smells, of the plants, the animals, the warm ground, seeped into her nostrils.

The dappling of the light through the tree crowns bathed her fur . . .

She soaked it all in. Closed her eyes, took a deep breath, let it escape. Ready.

That way . . .

— — — — — —

She circled upwind, to allow the beast to catch her scent, then looped back around, downwind, and waited.

What would he think when he sniffed and smelled her? She would be alien to him, and how would he react? Would he come to investigate? Or move away, beset with caution? Would he dismiss her altogether?

The bear was the top natural predator here, save for humans, and he wouldn't be afraid of her. And since he had killed humans? Probably wouldn't worry overmuch about them, either. Other than a bigger, fiercer bear, there was nothing for him to fear, claw-to-claw. He would be secure in his strength and speed.

After a few minutes, the bear's scent told her he hadn't moved. So, not curious, nor afraid, continuing his business.

Good. Time to move closer. Let him see her . . .

This close, the bear's musk was thick, and since she was approaching downwind, he could no longer smell her. She moved with care, slipping through the big trees, using them for cover. They were a few hundred years old, the larger trees, too big around to encircle with her arms.

She was eighty meters away, still concealed. The bear was feeding on something; she could hear the cracks of small bones being crunched. Before she could step out and let him see her, the crunching stopped. Was he done? Or had he somehow sensed her even though he couldn't see nor smell her? Sometimes, prey knew they were being watched; some innate, undefined sense warned them.

She moved from behind the tree.

The bear was looking right at her. He had known she was there.

He was on all fours, the remainder of his meal scattered on the ground, some medium-sized animal.

He moved his head from side to side, lifting it, sniffing at the air.

She knew that he had a much better sense of smell than she did though his vision was poorer, about that of a human, and he could hear better than they. At short distances, a bear could sprint faster than a man could run though maybe not as fast as a Vastalimi.

The bear stopped sniffing and watched her. Then it raised itself up onto its hind legs, continuing to look at her.

A display to make himself look more dangerous? Or a way to see better? Both?

The bear dropped back to all fours.

Kay stood as still as a statue.

A few seconds passed. The bear looked away from her, back at what it had been eating. Then it turned and padded off. In no great hurry, but not dawdling, either.

Kay smiled. He was not showing fear, but caution. Good.

Intelligent beings who did not hunt usually did not understand how prey behaved when it perceived a threat. They expected that an animal beholding something that might kill and eat it would flee as fast and as far as it could. That seldom happened. What usually took place was that the prey would move a short ways, out of quick reach, then stop to assess the situation. If the hunter didn't move to follow, as often as not, it seemed almost as if the prey forgot it was there. If the hunter was downwind and still, prey would often resume whatever it had been doing.

There were humans who hunted. Kay had met a few, including one who took other predators armed only with a spear or blades. She respected that; the prey had a chance of winning, the human could be killed.

There was no honor in hunting unarmed prey with a weapon that could take it from a kilometer away. If you were seeking meat, and that was the only consideration? Fine, use a gun. But there was no challenge in that. If you were smarter and better armed? *Pah.*

The real challenge was to hunt prey that was as smart as you were and better armed. That meant doing something highly illegal though there were sometimes arrangements made between hunters who wanted the risk. On Vast, where challenges to the death were not infrequent, few needed that spur, but she knew of places where that was not so.

She had known those who had hunted or been hunted by their own kind. They claimed it was the most exciting thing that could be done.

The bear was nearly two hundred meters ahead of her, about to break out of the woods into a clearing that bordered a shallow river. She had kept downwind of the bear, and taking him there would be harder—in the woods, the trees could be used to her advantage. She could dodge around and behind them, and while the bear could climb, she could climb faster and easily change trees, while it would be too heavy to do that readily. On the flats, she would have to depend on speed and agility alone if she elected to do claw-to-claw battle. Trickier.

The smell of the water grew stronger, but it was not just the river; the threatened rain had arrived, drops beginning to patter down into the treetops.

She slowed, as the rain grew stronger, the noise quickly masking other sounds. The bear's scent washed from the air. She couldn't see him, smell him, nor could she hear him moving, either.

She slowed. Something was not right . . .

The rain beat down, harder. The trees stopped some of it, but the light grew dimmer, and the rain itself was heavy enough to obscure vision.

The bear was watching her.

She knew it. Where was he, that he could see her?

She moved slowly, only her head swiveling, as she scanned the trees ahead and to her sides.

Behind her—

Now she heard him, as he ran, splashing through the fresh puddles, feet thudding on the wet ground. She could feel the earth vibrating under his strides, six hundred kilos of carnivore in full charge—

—She resisted the urge to scurry up the tree next to her but, instead, pivoted, marked the running creature, then darted to her left, putting a larger tree between herself and the bear. That done, she backed away, out of his sight—

—He didn't roar, and he was close enough that she could hear him breathing now, panting, the ground shaking more—

—The bear passed the covering tree, saw her, tried to adjust his direction. He skidded on the wet ground, scrabbled to turn, and his claws, as long as her fingers and claws combined, dug gouts of dirt and mud from the earth, spattering it in all directions—

—He slewed and dug his way toward her, and when he was five meters away and regaining speed, she leaped to her left and high, caught the bark of the fir tree with all her claws extended, and shoved off as the bear tried to stop, but slid past her perch—

—She came down behind him, hit the muddy ground, and swiped at his right rear leg, hard, trying to catch a tendon. Her claws cut bloody furrows into the fur and flesh, but too high; she didn't feel the snag of heavy connective tissue—

—Now he roared, an ear-smiting scream of outrage. He spun around, faster than she expected, and she backed up in a hurry as he swung a clawed paw that would have broken her spine had it landed, missing by a few centimeters—

—Kay jinked to the right, clawed her way up another tree, four meters, five—

—The bear came up, jumped, and his claws tore the tree bark just under her right foot, gouging out a chunk of the underlying wood as thick as her hand from the bole—

—She leaped, over the rampant bear, to the tree to his right, gained another meter, then sprang for the ground—

—He was faster this time; he turned, dropped back to all fours before she could claw him again. He charged—

—She spun and ran, the bear right behind her. She cut left, then right, gained another two meters as he roared again—

—She zigged, zagged, jinked back and forth, and gained more ground on him. He realized what she was doing and stopped trying to stay with her every move, but kept going in the same general direction—

—He was more canny than she had figured.

—She circled to her right, forcing him to change direction. The rain came down harder; the footing became more slippery. Lightning flashed, and thunder boomed almost immediately behind it—

—She spun 180 and screamed her own wordless hunting cry. It must have surprised him because he slowed. She charged right at him. That gave him pause, but he dug in to meet the challenge, galloping toward her—

—Three meters away, she leaped at him, but high, much higher than he was prepared to deal with. He tried to come up to bat her down, but he was a half second slow, and she came down on his back. She dug her feet's claws into him as she ran along his spine and leaped off his hindquarters—

—Lightning. Thunder. The bear screamed at her and turned—

— — — — — —

"Ah wonder how Kay's doing up there in the rainy north woods?"

"Probably having a great time," Jo said.

"Huntin' a big ole brown bear with nothing but her claws? Ain't you worried she might get hurt or killed?"

"We are talking about a trained Vastalimi fighter," Jo said. "I'm not worried."

In truth, she was, a little. Kay was her friend, and Alaskan brown bears were the biggest and nastiest wild animals still running loose on Earth. Something to take into consideration. David beat Goliath, but that was usually a sucker bet.

Unless of course David had been a Vastalimi in disguise . . .

"What are we talking about?" That from Gramps, who ambled into the mess hall and arrived at where Jo and Gunny sat.

"Bears," Gunny said. "Ah understand their gallbladders will cure impotence. Maybe Kay will bring that back for you."

"You got it wrong, Chocolatte. It's *my* gallbladder that cures impotence. I let the drug companies drain it every few months—that's what they use to make all the Cialagra they sell to treat erectile dysfunction, didn't you know? Watered down a bunch, of course."

Both Gunny and Jo laughed at that one.

"Ah'll give you that, old man. You got *gall* in fuckin' spades!"

— — — — — —

—Kay ran up the tree, jumped to a second one, then a third, confusing the bear. She was behind it now, and before it could turn to track her, she jumped again, onto its back—

—The bear tried to shake her off, but she dropped to her belly, extended her arms, and dug her claws into his neck. She ripped upward, shredding muscle and blood vessels—

—The rainy air went ripe with the metallic stink of blood—

—He dropped and rolled, a smart move, and she barely got off in time to avoid being crushed. She hit the wet ground in a shoulder roll, made it up before he regained his feet, and flew at him again—

—He got a paw up and swung it. It was a glancing blow, and only the tip of one claw found her flesh, over the ribs on her left side, but the force of the strike was enough to knock her three meters through the air like a batted ball, opening her fur and skin in a gash that bled but not too much.

She hit, rolled up, climbed the nearest tree. He came after her, and he climbed the tree, too. They weren't supposed to be able to do that well, adult brown bears this large, climb, but apparently, nobody told him he couldn't—

—She was faster, and as soon as she could, she leaped to a nearby tree. Almost missed and fell, it was farther than she wanted, but—

—The bear scrambled down, but she was on the ground ahead of him, and under him in time to claw his left leg. This time, she got the tendon—

—The bear roared and she leaped back as he got to the earth. He tried to charge, realized his left leg wasn't going to support him, and pulled up a second, then tried for her on three legs, the injured one raised slightly—

—His neck wound was bleeding freely, more so on the right side. She had gotten a big blood vessel, and it was gouting freely—

—She dodged, and he tried to claw, but the injury to his hind leg threw him off and he almost fell—

He stopped. Blood poured from the neck wound, soaking his fur. He gathered himself for another run, but only made it a few meters before he stopped chasing her.

He was running out of oxygen and the delivery method for getting more was damaged.

His breathing grew more labored; the rain had stopped, but the sound of his blood dripping onto the wet ground joined that of the water dripping from the fir needles.

He was almost done.

He looked at her, almost as if puzzled. He had been the master of his world, and this strange, small, and alien creature had come and beaten him.

After a few minutes, the bear collapsed, fell onto his side. His breathing grew more ragged. His final exhalation came, and he lay still.

With her joy at beating a killer so much bigger and stronger, Kay also felt a sense of sadness. The creature had been condemned; he would have died whether she had been here or not. She had given him a chance, and she had won, but he had been fierce and formidable.

"If there is an Other Side for you, hunt well when you arrive there," she said.

EIGHT

"Where do you think you are going?"

Wink looked at Jo. "Nowhere in particular. Just, you know, gonna do a little jogging, to stay in shape."

"Really? Since when?"

She didn't buy it, nor did he expect her to; a smart fem was a joy to be around, but sometimes also a pain. Still . . .

"Hey, is it a crime that I don't want to let myself get fat?"

"Four minutes of full-range myostim and watching your diet covers that."

"Yeah, but it's boring."

"Four minutes?"

"I have an active mind. I need to keep it stimulated."

"What you *need* to do is get rid of your adrenaline addiction and keep yourself alive, so we don't have to get a new medic."

"I'm only going to loop the base, not like I'm skying across country into the scouting zone. Any word from Kay?"

"She finished her hunt. The ranger posted an image of her with the bear. Look at your inflow."

He touched a control on his belt com's unit. The projection was a bit dim in the sunlight, but enough to see Kay standing next to a dead creature that dwarfed her.

"Holy shit. That thing is huge! Must be ten times her weight." He looked a bit closer. "She's got an injury, left side, on the ribs. It's been glued shut, but it dug a furrow there."

"Changing the subject, Wink."

"Kay is the one you need to be talking to about this. I didn't go hunting a monster with nothing but my knife."

"I wouldn't put it past you."

"Look, Jo, I'm just going to take a short run around the camp, not leaving the area."

"If you did, you wouldn't get far."

"What does that mean?"

"You're a smart man, Wink. Think about it."

He did. "Formentara."

"Yep."

"Our implant locators are not supposed to be triggered except in an emergency."

"Your leaving the base would be considered that."

"Yeah, well, if I don't leave the base—"

"It stays inert. But you know how clever Formentara is. Zhe has yours rigged with a proximity trip. Get outside the specified range? We get a tattle."

"Motherfucker."

"Just looking after our investment here."

"Does Rags know about this? This isn't in our contracts."

"His idea."

"I don't believe you."

"Well. He nodded his okay when I told him about it."

He shook his head. "I wasn't planning to stray."

"I believe you. But if something caught your attention on your run you wanted to investigate?"

"Can't fault a man for natural curiosity."

"Sure I can. Have a nice run."

"You know what? I don't feel like it anymore."

"I'm sorry."

"No, you aren't. I think I'll go and eat something. I'll myostim to work it off."

He wasn't really mad.

She knew it, too.

— — — — — —

Wink leaned against the wall of the little conference room and watched Gunny finish her coffee. "Doesn't it sound like fun?"

"Not really, no," Gunny said.

Wink said, "Come on, it's your chance to see local color, relax a little."

"Rags said you could?"

"Yes. Well, if somebody went with me."

"He doesn't trust you alone." Not a question.

"I need to get away, I'm getting cabin fever here."

"And you are asking *me* because . . . ?"

"Hey, you do this all the time."

"That's work. What makes you think Ah'd do it for fun? And why me? Jo turned you down?"

"I wouldn't give her the satisfaction of asking. She would enjoy being my babysitter too fucking much."

"Right. And Kay would draw a crowd, and neither Gramps nor Rags would go with you on a bet, so Ah'm it?"

"You wound me, Gunny."

"You say that a lot, and yet Ah never see any blood."

"Come on. I'll owe you one. And it'll be fun, really."

She thought about it. "Okay. If you promise to behave."

"Absolutely!"

— — — — —

As pubs went, Gunny had seen worse, but this one was not going to make anybody's list of great expressions of Terran architecture. It was a plain, prefab block that had weathered under years of Tejas sun and rain, edges smoothed, color faded, a crunched corner that looked as if somebody had slammed into it driving a cart at speed. Some bits of fresh graffiti here and there. The windows were small, high, cloudy, and pitted plastic, with glowing signs that advertised beer, ale, and liquors.

A country place, and picked because it was close. She'd been in places like it all over the galaxy. Local pub, mostly local people, and you could get into trouble or not, depending on your attitude.

A large, muscular, sleepy-looking fellow stood by the door, nodding at people coming and going.

No sign forbidding weapons she could see.

"Welcome to the Dew Drop Inn," Gunny said.

Wink said, "My kind of place. Shall we?"

"Ah don't know why Ah let you talk me into this."

"Sure you do. You were as bored as I was. How many times can you let Rags outshoot you before you get terminally depressed?"

"Fuck you."

"That would work for me, but I know your heart wouldn't be in it. How about we just get a beer and observe the locals in their native habitat? The war will kick off soon, then we'll have stuff to do."

Gunny shrugged. Getting away from a war zone for a cold beer? Lot worse ways to relax. And she had spent a lot of time in such establishments, that being part of her subrosa work for CFI all along. Need somebody to check out the local watering hole? Gunny is your gal . . .

The inside was no improvement on the outside. There was a long, black, scarred everplast bar that ran almost the entire length of the room, liquor bottles shelved behind that, in front of an unbreakable plastic mirror. Looked as if more than a few people had tested that unbreakable part; the mirror was dinged and scratched, and there were what surely were bullet holes here and there.

Gave the ambience all by itself, that mirror.

Of course, there was the smell, a pungent blend of cooked food, stale beer, dopesmoke, bodywash, sweat, perfume, and pheromones, as ventilators tried to, but couldn't quite, exhaust the atmosphere created by this many people doing things in this tight a space.

Gunny knew how it would be here: An hour after shift end on a fifth night, this place would be bouncing, stuffed to the doors, like a grenade with a the timer started. Not a matter of "if," but "when" before somebody got pissed off and started a fight . . .

The people inside were diverse, but there were a lot of mostly young men in faux-cowboy clothes—denim jeans held up with wide belts and big shiny buckles, tight shirts in various bright colors. They wore pointy-toed boots, and more than a few had wide-brimmed hats, either on their heads or hung on pegs nearby.

The younger fems were likewise dressed.

Among the young were older people, some of them looking as if they'd been outfitted for a Western period vid, some more conservatively.

It was early and not full yet, but maybe sixty people there. No aliens.

It was noisy, loud talk, laughter, glasses and bottles clinking. Music was playing in the background, some off-key singer lamenting the loss of his girlfriend, who had, apparently, left the planet with the singer's best old buddy . . .

Waiters and waitresses moved through the crowd, delivering or retrieving drinkware, and what looked to be greasy sandwiches and fried vegetables in plastic baskets.

"Just like Ma's home cooking," Gunny observed.

"It has a certain rough charm."

There were a couple of score tables with attached seats, securely bolted in place, and what looked like a slope to the floor that ran to a big, circular drain in the center of the room. She nodded at the drain, which looked as if it had a built-in disposal unit.

"Must make cleanup easier, spilled booze," Wink said.

"And maybe food and blood," she said. She had seen its like a dozen times around the galaxy. Great minds and all . . .

"That, too."

Gunny and Wink were in civilian dress, guns and blades tucked discreetly away, and they made their way to a two-person table toward the rear exit.

They sat. A couple of minutes later, a waiter appeared. "How do you do, folks, what can I get you?"

In the local accent, it came out: *Howdy, fokes, whutcannagitchu?*

"What's the house brew on tap?" Wink asked.

"Lone Star."

"We'll have two of those."

The waiter left.

"Lone Star?" she said.

"How bad could it be?"

The waiter came back a few minutes later and put two plastic steins on the table. "Five noodle," he said.

Wink handed him a ten coin. "Keep it."

"Thanks." He hurried off.

"Aren't you the generous soul."

"Hey, man is getting a nice tip, maybe he won't spit in our beer because we aren't locals."

Gunny sipped the brew. It was cold. Past that? "Well, this answers the question how bad could it be," she said.

"You've had worse."

"Not lately."

They sipped at their beers, listened to the music, watched the locals move and interact.

"Look at the size of the hat on that one."

"That's a *sombrero.*"

"What's that mean?"

" 'Shade,' Ah think."

"I can see why."

A couple of fights started to crank up, but there were a trio of big bouncers who appeared quickly to quell them. It was still early, not enough really drunk or stoned patrons to get really raucous. Yet . . .

A big, florid man dressed in his cowboy weeds and a big gray hat came over to the table and grinned down drunkenly at Gunny.

"Hey, there, little darlin', let me buy you a drink?"

Gunny smiled. "Ah have one, thank you."

"Well, then, why don't you bring it over to my table and set a spell."

Gunny looked at Wink. He shrugged. "Sounds kind of like your people, Gunny."

"Thanks, but Ah'm comfortable right here."

"I'd offer you my seat," Wink said, "but I'm not sure there's room here for that buckle. Of course, I guess the waiter could use it as a tray or something."

Gunny stared at him. "Ah knew this was a mistake."

The barroom cowboy's brain was pretty fogged by whatever he had been drinking or smoking, but something in Wink's tone must have seeped through.

"Say what there, pardner?"

"Oh, sorry, I was just remarking on what a fine-looking belt buckle you have."

The cowboy grinned. "Yeah, it is, isn't it? Ah won first place on the mechbull at Salty's last year."

"What did the guy who came in second get? Two buckles?"

"No, he didn't get—are you fuckin' with me, son?"

"Well, no, you're not really my type. Not hers, either."

The cowboy looked at Gunny. "That right, darlin'? You'd rather be with this micro-dick than a real man?"

"Got your number, doesn't he?" Gunny said. She smiled at Wink. "Micro-dick. M.D."

"Why don't you just run on back to punch your cows or

whatever, 'pardner.' My friend and I are trying to enjoy our beer. Though that's a lost cause with this snake pee."

"You insultin' Lone Star?! You outland asshole—!"

He drew back his fist for a punch—

Wink grinned and came up. He got in one good punch before the bouncers arrived, but that was enough to set the cowboy back on his heels. When he recovered enough to charge back in, Gunny stuck her foot out and tripped him, so he sprawled into the first bouncer and sent them both to the floor.

The second and third bouncers were not amused, and apparently, neither were the cowboy's friends; several of them came out of their seats and headed for Gunny and Wink.

"Time to go, Doctor Fool."

"So soon? I'm just getting warmed up."

"You aren't that good bare-handed, and if we pull hardware, we'll get cooked; half the people in here are carrying. Out, now!"

Wink headed for the door in a hurry, Gunny right behind him. The bouncers cut off pursuit.

"Got to go, folks," Wink said. "Maybe we can stay longer next time."

"Ain't gonna be no next time, Wink, you lyin' asshole."

"Thanks for your support," he said. "You know I feel better."

She grinned. That was true . . .

－ － － － － －

The days passed, and as they often did just before the action began, the time moved quicker as it approached.

Of a moment, it was only seventy-two hours out, and Rags called a staff meeting.

The stink of the ferrofoam, that hot-gun-lube odor, had faded some, but it was still obvious to Jo. Something you got used to when you lived and worked in such structures a big part of your life. Part of the military experience, the sights, sounds, smells. They faded and became the background.

Rags said, "Okay, let's have it."

Jo started. "We have completed our ranges, updated our maps, and interfaced with General Wood's staff. What we know, they know. Our gear is clean and ready, our troops are getting enough practice to stay sharp but not too tired. Come the fire, we are ready to cook."

He nodded. "Gramps?"

"Well, there is a new development, just in. I'm not sure what it means on the face of it, but my sense is that it means something we need to explore."

They all looked at him.

"What do you know about the Bax?"

Jo shrugged. "Probably what most people know. An intelligent species from an E2 world off a G-class, out the Orion Arm. Achieved N-spaceflight nearly a thousand years before we did, colonized a couple of stellar systems. Not particularly warlike, they do a lot of trade around the galaxy. Don't know any personally, but I've seen a couple here and there. I think they look like upright red wolves with more muscle and less hair. Why?"

Gunny said, "Where is this going?"

The older man said, "I sicced our C-AI folk into Galax-Corp's Legal Entities."

Jo looked at Rags. "Wow. You let him *do* that?"

"Sometimes you have to spend the money," Rags said.

"That's not what you tell me."

Rags shrugged. "He does the banking. He'd just do it anyhow. I'm surrounded by liars and cheats who take advantage of my good nature."

That got laughs.

"So what are we talkin' about again?" Gunny asked.

Gramps said, "I'll spare you the endless detail, fascinating as it is, the kind of questions they have to ask to properly narrow the search, the circular shell corporations and cutouts, but the bottom line is, there is an 87.6 percent chance, according to the C-AI runner, that UMex and thus Dycon LTD, are working for the Bax."

That gave everybody pause.

Jo got to it first: "The Bax? Why? What would the loopies want with water rights on Earth?"

"I haven't gotten that part yet," Gramps said.

Gunny said, "The other side is working for aliens. Don't that beat all?"

"Actually, no," Gramps said. "It doesn't beat all. Because our C-AI runners are passing diligent as long as you keep paying 'em, and I let them run for a while, there's something even more interesting."

He waited, a dramatic pause.

"You gonna tell us or just sit there grinning that shit-eating grin?"

"According to the AI, there is a 84.4 percent chance that *we* are working for the Bax, too."

That shut everybody up for a few seconds; then they all started to talk at once.

— — — — — —

Cutter calmed everybody down. Gramps had given him this intel only an hour ago, and while it was odd on the face of it, it didn't seem to have any direct effect on what they were doing here.

Probably.

Maybe.

Gunny said, "Not like there's any shortage of water in the galaxy, nor that the Tejano version is any better than anything you can make at home with a couple of gases and a spark. What are they gonna do? Pipe it onto ships and haul it off? Doesn't make sense."

"Something we might ought to figure out," Cutter said.

There weren't any dullards here. Wink picked it up: "Whatever their reason, they want it really bad. Because no matter which side wins, they win."

Jo said, "Maybe not. Maybe it's two different factions of Bax at odds with each other."

"And you say this because . . . ?" Wink said.

"Dhama's attempted bribe. Why would he do that if we are both working for the same people? They get the rights no matter what."

"Misdirection?"

Jo looked at Wink. "Seven million noodle on the off chance that we'd have somebody good enough to figure it out? No. In that case, it would be a complete waste. Makes more sense that it's two different sets. Likely the same reason, but competitors."

"Bax," Cutter said. "Trying to get property on Earth. That would contravene the ASA."

"My education is lacking," Wink said, "I thought ASA was the medical abbreviation for acetylsalicylic acid."

"The Alien Species Act," Gramps said, "a provision of which forbids members of intelligent species other than humans to purchase or own real estate properties on Earth, Luna, or Mars."

"Really?"

"Technically. There are some who have sneaked around the clause and used beards to buy parcels here and there, but if they get caught, it gets confiscated, there are huge fines, and somebody goes to prison. Several of the more intelligent sentients would apparently love to have access to Terran land."

"How come?"

Gramps looked at Gunny. "Back in the prespace days, when there were still more discrete countries than multinationals, one country would often buy property in another, for political, social, or financial reasons. Species that value property still do that. There are human landowners on other worlds."

"None known on Vast," Kay said.

"Death penalty?" Jo asked.

Kay nodded. "Just so."

"Maybe the loopies want to influence local politicians to vote for things that favor them in trade. Maybe they want a place where they can seduce our women—or men—drink the local wine, pee on the ground. Maybe just to be able to point at it and brag to their friends? Who knows why aliens want what they want? Who knows why anybody wants what they want?" Gramps said.

"Ain't you ever the long-winded philosopher."

Cutter said, "I don't want us to have any part of this, but we are on the ground, and if we just report it and walk away, that maybe doesn't fix things enough. General Wood knows what we know, and she has people who will pursue it, too."

"You think they know about each other? The Bax?"

"I would not be surprised."

Cutter thought, *Well. One more variable to be taken into account . . .*

Gunny said, "Well, sheeit. So much for having a nice, plain shooting war on our plate. Ah hate all this fuckin' intrigue."

Jo said, "Knowledge is power."

"And ignorance is bliss," Wink said. "Except if it might get you killed."

NINE

War Day arrived:

"HOSTILITIES WILL COMMENCE IN TEN SEC-ONDS," the Monitor broadcast announced.

Jo, leading her team, looked around as the Monitors did the countdown:

"FIVE . . . FOUR . . . THREE . . . TWO . . . ONE . . ."

The oogah horn sounded.

"Okay, the war is hot, people, asses and elbows!"

The cart accelerated, rolled past the Monitors stationed on the road.

One of the Monitors behind her camera waved.

Jo shook her head.

The entrances to the battle sites had been divided into two 180-degree sectors, and those randomly assigned. Neither side offered any overwhelming tactical advantage, but their assignment put them almost a kilometer closer to their destination, and since it was the only high ground in the area—such that it was—and it overlooked two of the main roads in and out, they needed to get to it first and occupy it.

Easier to protect your people on the flats if you had the high ground.

"High ground" in this case was something of a reach; this was mostly dead-level terrain, some river and lakes. Save for the planted forests of the mineral-laden cypress trees and some fast-growing black cottonwood pulp-crop plantations, it was nearly all scrub, with scraggly bushes and grasses. Once upon a time, this had been territory primarily farmed with cotton, corn, wheat, and the raising of bovines. They still grew a lot of grain, not so many cattle.

Their destination was not a natural rise, but a man-made trio of hills, constructed from excavations that made a reservoir nearby. A hundred years ago, they had dug a big hole and piled up the dirt. The elevation of the tallest hillock was only 150 meters; the other two were slightly lower. The newly created real estate had quickly sprouted some expensive houses, but during the Mutant Plague Years late in the previous century, the rich people who owned those houses had somehow suffered infection worse than the poorer folks around them. The houses were, according to local superstition, cursed, and while some of the structures were still there and more or less intact, home to a few squatters, the enclave had become mostly a ghost town.

The squatters had been kicked out for the duration of the war.

The name of the fake mountains was ironic: *Montoncillo de Habas*. Which meant, more or less, according to Gramps, "Hill of Beans . . ."

Singh drove, having shown a talent for operating small armored vehicles. On the field, nobody trusted the computers to pilot if they didn't have to do so.

The road was narrow, barely wide enough for two lanes of traffic, though both lanes were one-wayed toward the upcoming action, and the column Jo led was double-stacked and rolling fast. Twelve vehicles, two of them troop carriers, the rest lightly armored, some heavy machine-gun platforms, 10mm-caseless Fraleys, and supply transports.

High ground didn't mean as much as it once had, given aircraft and satellites, but water still ran downhill. It was harder to ascend than descend, and the ability to eyeball incoming traffic was sometimes critical. One of the first things that happened in combat, even a small war, was that high-tech gear went wonky. Coms failed, sat overflies that could pick out individual troops taking a leak somehow missed a column of tanks, drones developed engine problems. The fog of war obscured everything.

If you looked out over a road and saw infantry marching in your direction with your own eyes, that was probably closer to reality.

"Singh," Jo began.

"Six minutes, sah."

Jo activated her opchan. "Gramps, how—"

"Nine minutes before they get there," Gramps said. "You'll have all kinds of time to set up and start plinking."

"Big talk, old man," Gunny said. She was in the caboose, bringing up the rear. "Takes you three minutes to find the Velcro to untab your fly."

"Yeah, but then I have overwhelming firepower."

Jo grinned.

– – – – – –

Kay ran, working her way through the forest. Her com was shut down. Even though it was encrypted, using it would produce a signal that might be detected, and that was more information than she wanted to reveal, and she didn't need to talk to anybody yet.

Yes, they would know enemy scouts were in the woods, but they might be able to determine some kind of location using field-strength metering, and she didn't want to give them anything.

The enemy had ATVs, small single- and double-wheelers, a couple of two-person quads, but no GE or hovercraft— the woods were too thick to operate those safely. Kay's side also had similar vehicles, but she was faster on foot than most of those in a wood this dense.

There was a choke point half a kilometer ahead, a deep stream that would have to be bridged to allow vehicles and troops to move over it quickly. Kay's assignment was to get there as soon as possible and slow the construction of a crossing until more of her own troops could arrive.

Control of the stream was not likely to win the war, but it was a factor.

The enemy had the advantage in that their entrance to the forest was closer, and they should reach the stream first. Control of the forest might be key since the wells themselves were just past the northern edge. It was not critical for Kay's army since their plan was to approach from a different angle; however, it seemed that the opposition had elected to work from this venue.

The rule was simple: If an enemy wanted something, it was generally best to deny it to them if you could.

She heard the hum of gyroscopic motors in the ATVs before she heard the sounds of human engineers. They were at the stream, only a few minutes ahead of her, but they would have support infantry. Not too many, since the limits on combatants were strict, but at least a squad or two, maybe a platoon.

Kay slowed, moved more cautiously, heading for the first-choice spot she had selected on the recon of the area earlier. There were three good vantage points on her side of the stream, and if she could get the first, she would have the best field of fire.

The enemy had two men in the water swimming when she got to her spot, and those were her first targets.

She unslung her weapon.

The unit had computer-assisted-targeting sniper rifles, the CATs were accurate to a thousand meters, and you had to get in its way to miss a human-sized target as far as they could reach. The computer's cam could spot, ID, and paint a target with a tiny dot of light, and all one had to do was point in the approximate direction; the inbuilt gyros would hold the weapon rock-steady. It could be programmed so that you didn't even have to trigger it yourself—it would fire automatically as soon as it was lined up. It would seek the nearest target after that and repeat the process until all the targets were down or it ran empty.

On the other hand, CAT rifles were expensive, heavy, loud, slow, and their tactical choices weren't always correct. Sometimes the target selection was wrong—the computer didn't differentiate between a man with a gun pointed in your general direction and one dialed onto your heart.

Kay was not the best shooter in the unit, but she was certainly adept enough to use a manual weapon at short range effectively, and she trusted her sense of who to deal with better than she did the computer's. Always her choice when it came to machines. A gun might misfire, a claw was always there.

Cutter Colonel left it to her, and she had elected to use a lightweight carbine with a suppressor and simple-glass. At 150, it should be more than enough. She had ranged the sights in practice to this distance, it was a dead-on center hold, and the scope was preset for a cold shot at that range.

The first enemy soldier achieved the near bank of the stream, wading onto the shore, as Kay lay prone and lined up. His armor was minimal—it was hard to swim in Class IV—and even with the suppressor, the restricted hardball should punch through a standard trauma plate. He had his helmet off for the crossing, and she knew the round wouldn't be slowed much by his skull.

She lined the crosshairs up right between his eyes and stroked the trigger.

The sonic boom happened some meters in front of her.

The target's head blew apart.

Even as he fell, she swung the sights to cover the second swimmer, but he was quick and smart. He submerged, still five meters from the bank, leaving ripples in the slow-moving stream.

Kay adjusted the carbine. She knew which way the water flowed, and she had measured the speed. She reasoned that he wouldn't keep swimming toward her, and swimming against the current would take more energy and oxygen, so it made more sense for him to go downstream. He would want to get as far away as possible before he had to come up for air, then he would expose as little of himself as possible. Were it she, she would roll onto her back as she rose and put no more than her nose above the surface. She would have already exhaled, so all she'd have to do would be suck in a fast breath and backstroke herself down again, less than a second, and at best, that would be a nearly impossible shot for an expert. Taking off a nose wouldn't be useful in any event.

Shooting at a target underwater at this shallow an angle was a waste of ammunition. The bullet would skip across the water like a thrown stone.

The soldiers on the other side of the stream began making a lot of noise as they realized their swimmer had been shot. They would be seeking cover, but that didn't matter; from where they were, they weren't a threat unless they knew her position, and they didn't yet . . .

The second swimmer came up, and his mistake was that he didn't roll onto his back but stuck most of his face up.

Kay was almost exactly on target, a couple of centimeters off. She fired again, and immediately rolled to her left, five quick revolutions. She crawled quickly forward, then angled farther to her left.

Either they spotted the suppressed muzzle flash or backwalked it with spotting computer because her former position was raked with full-auto fire. The bullets chewed up the ground and bushes, but she was eight meters away and moving toward her second-choice location.

She didn't have to hit any more of them now, only make them keep their heads down and stop trying to build their bridge.

As she crawled toward the cover of a tree, she glanced at the water.

The second swimmer's body floated downstream.

Enemy troops were dug in.

She toggled her com on. No worry about them knowing she was out here now.

"On-station," she said. "Enemy advance delayed."

– – – – – –

"Park it behind that stone wall, right here," Jo ordered.

"Sah."

A meter-and-a-half-high wall of natural rock surrounded one of the larger houses, a two-story monstrosity that had boarded-up windows and part of the roof on one end collapsed. Somebody had tacked a gray tarp over the sunken section of roof, and there was a small garden planted to the rear of the place, rows of assorted plants, some of which bore green and red fruits or vegetables.

Stone wouldn't stop big artillery, but there wasn't going to be any big artillery, and it would keep small arms and machine-gun rounds at bay.

Singh parked the cart.

The other vehicles moved into their assigned locations, and within a minute, everybody had exited.

The grenadiers scrambled to their positions, and the two mortar teams hurried to set up.

Jo saw the enemy column approaching on the road from the other direction. They were moving fast but by now must know they were beaten. Jo saw several drones crisscrossing the sky over the enemy convoy, some of them theirs, some hers. As she watched, the drones fired at each other, and some shot at the vehicles below. Probably those were hers, but you never knew. Friendly fire—an oxymoron—was always a danger once the war went hot. Excited troops would sometimes shoot at anything that moved without worrying if it was their own.

"Mo?"

"Dialed in, Cap," came the mortar-crew chief's vox.

The weapons had been preset to hit at a certain distance, and the flight time for the shells calculated in. In theory, as soon as the lead vehicle reached a predetermined spot, there would be an explosion waiting for it . . .

As she watched, however, the dozen vehicles on the road below began to split. Several of the smaller ones veered off the road and began evasive maneuvers across the flat dirt, kicking up clouds of dust. The leading vehicles stopped.

"Recalibrating," the mortar CC said.

That would have been too easy, wouldn't it? That they would have just driven right into the hard rain . . .

On com, Jo said: "Who is running our drones?"

"Why, that would be me," Gramps came back.

"I wouldn't be upset if you stitched that lead APC some before it gets to those oak trees."

"Your wish is my command."

He was dozens of klicks away, but that didn't matter; you could run a drone from halfway around the planet and then some—hardly any appreciable time lag at such short ranges.

Jo watched one of the drones bank and zoom to follow the APC bouncing across the scrub toward a grove of pin oak trees nine hundred meters south of the hill.

A second friendly drone peeled away from the air-to-air shooting to circle around from the opposite direction.

The lead drone's light machine guns blinked, the sound arriving a few seconds later, and the bullets thunked and spanged off the vehicle's top armor. It kept going.

"Help if you would hit the sucker," Gunny said.

"I *am* hitting it, open your ears! It's the crappy low-powered ammo."

The second drone came in from the front and opened up, and either clouded the windshield or busted it. The APC slewed to a stop in a mushroom of reddish dust.

"Gotcha!" Gramps said.

The drone went into a hover and continued to fire for a couple of seconds, but then a thin tracer line arced up from the ground below and connected with the drone, which blew up in a spew of fire and pieces.

"G2A," Gunny said. "Under the size limit."

"Big enough," Jo said.

"Might want to hose 'em before they get the other one," Gunny said.

"Teach your grandfather how to use a fork," Gramps said.

The second drone chattered.

Jo accessed the drone's feed on her heads-up. The troops were out of the carrier and moving under the cover of the dust though the drone's IR saw them just fine. Eighteen, twenty, still on their feet. They were shooting at the drone with carbines, and another G2A rocket went up—

"You'll want to move your aircraft—" Jo began.

Too late. Even as Gramps banked the drone, it blew into incandescent smithereens.

"Well, shit," Gramps said. "Hope Rags doesn't take that out of my pay."

"Gunny?"

"Ah'm already on the way."

Gunny led two squads a short jaunt to the viewpoint. She had twelve riflemen, one light machine gun, a rocket launcher, and two grenadiers. Somebody had put a steel bench there, on a carved-flat section of ground next to the path that wound down the hill. A place to sit and rest, watch the sunrise, maybe. Probably they never figured it would be used by an army to cover enemy infantry coming up the side . . .

"Make some noise," Gunny said.

The grenadiers unshipped their launchers, 6x40mm Milkor M9s. Built like old-fashioned revolvers, they were reliable, cheap, and accurate, effective to four hundred meters with the ammo they were being allowed.

They started shooting, multiple small explosions followed, and anybody down there who thought they were just going to storm the hill and kick ass had a fast change of heart.

"Gunny?"

"Ain't nobody coming up unannounced, Cap."

"You need any help?"

"Sheeit."

Gunny raised her carbine, spotted somebody a hundred meters down who poked his head up. Bad move on his part.

She didn't smile as he fell, but she felt pretty good. The war had begun, and this was what she did. They had this under control. This was why she got up in the morning.

Jo shook her head. This was not a com she was happy to hear.

"A hurricane?"

Gramps said, "Yep. Churning along in the Gulf of Mexico and all of a sudden headed right in our direction."

"I don't recall seeing that in our background briefing."

"Because it wasn't. Our field of battle is just over 160 from the Gulf, and even storms that move directly this way tend to fall apart when they hit land. Generally, this results in some breezes and a lot of rain dumping in a short time, nothing an anchored spray-frame igloo can't handle."

"But . . . ?"

"But the bad weather that was heading south of here took a turn in our direction. They give them names here, and Hurricane Bruce is a Category 5 storm, which means it is as big and bad as they get. At the moment, there are winds gusting to 275 kilometers an hour near the center, and if it continues on its present course, it will start raining and blowing here in twenty-four hours. It will slow as it reaches land, but it will have enough momentum to pack a hefty punch by the time the eye reaches us. Sustained winds of 150 kph, gusts to 185 or so. Plus the odd tornado spun off there and there."

"Wonderful. Whatever happened to the promise of weather control?"

"Well, they managed to halt global warming but not reverse it, and the technology for preventing these kinds of storms is iffy at best. Sometimes it works, sometimes not. Once a hurricane or typhoon gets this well organized, it is, pardon the expression, pissing into the wind to try and break it up. Too much power to stop."

She didn't say anything to that.

"Hey, it's not my fault, I didn't do it. When we got here, it was a tropical depression two thousand klicks away; nobody knew it was going to do what it did. The predictions were wrong."

She shook her head. "Crap."

"Well, the rain falleth on the just and unjust alike."

She nodded. That was true. Whatever problems it caused them, it would also cause the enemy; still, bad weather could be worse than anything the other side could throw at you.

"Are these houses up here structurally safe?"

"For the weather coming at us? In a word, no."

"Okay. We'll set up the igloos."

TEN

The heat of the day was little abated by darkness; near midnight, and still hovering around body temperature, plus the humidity must have been near 90 percent. Hot and muggy, and the threatened rain that might have cooled things off passed well north of them. Gunny saw the flashes in the distance, but the thunder didn't reach this far.

Of course, there was more rain on the way, according to Gramps. Big rain. Come the morrow, the field of battle was going to get soggy.

She'd held off eating until her watch was over. Field rats were never a reason to look forward to supper.

Her choices had been soy-chicken à la king, saitan beefsteak, or pasta with red sauce. Or the classic favorite, mock-tuna potpie. She had gone with the saitan. It wasn't the tastiest faux-meat in the galaxy, but it had a real texture.

She came off her watch to find Singh tucking into his own field rations, eating as if it was the best thing he'd ever tasted.

"You *like* that shit?"

He smiled around a mouthful of something not quite recognizable. "Sah. When I was in the army at home, the joke was that if the choice was between our field meals and our boots, the boots would cook faster and taste better. Compared to that? This is a gourmet dinner."

Gunny laughed.

Jo drifted over.

"Hey, Cap. You want a bite of delicious fake steak?"

"Thank you, no. My pasta is still deciding if it is going to send me to the latrine with the FR runs. What Rags buys for us to eat is probably surplus from that war for the Alamo, back in the day. I think there was some dinosaur in mine."

The house turned out to be in pretty good shape. Whoever had squatted there had taken good care of it. The interior walls had been painted in the last couple of years, the floors were clean, no trash piled up. There wasn't any running water, nor electricity, but the outhouse out back wasn't too bad. Except for the one section of collapsed roof covered with a tarp that kept the rain out, it seemed sound. But the air circulation was for crap. Even with all the boarded windows and doors swung open, it was like an oven in there.

They could have rigged one of the vehicle ACs to pump cold air into the house, make it easier to sleep, maybe, but that would take a lot of fuel, and that wouldn't solve the problem of walking outside and getting hit in the face with the heat. Better to acclimate yourself to the climate and live with it. Moving from a cool building into a hot summer and back was bad for the respiratory system. Contributed to lung and sinus problems, least that's what Wink said.

Of course, so was breathing gun smoke and fuel exhaust. Plus the storm coming in would get here tomorrow and start cooling things off. Assuming they were still here.

Jo said, "Remind me again of why we do this?" She waved at the hot night.

Gunny grinned. The insect repeller's hum was low and constant, but it did keep the mosquitoes at bay, mostly.

Step outside the repeller's field, and the little vampires would be all over you, even with the confuse 'em patches. You would think somebody here in the cradle of human civilization would have figured out how to get rid of mosquitoes by now, but apparently no matter what they tried, there were always bugs that didn't get the memo. *Mate with that sterile male? No, thank you, I don't like his looks. Death hormone in the DNA? We'll evolve our own. Poison? Yum!* Now and then, one got past the repellers, too. Too stupid to die out . . .

Gunny said, "The glory, the adventure, the chance to travel the galaxy and meet exotic people and aliens!"

Jo laughed. "I remember that recruiting earworm. Always a new batch of young and ignorant cannon fodder stepping up. The road to victory is paved with newbs."

Gunny chewed on a bite of the meat substitute. This particular delight had a consistency somewhat like warm rubber, but with half the taste. She set the FR plate on the foldout bench next to her, drank tepid, but pure, water from the vacon bottle. Now there was a useful, and mostly workable piece of technology, and one that performed all the better for the high humidity. It condensed pure water from the vapor in air, and would fill itself to capacity here in twenty or thirty minutes. In a desert, it would take an hour or longer to do the same, but as long as there was any moisture in the atmosphere at all, it would work. Solar and motion powered a rechargeable e-cell battery good for what, thirty years? And the failure rate on the things was near zero.

Drink it dry and pretty soon, you'd have a fresh liter of water anywhere you went, long as you didn't lose the sucker. One of the first things you learned to do was keep track of your water bottle. Drink, stick it back into the belt holder. Whoever invented this must have made a fortune. Gunny took another sip and raised her bottle in a silent salute. Then she holstered the flask.

Too bad the wick-away-moisture clothes didn't work as

well. Fungal infections were always lurking on hot and wet battlefields, even with the chems circulating.

There's a fungus among us, and he noshes on our crotches . . .

Crickets sawed away in the darkness, and Gunny remembered that there was some kind of formula connected to the speed of their noise and the temperature. Hotter it was, the quicker the chirps, but she couldn't remember the numbers. Didn't matter. She knew hot when she felt it.

"Anything new?" Gunny asked.

"Nope. We're up here, the enemy is down there. We have the hill, they want it, and each of us has enough troops to make the swap unlikely. They'll probably bring up reinforcements, we'll bring up ours. Maybe somebody starts shooting, then we see how it goes. Simple. We've had a lot worse duty."

"Maybe we should build a campfire and roast something, tell old war stories," Gunny said.

"Right, give them a focus for a heat-seeker if they want to try one. Not to mention warming up the night more than it already is."

"Our part of the glorious war."

"I talked to Gramps," Jo said. "He's still poking around the whole thing with the Bax."

Gunny shook her head. "Why is it lately that no matter where we go, there is some kinda fucking *intrigue* we have to deal with? Can't we have just a plain old shooting battle where all we have to do is drill holes and take names? All this wheels-within-wheels shit gets old."

"Man proposes, God disposes," Singh said.

Both fems looked at him. He shrugged. "Whenever you run into a situation that you cannot control, we on Ananda often find it convenient to blame it on God."

Both fems grinned. Jo said, "You don't sound like much of a believer, Singh."

"Sah, I was, when I was young. One only needs spend a short time looking around to find examples of ugliness that no benevolent god would reasonably allow. Faith falters in the living of life."

"But the gods don't work by the same rules as people," Gunny said, "so we can't understand their bigger picture."

"An old argument, sah. If we are but insects in the sight of a god, then there is no point in our worshipping or trying to understand them. If they exist, I cannot see them as anything remotely like us. The priests might believe they can translate to the rest of us, but I cannot believe it. Not to offend any beliefs you might have."

Jo chuckled. "Contrary to the old saying, there *are* plenty of atheists in foxholes. Gunny and I haven't spent a lot of time in temple or church."

"You look thoughtful, Singh. Somethin' else?"

He looked at her. "I was wondering if you were going to eat the rest of that?"

Gunny laughed. She handed him the FR. "Have at it, my young philosopher."

– – – – – –

Once her support troops arrived, there was no need for Kay to remain at the stream. Her side's troops could patrol the area, and until the opposition decided to send more of their soldiers, if they did, crossing the little waterway would be a losing proposition.

Kay faded back into the trees and began a steady trot away from the site.

Much of war consisted of holding strategic territory, and sometimes, an hour or two was sufficient to tip the balance your way. An entire battle could turn on a single action, a second faster, a bullet dodged, a claw deflected.

There was a different smell in the air. Distant rain? That would go with the forecast Demonde Captain had tendered earlier. A storm. It had been too long since she had defied a storm . . .

She had accomplished her mission and could return to base and rest if she wished. She didn't need rest; there had been no great output of energy required. She would instead find another action to attend. If Jo Captain was involved in such, she would join her.

As she worked her way back toward her chosen exit from the forest, she suddenly caught a scent she recognized.

The male Vastalimi. Not far.

She slowed. This was not a sector controlled by the enemy. What was he doing here?

Curiosity was not as strong a trait among her kind as it was humans, but still. One of her kind, perhaps the only other of her kind on this world?

She had to go and look.

- - - - - -

Kay stepped into the clearing carefully though she knew that the male knew she was there.

He waited until she was twenty meters away before he turned around. He did it slowly and made no move toward his holstered pistol, his hands wide of his body, claws retracted, to show his lack of killing intent.

Her own rifle was slung, her pistol holstered.

He was tall, well muscled, his fur lustrous and thick, and his body set balanced.

"Ah," he said. "At last. I scented you earlier." He spoke in *Govor*, which was her own first language. It was not the most common tongue among The People.

They were from the same region? Interesting.

"And I you," she said. "I am *Kluth*fem. My humans call me 'Kay.'"

"*Grey*masc," he said. "You want family history?"

"Not necessary, given the circumstances."

"Agreed."

He paused, then said, "There was another fem. I understand she died."

"As did the one who killed her."

He nodded. "That one has not been found."

"Good luck with that."

They regarded each other. She caught a hint of his musk, and it indicated . . . *interest* . . .

Kay was a long way from Vast, and outside of a brief, if enjoyable liaison with Wink Doctor, she'd had no sexual contact with another for quite some time. Her last lover on the homeworld, Jak, had been satisfactory in that regard, but that had ended badly for other reasons.

She felt her own hormones rise. Too bad this male was with the enemy. Good that she was downwind, so he didn't catch her own interest . . .

"You have been with your humans long?" he asked.

"Some years."

"I have been with mine but a few months. They respect my abilities, but that is overlaid with fear and suspicion."

"Sad for you."

He shrugged. "We are hired claws. Outlanders among aliens. It is the way of such."

"I regard my humans as family."

"Really? How delightful for you."

For some reason, that statement resonated well. She felt compelled to tell him a personal truth: "When I left Vast, it was because I was considered a troublemaker. I made political waves. I did not expect to be with family again. It has been an unexpected reward."

"Then we have something else in common. Few were unhappy to see me depart the homeworld. Well-adjusted People don't leave Vast, do they?"

"Mostly not, no," she said.

He smiled. "So here we are, two malcontents working as warriors for a species not our own, and on opposite sides of a conflict. Sad for both of us, given the rarity of our kind out here. It precludes more . . . pleasant activity."

She matched his smile. "My mother warned me about smooth-tongued males like you."

"I should hope so. Tell me, how do you see this conflict?"

"Brief, bloody, and our side victorious."

He laughed. "A fem after my own heart! I can agree with the first two, but I wonder why you offer the third, save for a general optimism?"

Sharp, this one. She said, "I have been in many engagements with my humans. They are more adept than most. There have been times when outright victory escaped us, but we have not lost outright, either."

"Ah. I cannot say the same. Mine are not particularly inept, but they have sometimes performed less than optimally. Still, win or lose, I get paid."

"No victory bonus?"

"Yes, but the rate without that is sufficient. Why would I need more?"

She nodded. A sensible attitude. She liked that.

"I take their pay, I serve to my ability," he said. "Yet I confess that, even having just met you, I find in this moment that I would feel somewhat . . . bereft if I had to kill you."

"I would strive to keep you from such misery, so far away from home."

He laughed. "Oh, a fem with a sense of humor is a jewel beyond measure!" He regarded her for another moment. "Will you offer *prigovor*?"

She considered it. She didn't want to kill him, either, even though it would be to the Cutters benefit. "Not at this time," she said.

"Good. Nor shall I. Perhaps if we both survive this conflict, we might speak again, when we are not paid enemies?"

"I would like that," she said. And she found that notion to be a happy one. Something about him . . .

"As would I. Survive, *Kluth*fem."

"Survive, *Grey*masc."

He turned and padded away from the clearing. He definitely moved well.

Jo felt as much as she heard or smelled Kay when she arrived. That the Vastalimi could wend her way past enemy sentries outfitted with spookeyes or EV augs was no surprise.

That she got past *their* sentries unnoticed pissed her off.

"Don't we have anybody on fucking guard duty?"

Kay said, "I did not think it necessary to disturb them."

"Yeah. Don't worry, I'll disturb them later."

The hunters on Vast were considerably more adept than humans. Ghosts in the night.

"Well, it's still good to see you."

"And I you, Jo Captain."

Dawn was still a couple of hours away. "You came from the other end of the area?"

Kay shrugged. "No more than a dozen kilometers. Not much of a run."

Jo imaged making that trip at a jog in a fur coat. She shook her head.

"I have news," Kay said.

Jo caught the quick flash of a smile.

"Yes?"

"It concerns the male Vastalimi. We met, he and I, in the forest."

"Really?"

"Yes."

"And . . . ?"

"And . . . what?"

"Come on, fem. He's probably the only male of your species for a dozen parsecs. What did he look like? How did he carry himself? How was his musk?"

"He looked like a male. He walked on two legs as we all do. His musk . . . well, it was sufficiently masculine."

Jo shook her head. "I know you aren't that dense!"

Kay grinned. "His name is *Grey*masc. We spoke for only a short time. He was . . . not unattractive. He laughed at my joke. He allowed that he would feel bad if he had to kill me. He moved well."

"All that?" Jo paused. "When is the wedding?"

Kay regarded Jo as if her skin had shifted to flaming purple. "Wedding?"

" 'Not unattractive,' you said. With a sense of humor? And he moves well? Sex, at the very least? Tell me the thought never crossed your mind."

Kay grinned again. "I cannot tell you it did not. And it was . . . not an unattractive notion."

Jo laughed. "Life is short, fem. You need to make hay while the sun shines."

"I don't understand the metaphor."

"Claw while the prey is in reach."

"Ah." Kay laughed. "Perhaps if he survives. It would not do for us to . . . do anything while we are on opposite sides of a conflict."

"Okay. I won't kill him if you won't."

They smiled.

ELEVEN

It was late, just past midnight. Cutter was crossing the quad when he felt the pressure—somebody was watching him.

It was a public space, lots of troops went back and forth between the camp's buildings at all hours, so somebody noticing him wasn't a big deal, but this was different.

Somebody was *watching* him. With *intent*.

There were plenty of people who didn't believe you could do that, sense somebody watching you, but he had learned to trust that feeling over the years. It wasn't always right, but it was right more often than not.

He kept walking. He raised his left arm and pretended to look at his ring chronometer, but instead did a quick and surreptitious scan ahead and to his left. He stopped, as if he had suddenly remembered something. Shook his head, as if in irritation at himself, turned around, to the right, and took in what he could see that way.

Nothing amiss. He headed back toward the HQ module. Nobody else in sight, and he had done a 270-degree scan.

Either they were hidden, too far away to see, or in that last quadrant, now to his right front.

He flicked a glance that way . . .

There. Was that a hint of movement, in the shadow of the cantina?

The pub closed at 2330, and the building was dark; no light spilled from the windows.

The camp lamps on eight-meter-tall poles bathed the compound in a functional, if not all that bright, yellowish glow, save for a brown corona around the LEDs themselves. A few moths or other night insects who didn't realize they weren't supposed to see and be attracted to the glow flitted around them, casting fuzzy, pale shadows of themselves here and there.

It was more that he felt a presence than saw it.

In another five meters, he would be as close to where he thought somebody was as he was going to get; after that, his back would be toward the spot, and of a moment, he knew if that happened, somebody was going to try for him.

Knew it, absolutely sure.

Who was it? An enemy infiltrator? Somebody come to take the head off the opposition's leader?

Should he wait and see? Was his ability to track and shoot enough to beat somebody firing first from less than ten meters away, if that was what they intended?

Was anybody even there? Was he seeing ghosts in the night?

Something changed, something in the air, what he couldn't have said. He didn't see anything, he didn't hear anything, but he didn't wait—he snatched his pistol from its hip holster, thrust it toward the darkness under the cantina's overhang, and fired three rounds—*pop-pop-pop!* moving his wrist a hair between the shots, left to right, drawing a line. At this range, it would be a spread just under half a meter where the missiles would impact.

"Fuck!" somebody screamed.

Muzzle blasts sparked in the darkness, but even as he dived and rolled to his right, he knew those shots went high and to his left—

—Cutter landed prone, the Willis 4.4 lined up on the place where the shooter's muzzle had been. He fired five more times, tracking from chest height at a slight angle to the left and downward, in case the shooter had ducked—

Somebody started yelling "Who goes there!" and "Show yourself!" behind him.

Their guards.

Cutter lay quietly, waiting.

Somebody punched in the crisis lighting, and the compound lit up like it was daytime.

There was a body on the ground under the cantina's overhang.

Cutter voxaxed his command com onto the night's opchan. "This is Colonel Cutter. I'm prone on the ground eight meters from the cantina's front window, don't spike me. There's a shooter down next to the building. He's probably out of it, but approach with caution. Shooter might not be alone."

He waited, and pretty quickly, a quad moved toward the cantina, carbines leveled.

They bracketed the downed shooter. One of the guards moved in carefully, bent to examine the shooter.

"DOA," the guard's voice came, both over the com and through the warm night air.

Cutter stood, pistol still in hand.

He felt somebody come up behind him.

"An assassin?" Gramps.

"So it would seem."

"Guards are doing a perimeter check."

"I hope they do a better job than last time. Find anybody, try to bring them in alive."

Cutter moved over to look at the dead man.

Nobody he recognized. The man lay on his right side, blood from multiple wounds on his torso and neck pooling on the ground, a silenced pistol near his outstretched hand.

Wink arrived, half-dressed, carrying a medical bag. "Somebody need a doctor?"

"Not unless you have a miracle in your sack of tricks," Cutter said.

Wink bent and looked at the corpse. He did something with a small reader. "Three . . . four . . . five, maybe a key-hole . . . I count six hits. How many times did you shoot?"

"Eight."

"Getting old, Rags."

"Bracketing, you miss some. Better safe than sorry."

"Do we know who this is?"

"Never saw him before, I know of."

Gramps said, "I-team says the perimeter is clear. Who's the dead guy?"

"Don't know."

"He aiming at you in particular?"

"I think so. I think he meant to backshoot me. I spotted him before he could."

"Got any enemies?" Wink said. He smiled.

Cutter smiled back.

Gramps came round. "You get a DNA?"

"Already logged into the system," Wink replied. "No immediate comeback, so he's not one of the opposition's registered."

"And yet, who would want to see our commander dead more than they?"

"The list is probably fairly long," Cutter said.

"Piss off anybody lately?" Wink asked.

Cutter and Gramps exchanged looks. Gramps picked it up: "Junior."

Wink looked up. "Junior?"

Cutter said, "I'll fill you in later."

The I-team leader joined conversation oncom: "We got a shielded fuel-cell trike outside the fence. Probably what our visitor rode here on. I will check local records."

"Stet that," Cutter said.

Well. Never a dull moment.

— — — — —

The sweep came up empty. If there had been anybody else, he or she was gone, and there was no sign of another trike, so it would seem to be just the one shooter.

Wink told them there was no record on Earth of the shooter's DNA, at least not one they could access, and he wasn't carrying anything that would ID him. Interesting, and moderately impossible. You couldn't move around on Earth without leaving a trail, and if you were from offworld, there should be an entry tag somewhere.

No match to the dead guy existed. Which meant he was protected by somebody.

Gramps said, "Could be some kind of sub-rosa op, shielded identity."

Cutter nodded.

"I wouldn't think Junior would have any trouble importing a killer without leaving a trail."

"Probably not."

"You'd think he'd offer you a little more respect by hiring a better one," Gramps said.

"Given how things went back on Morandan, maybe not. He caught me flat-footed."

"We don't know it's Junior. Could be the opposition. Or an old enemy."

"Could be."

"You don't sound too worried."

"He missed, I didn't."

"They might send somebody better next time."

Cutter shrugged. "Or not. See if it happens."

- - - - - -

"Captain?"

Jo came awake at once. Her internal clock told her it was 0320. The sodden night smelled of mold and moths, which, until she'd had olfactory augmentation, she'd never known, that moths had a kind of . . . powdery-rot odor.

It was Singh. "Yeah?"

"Pradar op says we have aircraft incoming."

Jo stood, stretched, moved to the craft's computer board. She called the pradar op even as she toggled the image onto her control screen.

"Hey, Prop, what do we have?"

He said, "Two craft, masked sig and stealthed, but from the size and speed, I'm guessing troop copters, probably Howard 120s."

Jo nodded to herself. H-120s would carry eighteen troopers with chutes or twelve with flysuits. If they could drop two dozen on top of them, that would make things interesting.

"They have to know we know they are there," Jo said. "Reach out, Prop, see if there's anybody else flying our way."

"That's a negative out to one hundred klicks, Cap."

"Stay alert. Let me know if anything shows up."

Jo opened the command opchan. "Heads up, people. If you haven't already noticed, we have enemy aircraft approaching. The G2A spikes are ready to go, and we'll hold off until they are close enough so they can't duck 'em; but meanwhile, everybody scans everything else, this might be a decoy."

H-120s were slow; unless the enemy had some way of stopping tight-beam-guided ground-to-air missiles, they would be easy targets once they were within range, and they almost were there. They couldn't get close enough to drop parachutists that could reach 'em unless they were a lot higher, and the missiles could stretch to an H-120's ceiling.

If, however, they were carrying troops in flysuits, they'd drop them before they got within missile reach. The suits— essentially stubby wings with small turbojet engines—were slow, had a short range, and were harder targets. The fliers could drop into the ground clutter and be hard to spot on pradar or Doppler. This was risky, since the controls weren't all that precise on issue flysuits, and if you leaned crooked at two meters up, you'd auger into the ground at speed or bounce along the dirt like a stone skips on water; still, trained troops might get to a target without being shot down. It was something to worry about.

"Cap, they are holding just outside maximum range, and I'm getting e-chaff."

Jo noticed on her own scope. "So they are using flysuits."

"That's my guess."

Be a waste of missiles trying to spike those, Jo knew. They might snag a few, but their standard G2A systems weren't rigged for cold, human-sized targets.

"All stations, expect troops in flysuits incoming."

"Oh, boy, wingshooting!" That was Gunny.

Jo shook her head. Time to go outside and have a look.

"Inbound," somebody said. "The leader is eleven hundred meters out, speed . . . 180."

The machine guns had enough onboard brain to calculate the lead. An ape could hit them if he pushed the right button.

"Targets of opportunity," Jo said. She scanned the skies. Her optics were first-class, but she didn't see anybody yet.

"Soon as you can hit them."

"I got four more, I think," another voice said. "Oops. One of them disappeared. Bad flying."

"That just means the more dangerous ones are still coming," Jo said.

The first machine gun opened up.

Jo saw the tracers zipping up from the emplacement into the night.

"Leader is down," the gunner said. "The next three have separated—"

"—and the one farthest north is mine," Gunny said. "Come on . . . come to Mama . . . Gotcha!"

The second machine gun chattered; more red streaks arced through the darkness.

That shooter must have put a round into one of the fly-suit's engine intakes; there was a small flash of orange light as the engine blew, followed a few seconds later by a screech of metal tearing.

Time that sound got to Jo, that flier would already be dining on dirt.

More carbines fired. Even if the suits had been pradar-shielded, which they weren't, troops on the ground wearing spookeyes could see them well enough.

And if Jo were one of the fliers, right about now, she'd be tossing some kind of photonic to make shooters on the ground blink—

The thought was the deed: Photon flares on glide foils erupted, lighting up the sky. That made the nightscope shutters automatically shield, but it also gave plenty of illumination for naked eyes to see the fliers, a couple of which were no more than five hundred meters out.

Jo raised her carbine. She didn't use the sights, but let her training tell her where to point. Human brains were exceedingly accurate when it came to tracking motion. When it felt right, the position of her weapon's muzzle and that of the target, she pulled the trigger and let go a full-auto blast, fifteen rounds, continuing to track the target without conscious thought.

Years back, she'd taken a seminar given by a professional trick shooter. Don't think, the woman had said, just feel. There will be a connection between you and the target, and once you feel it, fire. Have that, you won't miss.

That woman could borrow a ring from somebody in the audience, put a paper sticker over the opening, toss it into the air, and thread it with a pistol round without scratching the ring. As far as Jo could tell, the trick shooter didn't have a single aug running, which made it even more amazing.

Her target didn't slow, but it changed direction and flew into the ground.

"Where *you* goin', birdboy?" Gunny's voice came over the com. "Nobody excused you! Eat this!"

Somebody said, "Cap, I think we got a couple made it to the ground, south side, on the hill."

Kay seemed to materialize from nowhere. "I will check," she said.

Jo nodded. "Go." If there were a couple of enemy soldiers there, they'd be shedding their suits and looking for cover or a way up. Kay was on it, and Jo wasn't worried about a threat from there . . .

"Captain, the H-120s are making a run."

"What? That's idiotic!" Jo said, half to herself.

Might be remotely controlled and full of explosives. That would be spendy, but it could make a big enough bang to draw attention away from the incoming flysuiters.

"Spike 'em as soon as you can," Jo said.

The first copter blew ten seconds later, and it was indeed a big boom. The light turned the night into noon for a brief moment, and the sound, when it got there, was a lot more than a G2A missile and a fuel tank would make.

"We have the big birds," Jo said. "Don't let the little ones get past!"

A second later, the second Howard exploded, with equally bright and loud results.

Seemed like a lot of sound and fury for what they had to know wouldn't amount to much. Why?

Assuming stupidity on the part of an enemy was seldom the safest way to bet. It might be the case—she had seen a lot of foolish enemies—but you were much wiser to go with the notion that the enemy wouldn't make any bonehead moves. If they did, that was good, it was a gift, but if they didn't, and you were ready, you were much better off.

There were a lot of people run through the military crematoriums who had underestimated their enemies.

The copters and the fliers were low-percentage attacks, and anybody with any experience had to know that. And if they did, what were they really up to?

"We have incoming rockets," the prop said. "G2G from down the hill."

"AR spikes auto-launched," the prop continued. "They are wasting a lot of ammo. They ain't gonna get shit that way."

"That's what I want to hear," Jo said.

As dawn approached, the theater was quiet. Whatever the enemy had intended from the three-prong attack, they had indeed been wasting their ammo. No casualties on CFI's side, and at least a few of the enemy were pushing up daisies, and probably more decorating a surgical suite in the flatlands.

Jo called base. Gramps was up, and he took the com. She filled him in.

"Why are you awake, aren't you off duty until 0700?"

"Had a little ruckus here. Somebody sneaked onbase to take a shot at Rags."

She felt a sudden stab of alarm, but before she could ask, he said, "Rags shot first, no problem. Well, except that the guy is dead, and we can't question him."

"Junior," she said.

"That thought had crossed our minds. And since the shooter was not particularly adept, that makes it an even better guess—Junior is not the sharpest blade in the drawer, and cheap, too."

"Crap. We don't need Rags getting tagged."

"We will take better care of him in the future. You might want to get some sleep. The weather guys are a half step slow—you are gonna get rained on pretty soon. If you aren't battened down yet, better get that way. Noon on, you are going to get wet, and come dark, really wet. By midnight, you are apt to be blown off the hill, you aren't tied to something."

"Great."

"A soldier's lot is not always a happy one. Want a couple verses of 'Field Rat Blues'?"

> *I got the field rat blues, baby, got diarrhea runnin'*
> *into my shoes*
> *Yeah I got the field rat blues, baby—*

"Seal it," she said. "It's too close to the truth. I'm the poster girl for Immodium now."

"Sorry."

"Right. You're thinking, 'Better her than me,' aren't you?"

"Not I."

"Liar."

"I'm gonna see if I can get Formentara to install one of them mind-reading augs in me, too."

"Careful, it has a bad side effect; you can read minds, but you also have to tell the truth."

He laughed. "I'm workin' the FCV starting tomorrow night," he said, "so I'll be a little closer to the action. Stay dry, Jo."

"Stet that."

TWELVE

Bright and early, Gramps cranked up the shielded lines and made some calls.

"Ah, the infamous Junior Allen," the speaker on the other end of the shielded com said. "'The Butcher of Morandan,' though if you say that aloud in public, his lawyers will be on you like stink on a spooked skunk."

Gramps smiled. He hadn't heard that simile in a while.

The speaker, Max Tigre, had retired from the GU Army and moved into private military intelligence twenty-some years past. They went way back; Max had been a sergeant when Gramps had started basic training, and he had to be at least seventy-five by now. The heuristic was, anybody who had fifteen years on you? They were old . . .

"How's the Chapman Stick going?" Max asked.

"I do my daily diligence. You still paying squeezebox in that bar band?"

"Now and again."

Max was an accordion player in a Norteña Espacio band that had a chart hit a few years back, a little ditty about narcotic traffickers working the lanes around Jupiter's moons.

"So, tell me what else you know about Junior."

"Not much. He's idling a peacetime command here until they can force him to retire," Max said. "Anybody with two neurons to spark at each other knew it was Junior's fuck-up, and that Rags took the hit for it. Knowing and proof aren't the same, but the uplevels put a black mark next to Junior's name, and those don't ever go away. He's had a completely undistinguished career since, a series of do-nothing stations, shuffling equipment and guarding empty bases, like that. Along the way, there were some questionable activities out in the boonies where nobody was looking over his shoulder. A little nest-padding, some troops complained of poor treatment. I think the current post is probably the best he's had in ten years, and it's only because they can keep a better eye on him here."

"If it was that well-known, I'm surprised nobody from Morandan has made a run at him."

"Oh, they have. Couple–three times we know for sure, somebody took a shot or threw a bomb his way. He doesn't go outside much, and when he does, he's armored up the ass, with bodyguards left, right, and center. Closest anybody got was a piece of shrapnel in his back, but it was minor. He was running pretty good when the grenade went off; took out a couple of his guards, and that because he was well ahead of them, and gaining. Got a Purple Heart for that, go figure.

"He doesn't travel anywhere that isn't cleared these days, and you need an engraved invitation to get in to see him if he doesn't know you personally. Must be kind of funny to see a full-security sweep of a locked-tight warehouse full of tents and sleeping bags before Junior will set foot in it. Man has to look over his shoulder taking a piss in the base latrine."

Gramps said, "Not much chance a sniper will plug him out taking a stroll?"

"Not much chance, no. You thinking about it?"

"Me? Why, no, that would be illegal."

Max laughed. "The GU Army is letting him fade away, Roy. You know how they are; better to let all that stuff stay swept under the rug than risk big sneezes trying to clean it up. Another few years, Junior will find himself in command of a barren moon somewhere where the sun don't shine, and he'll get tired of it and put in his papers. They'll let him go with an HD, he'll collect his pension, end of story.

"Eventually, everybody directly connected to the slaughter on Morandan will die off, and it'll be another bit of ugly military history that'll get spun in the texts as an unfortunate event laid to the fog of war."

"Yeah, but in the meantime, Junior can be a pain in somebody's ass."

"He make any threats at Rags?"

"Nothing actionable. He's watching, looking for a reason to stomp us. If we are careful not to give him one, he'll invent one. We'd rather not worry about him backstabbing us while we are in a shooting war on the ground down here in Tejas."

"In your boots, I'd feel the same way. But I don't see a lot you can do. He'd have to make an illegal move in your direction, and it would have to be documented out the wazoo. They won't want to act on it no matter what you have because that means opening an old can of worms nobody wants to look into. Unless he murders the GU Military Commander on the front steps of HQ in front of a hundred witnesses and the evening news cams, they ain't gonna do shit."

"I hear you."

"I wish I could help."

"You did, Max. Never hurts to have a little more intel."

After they discommed, Gramps thought about it. About what he expected, given the flow of history. They were going to have to come up with a way to deal with Junior, and that might be difficult. Difficult wasn't impossible, though.

He stood, stretched, and walked outside into the already-warm and sunny morning.

The sun wasn't going to last, though.

Scudding clouds raced across the sky, and it was darker to the south and east. Looked as if that hurricane was arriving.

Well, a good soldier could stand a little rain and breezes.

- - - - - -

The Base Medical Trauma Suite was fully functional, everything humming along as it should. It had eighteen beds, room for another dozen gurneys, and six D&T full-ride units. That wasn't the same as having six live doctors, but with the diagnose-and-treat systems running, the supervising medic could monitor and deal with problems the meddins couldn't manage, which, truth be known, weren't apt to be many for combat injuries. There were only so many ways soldiers got hurt during a battle in a gravity well. People got shot, electrocuted, cut, burned, sometimes gassed, hit with shrapnel, injured by explosives. There were vehicle accidents. Troops might get otic or ocular damage, induction-neuritis, sonic CNS shock. Now and again, somebody would OD, drown, fall off a building, or step in a hole and break a leg. The dins could deal medically and surgically with most such patients, and certainly triage them so he could attend the worst first.

Hell, most of the time, the place could be run by a couple of orderlies who were smart enough to load patients into the D&Ts. The units were automatic, self-regulating, and if they couldn't handle something, would flash and beep until somebody came to help.

Wink did another system check, but that was unnecessary. He was antsy.

He was also bored.

Yes, the medics would probably be transporting wounded his way soon enough. Plus field medicine had continued to advance. Trauma that would have killed people even ten years ago could now often be stabilized for transport, and once he got them here, Wink and the dins could save most of them. Every conflict was different, of course, but his numbers were good: Assuming they didn't bleed out or have irreparable CNS damage when they arrived, Wink could cut-and-paste 'em back together well enough to achieve a 93.7 percent survival rate for those not too far gone. There might be combat doctors who were better, but they would be few and far between.

The action had just begun, and so far, nobody had been hurt bad enough to get sent here; the medics had patched what had been minor injuries and sent soldiers back to work. That probably wouldn't last, but in a shooting war that only ran a week, and with his responsibility limited mostly to a short company of CFI troops? It might not ever heat up.

Of course, he was overflow for the other units; if their stations got filled, he'd deal with that, but sometimes, there were a lot of shots fired but not so many people hit. Didn't speak well for training, but it did make for a snooze at work.

His com chirped: "Doc?"

The sig said it was Dolan, one of the medics.

"Go ahead."

"I got a man tripped a flying fryer. He's stable, vitals are good, but his left side is cooked pretty good—arm, torso, upper thigh, and hip, 15 percent second-degree; maybe 3 percent full-thickness third; got a 5cm-diameter fourth char on the iliac crest. Medical hopper just picked him up, ETA nine minutes."

"Stet that, Dolan. Why so long?"

"Weather is getting nasty out here. Nancy says slow and steady is better than plowing up dirt."

"Copy that."

"Meds are 0.4 Keph IM, multicillin 500, and antishock single dose, IV push. I'm uploading the file now."

Wink had moved to look at the medcomp, and the flow of information from the field popped up onto the holoproj. Respiration, heart rate, blood pressure. All pretty good for a patient who just got flamed by an antipersonnel mine. "Got it. Good work."

"Yeah, and best I get back to it. Discom."

Wink didn't much like burns. When he'd been doing his burn-unit rotation back in the day, he'd had a patient who'd been really bad, and it was not a pleasant memory.

He looked at the chart. The trooper, whose name was Marco Novo, was twenty-eight, in good health, and had a good fitness report. He could recover from less than 20 percent with most of his function and shiny new skin in a few weeks, assuming no complications, infections, like that. The D&T could handle it.

He needed to find a way to get into the action.

The building vibrated, and it took a second for him to realize why: The weather Dolan mentioned, the storm, was arriving, and the wind gusts were rising.

Now that he noticed, he could hear it blowing out there. He wasn't worried; the BMTS, when pegged down, could, in theory, shrug off an EF-5 tornado. Wasn't anything a hurricane could throw at them this far inland worse than that.

It would make patient delivery problematical, though. Past a certain point, nobody would be allowed to put any kind of craft into the air, so transport was going to be in a crawler, and there were locations where those would have trouble.

The storm might also make hot conflict a little soggy. If you were worried about being picked up and blown half a klick up the road, you might hunker down instead of waging a firefight.

Then again, that might also be just the time to do it, when the other side was hunkering down.

The building vibrated again. Wind moaned over a hollow somewhere, like blowing across the mouth of a bottle.

Well. At least the weather would be dramatic even if business here was slow.

THIRTEEN

"Rain is coming down pretty good now," Gunny observed.

A gust of wind measuring 90 kph, according to the crawler's sensors, sheeted rain almost horizontally over the vehicle.

"Like bein' in a truck wash," she said.

Jo nodded. The storm had begun to arrive a little earlier than forecast, and as the afternoon headed toward dusk, the rain and wind increased. Even though sunset was still an hour away, it was as dark as midnight under the roiling overcast.

No place to go, nothing to do; the rain was here.

No major problems though Jo was concerned with the sensor array on the southwest side of the hill. A couple of times, the IR images had blinked off, then back on. Even as she looked at the tactical comp's screen, the IR for that section winked off.

And stayed off.

"Shit."

"What?"

"IR on the SW quadrant just went down."

"Maybe the manufacturer will send a tech out to fix it. Probably no more than six or eight weeks for them to get here. We got spares, right?"

"Yes."

Kay said, "I will go and replace the sensors."

"You aren't a tech," Jo said.

"How difficult is it to set up the array?"

"Well, it's pretty complex: You have to remove the malfunctioning units, mount the replacements onto the ground spikes, and make sure they are pointed in the right direction."

"That is all?"

"Yeah. We can turn it on from here."

"I think I can manage. I will go."

"You gonna get wet," Gunny said.

"I have been wet before. It will be invigorating. And it is preferable to sitting here doing nothing."

Jo shrugged. "Suit yourself. The spares are in the locker by the aft door. Gray everplast box about so big." She formed an imaginary rectangle with her hands the size of a brick. "It says 'Aimed IR Sensory Array M-3A' on the box."

"I will endeavor to locate it."

Kay left, and Jo smiled to herself. Vastalimi didn't much like to sit still for long. She understood the feeling though she had learned how to be patient when the need arose. Part of being a commander in the field was knowing when to sit and when to run, and doing them in the wrong order could be a problem.

Nobody down the hill seemed interested in coming to visit, and they weren't getting any more troops by air for a while, unless the pilot was less than sane. The igloos and crawlers should be fine in the bad weather, but running around outside, while doable now, would get more difficult as the winds increased. Every day that went by was a big chunk of time in a limited-to-seven war.

Kay enjoyed the blasts of rain and wind that tousled her fur as she moved toward the dysfunctional sensors. The swirling water and wind made it hard to catch any kind of discrete scent, and she had to slit her eyes against the weather in the stormy darkness. She could have printed and worn sheeting goggles that streamed the rain into relatively clear viewing, but she didn't like the feel of them on her face, and it would take half an hour for the printer to make a pair that would fit a Vastalimi.

She picked her way toward her goal. Detritus blew past, leaves, small branches, items missed during the tie-down preparation, or peeled away from the ancient houses. Nothing large yet. She had storm-walked in fiercer conditions.

As she approached the malfunctioning sensors, there was nothing to trip alarms. The wind and rain masked sights and sounds and odors, but nothing seemed out of place.

She circled, as to approach the sensors from downhill.

Fifty meters short of her goal, she stopped and crouched low, motionless.

Most likely, the sensors had been damaged by wind or rain, maybe hit by something bouncing along the ground; but, there was a chance that the failure was due to intent.

On Vast, hunters were familiar with traps. Prey were sometimes canny creatures and able to successfully hide or outrun pursuit. Good hunters had other tricks, and beguiling prey into a place where they could be more easily taken was a useful skill.

Part of that came from an ability to understand how prey saw the world, how they thought. If you had an idea of what would draw, or frighten your quarry, you could use that to your own end.

She crouched, statue-still, watched and listened and sniffed.

Nothing amiss. Hard rain, moderately hard wind.

She remained motionless.

Enemy soldiers could be considered prey. And being able to put herself into their minds was not so hard.

Were she on the other side, how might she use this situation to her advantage?

If she were able to approach and deactivate the sensors without being detected, then shutting them down would draw the attention of those monitoring them. They would deem them necessary and likely send somebody to examine and repair them. Were it her? She would find a place to watch for such an approach, and when the opposition's tech arrived, she would take her down. But to what end? Killing a single technician would make little difference in this kind of engagement.

So, the trap, if there was one, was to effect a larger goal.

Knock out the IR sensors, then kill the tech, and what did that buy you?

Time.

Those monitoring would wait some amount of it before becoming worried about their tech and the resulting situation.

The longer the sensors were inoperable, the longer an opponent would have to sneak a team undetected up the hill. IR could see through rain and darkness, but unaugmented human eyes were less able. A few minutes might be enough.

And then? How best to continue?

Sappers?

The size of the explosives allowed in this war was constrained, but soldiers of any worth knew how to get around that because the numbers of smaller explosives were not so limited. A score of small charges carefully placed could be made to equal one large one.

Apparently, those in charge of limiting the wars had not considered such a thing. Must have been humans . . .

A three- or four-person team could deploy multiple small

charges in a short amount of time. In the confusion following a major detonation, along with the inclement weather, a successful attack could be mounted. It would be risky, but the element of surprise might be enough to give one an edge. It could be done if done right.

With a competent team, Kay could do it.

She should call Jo Captain. But it was no more than a hypothesis. It needed to be tested . . .

She waited. She was a rock in the dark deluge.

There . . .

A small movement, no more than a man might make twitching against a hard slash of rain.

The hunter in her wanted to bare her claws, to charge and leap. The training she had as a soldier made her reach instead for her pistol. Personal satisfaction came from many things, and a job done properly was one.

Fifty meters was a long shot, in the rain and dark and wind. She would need to creep closer.

She would also need to let Jo Captain know the situation. As soon as she ascertained what it was.

She was about to move when another thought arose.

What if the saboteur was not alone? What if there was someone guarding the rear?

Vastalimi preferred to hunt solo, but humans were much more likely to do it in groups.

So. Even though it might delay her com, best she check it out.

She dropped to her belly in the mud and slowly crawled up the hill, angling back and forth. She stopped, froze, then started again.

Five minutes later, she was sure there was one person there. Large, probably male, but too dark to tell, and the wind swept his scent away from her. No sign of a second enemy. And yet, some sense tingled, warning her of unseen danger.

From the set of the soldier ahead of her, he was prone and facing up the hill, a dozen meters away from the sensors. Of course, anyone coming to inspect the sensors would reasonably come from that direction.

Kay's pistol had a flash- and sound-suppressor, and in the stormy evening, such a device would likely hide her unless somebody was looking directly at her when she fired.

The suppressor was in her pack, back in the crawler. She had not foreseen the need.

An error.

She angled to her left, set up for a side shot on the prone man. Maybe he would be wearing armor, but since stealth was more important in such a situation, maybe not.

She slowed her breathing, aimed at the center of mass, and fired five shots, as fast as she could pull the trigger. By the time the fifth shot left the barrel, she was rolling in the mud to her right, fully prone.

Good that she had done so.

The second soldier came out of the ground itself ten meters behind the one Kay had shot. With a carbine on full auto, he raked the spot where she had just been, slaying the mud. Before he realized his error, she indexed her pistol and shot him, two to the torso and one to the head. He fell, and if he wore armor, it wasn't enough. She waited.

No movement not driven by the wind.

She moved forward to check the downed pair.

The one who had come out of the ground was dead, hit three times. He had a trauma plate over his heart that stopped the first two bullets, but the third had entered his skull just above his right eye.

He was also wearing a thermosuit, an outfit that circulated coolant through a mesh and reduced the temperature to match ambient conditions. That's why the IR hadn't picked him up.

Kay would bet that the sapper team likely crawling up the hill also wore such suits.

Kay looked at the ground. It was dug out long and wide enough to encompass a prone human. It was partially filled with water, and there was a deflection tarp under the dead man. A simple hiding place, showing nothing but a slight rise in the earth when the tarp was laid but effective enough in such conditions.

She moved up to the second enemy soldier.

The prone man was thermosuited, too, hit twice on the left side, then three times on the ventral torso as he rolled away from the first impacts. His simple trauma plate hadn't stopped any of her bullets.

As she watched, he shuddered and blew out his dying breath.

"Kay? Is somebody shooting out there?"

"Yes. The sensors were disrupted by two enemy soldiers in thermosuits. Both are dead. I expect there is a team of sappers crawling up the hillside below this position. It might be wise to add bite to the rain in that direction."

"Stet that. Gunny, get some shooters there, and let's light it up. Flares coming, Kay, watch your vision."

"Understood."

A moment later, photonics went off above her. They were less effective in the wind and rain, battered this way and that, but shed enough light as they were blown away to see that there were indeed human forms eighty or so meters down the hill from where Kay crouched. She counted five before the light faded.

Gunny arrived with two grenadiers as the last flare blew away.

"Eighty meters," Kay said. "That way, and if they are smart, probably scrambling back down."

"You heard the fem. Eighty and walk 'em."

The grenadiers adjusted their sights and began launching the grenades. They shot, moved to avoid being stationary targets, fired again.

The weather was growing worse, and several of the missiles went wide, but the shooters corrected their aim and walked the pattern downward.

Below them, somebody opened up with a carbine, to return fire, but that just gave the grenadiers a target, and the first grenade to land close to the muzzle flash silenced the carbine.

Out in the open, no cover? Bad for the sappers. Those who would survive would have to retreat in a hurry or be blasted.

"Put a few more farther out and down," Gunny said. "Just in case there's an assault team staged there."

FOURTEEN

It was near midnight, and the storm had come to play, hard.

Gunny said "Oh, man!"

A section of roof torn from one of the houses blew past, a ragged chunk maybe a meter by two, including wooden supports as big as her arm. It had a ghostly look under the IR camp lights, dim even with Jo's enhanced vision in the heavy rain and night.

As they watched, it banged into one of the igloos, bounced off, and whirled away into the thick gray rain. The igloo mostly held, but the top was definitely dented.

"Somebody is about to get wet," Gunny said.

"They can patch it from inside," Jo said.

"Check out Kay."

Jo looked: Five meters away, Kay stood facing into the wind, leaning forward, her arms outstretched. She was using her hands as spoilers, tiny wind foils, to help keep herself anchored to the ground. She was soaked, but her wet fur streamed in the storm winds. Jo could see the vortex eddy behind Kay as the rain swirled past the obstacle, creating a complex pattern in the air.

Vastalimi in the rain. A song or a story, maybe a poem there . . .

Even over the constant roar of the storm, Jo's otics picked up the sound of Kay growling. Low, sustained, and fierce.

The Vastalimi fem ducked as something blew past her. She came back up, teetered for a moment, then regained her stance into the wind.

"Why's she doin' that?"

"Defying the elements. Goes to an old ritual on Vast, where they get some big storms during their monsoon season."

Gunny shook her head. "Like the night hasn't already been interesting enough. Probably no other sappers going to try us again in this."

Their vehicle faced into the wind and was designed to resist that, along with rain, sand, pretty much anything short of a volcano spewing lava. Bits of this and that spanged off the armored denscris windshield and windows, sounding like small-arms rounds ricocheting. Even the raindrops made a hammering racket.

There was plenty of room for a couple of passengers to stretch out and sleep, and even with the loud noises, any soldier worth her salt could drop into a snooze; it was one of the first things you learned how to do when you put on a uniform.

Not that they would be sleeping since they were on duty.

And not that they were worried about any of the bozos down the hill trying to mount any kind of attack in this. Step crooked, and the wind would pick you off the side of the rise and drop you somewhere else. Made for interesting logistics: *Whoa, there went Henri! Somebody see if you can find his machine gun . . .*

Kay stopped growling, and when Jo looked, she was gone. There was a moment of worry, then the rear hatch opened, and Kay climbed into the cart. She shook herself like a dog, slung water off.

"Havin' fun out there?"

"It was invigorating, yes."

Gunny shook her head. "Loony as a latrine lamprey."

Kay grinned.

The cart shook, seemed to rise a couple of centimeters, then settled back.

Jo glanced at the sensor image. "That gust was 183 kph and the eye wall is not here yet."

"We are on a hill and exposed to more of the storm," Kay said. She had a towel, sponging the rest of the water from her fur.

Gunny looked at the sensors. "Nothing on the pradar or IR except detritus blowin' in the wind out there."

"It would not be an ideal time for an attack," Kay allowed.

"Yeah, being worried about being blown twenty klicks away to land head down in the scrub will do that. Not something Ah would be keen to try."

"It still might be done if the attackers moved with care."

"Which is why we are here watching," Jo said.

Another piece of building pinwheeled by, and Jo caught only a glimpse of it. Looked like part of a window shutter. More small bits rattled against the cart. She waved at the sensor controls, crooked a finger to bring up the weather sat. Their location appeared as a pulsing green dot. There was a lot of storm surrounding the dot.

"Something just took down those IR sensors you replaced," Jo said.

"Shall I go and replace them again?"

"No, I think we're good for now.

"The eye is approaching. Another few minutes. This should be interesting."

"Why interesting?" Kay asked.

"Well, I've never experienced it, but the center of such whirling storms is the axis and mostly calm. Little or no wind and rain, low pressure. This storm's center is relatively small, under thirty kilometers in diameter. Just before it gets here, the winds will be their strongest; when it arrives, in theory, it will be almost calm and cloudless, you could look up to see the stars. When it passes, the strongest winds will return, but from the opposite direction, so we need to orient our vehicles the other way for optimum wind resistance. According to the chart, the speed of the storm should give us about ten to fifteen minutes of calm. Plenty of time to turn the carts around."

Jo had worked that out when she'd gotten the briefing on what to expect.

Kay said, "And while in the eye, there will be sufficient time for an opposing force that presumably has the same information, to mount a quick attack. If I were in their position, that's when I would do it."

Jo and Gunny both nodded. "We already kicked their asses pretty good once this evening," Gunny said.

Jo said, "The wind and rain would play hell with grenades and mortars, even small-arms rounds get deflected or pushed off target. But in a dead calm . . . ?"

"Maybe they don't want this hill that bad," Gunny said.

"Do you believe that?"

Gunny shook her head at Kay. "No. The clock is tickin'," and the conditions are going to be nasty for the next couple of days. Probably won't have a better chance."

Jo toggled her com's opchan on. "Listen up, people, it's going to stop raining and blowing here in about . . . nine minutes. If company is planning on dropping by unannounced, there's a small window when that is most likely to happen. Anything not IDed with our sig is a target. Shoot and report, in that order. Stets?"

Jo listened as the troops toggled message-received blips.

"Be a hard slog up that wet hillside," Gunny said. "Ten minutes might not be enough."

"But enough to get close enough to throw things at us.

We'll make it rain harder than water to give them something else to think about if they try it. Though the wind will blow our fire all over the place when it cranks back up."

"I should go and scout."

"Negative. I don't want to see you flattened by a chunk of somebody's greenhouse. You already had your conversation with the storm. Wait until the wind dies."

Kay nodded. "Understood."

The opchan alert blipped on the console.

"Hey," Gramps said, "I don't know if you have noticed, but there's a little rain and wind happening."

"Listen to the old man, Ah can't believe he can still put his shoes on by himself."

"Hey, Chocolatte, I miss you, too. But for those of you thinking that you are going to get a package from home or anything in the mail tonight, forget it. Air support is grounded.

"Nancy would fly if the colonel would let her, but we've got tornado alerts, and taking aircraft through those is generally considered unwise."

"Tornados," Jo said. "Yeah, I see 'em on the weather radar. Doesn't look like they are a threat here, they are already past us."

"Yep, but it's early in the evening and those can pop up anywhere in a hurry. You know the eye is about to reach you?"

"Yep. We're geared up in case somebody thinks that's a good time to mount a charge."

"Mount a knee-deep-in-the-mud wade, you mean."

"They have some small treadware down there, might could move quickly enough to get up a ways before the wind comes back."

"I trust you are prepared for such an eventuality."

"We are. How are things on the other fronts?"

"Mostly shut down. Not a fit night out for man nor beast. I'm running the FCV on the edge of the woods about twenty klicks from where you are."

"You should have been here a few minutes ago, seen

Kay out there leaning against the wind; she was havin' a
fine ole time."

"Mad dogs and Vastalimi," he said.

Jo chuckled.

Kay said, "I don't know the reference, but it sounds pejo-
rative on the face of it."

"It is. By our standards, your behavior sometimes can
be classified as insane."

"We feel the same way about your species."

"Said the fem who tracked and killed a carnivorous
monster the size of a troop carrier using only her claws,"
Gramps said.

Kay smiled.

"She's smiling, isn't she?"

"Like a stoned baboon," Jo said.

"Okay. If the opposition comes to call, drop a few rocks
on their heads. Keep us in the loop."

"Done."

"I'm gonna go see if I can make a kite. Great weather
for flying one; been a while since I did that."

"Back when you made 'em from dinosaur hide and bones?"

"I told you about that?"

Gunny shook her head, but she smiled.

"Discom, fems. Have a nice night."

Kay noticed it first, Jo and Gunny right behind her.
"Listen," Kay said.

"I don't hear any—ah, yeah," Gunny said.

The wind and rain had slackened. Even as they noticed,
the sounds dropped again, almost as if somebody had
waved a volume control to a lower setting.

"Heads up, people. Stay sharp."

- - - - - -

As soon as the wind died, Kay exited the vehicle and
headed for her vantage point. The area was strewn with
debris, tree branches, parts of buildings, bits of plastic, and

uprooted bushes. There was a chunk of frame-igloo material the size of her head just there. Pieces of what looked like glass and other glittery shards of unidentified material shattered by the storm lay scattered about, visible in the starlight that shone down from a mostly clear sky.

Most interesting, this effect. From storm to nothing in only a few moments.

She felt pressure in her head and eardrums, and she equalized it, yawning, feeling a *pop!* as she did. She splashed through puddles of warm water, treading carefully to avoid stepping on something sharp. Her feet were leathery tough but not invulnerable.

The air smelled of torn and crushed vegetation.

She made her way to the edge of the hill. There was a smallish tree and some shrubbery there, and it seemed to have withstood the wind and rain. It would break up her outline, offer some concealment, as she peered over the edge. The enemy would have night-vision augmentation, but it would be no better than her own night sight.

It felt eerily quiet.

She saw movement almost immediately, no more than two hundred meters away. There were bushes down the slope blocking a clear view.

"We have enemy approaching," she said.

On her com, Jo Captain said, "We have them on the scope. They must have started before the wind stopped."

"What I see appears to be a small multiwheel crawler. Wait—there is a second, just behind it. Ah."

"What 'Ah'? What?"

"They are drones—no riders."

Jo said, "Fuck! Crawling bombs. Somebody got a bead on these suckers?"

"I have them." That was Singh.

"Spike them now."

A minigun opened up to Kay's left, eighty meters away. The tracer rounds revealed the trajectory, and a grenade launcher *whumped!* arcing down to follow the tracers. Of a moment, there came a bright flash, followed by the sound of the explosion—

"One down," Singh said.

More tracers flew down the hill.

Kay looked away, to preserve her night sight. She smelled a feint. She moved from her concealment and edged away from Singh's firing—

The second crawler exploded, much louder and brighter. Must have triggered the onboard bomb.

"Both targets hit," Singh said.

Kay was fifty meters away now, staying low, searching . . .

Here came five, six . . . nine troopers in electronic camouflage, almost invisible in the darkness."

"You see them?" Kay said.

"Stet that. Ten?"

Kay frowned. Ten? Had she missed one? Where—

"Sorry, I see nine. They are approaching the AP mines—"

As if to punctuate her comment, one of the antipersonnel mines went off, and somebody screamed.

The enemy advance stopped.

"Grenadiers, dial it in, let's give them something else to chew on."

A pair of grenade launchers behind Kay began firing.

Two . . . four . . . eight . . . ten rounds arced over her and fell, and their shooters had the range. The grenades began going off, and there were more screams from those being hit.

Not a good night to be a Dycon soldier in these parts.

Kay had her carbine, but she hadn't unstrapped it.

The soldiers below began a retreat.

It was a high cost for no gain.

Kay frowned again. This seemed an unwise attack. Could they be that stupid?

She lifted a bit higher, to get a better view—

"Down!" Gunny yelled.

Kay dropped flat, face-first into the mud.

The bullet passed over her close enough to stir the fur on her left shoulder—

Gunny fired a triple tap from her carbine—

"Clear!" Gunny said.

Kay raised her face and looked down the hill to see the shooter still falling.

She came up. The tenth one. "Thank you. I made an error."

Gunny moved closer, still looking for targets downrange. "Sniper. I bet he came up while the storm was still raging. He was set up when the others got here, looking for a target of opportunity."

"They are determined."

"Yep, and that and a noodle will get you a cup of bad coffee."

The wind started coming back, but from the other direction.

"Time to go back inside," Gunny said. "Ah'm guessing we are finally done for the night. They gonna need some new soldiers to replace the ones we tagged, and Ah'm guessin' they won't be coming anytime soon."

FIFTEEN

Gramps was dry and tight in the FCV when his displays splashed warning icons, and an alarm chimed: He'd just lost the last satellite feed.

The brunt of the storm was past, and some of the trees ahead on the edge of the forest hadn't survived it; they were splayed and downed, mostly leaning in the same direction. The big clearing where the FCV was parked was littered with debris the hurricane had brought and left behind. Branches, trash, odd things he couldn't even identify in the darkness. Quite the meteorological drama. He'd been through other storms, but none quite as big as this.

He shut off the alarm.

Shit, he thought, *there goes the last link unit.*

It was the third of three modules he'd set out before the storm. Each was connected to the FCV by optical cable instead of a wireless pipe. Wireless transmission could get iffy during bad weather, and especially as far out as he'd set them. The links had been designed to stay close to the

FCV's transceivers because nobody thought they might need to be anywhere else.

When the military-hardware folks designed things, they usually had something particular in mind, and flexibility in function was somehow never high on their to-do list. And their responses when queried about such things?

No, that is not within our design parameters. Do not attempt to utilize it in such a manner.

The first had died an hour into the storm. The second lasted two more hours.

Now the third was kaput, and that's all they had.

Which was fine for REMFs who didn't have to use the stuff with expressed murder blowing past your head at hypersonic velocity, or huge fucking wind and rain, but in the field, you had to make do.

Cable was really old-school, but hardwired sigs were better. And, he could switch his signal among the three squatty boxes and down- and uplink his ELINT profile geographically, as well as spread-spectrum, which was also easier. Wireless sometimes got confused at multiple sigs and would start to cry and keep rebooting, which was a pain in the ass. Plus the proximity of the signal-blocking trees was just one more brick on the load. He had found some relatively clear spots to set the links, but the wind moved all kinds of crap back and forth . . .

The squad that usually walked shotgun on the FCV would normally attend needed repairs, but they had to stay inside. No way they could roam around in that blasting wind and shrapnel-like rain anyhow.

He ran a diagnostic on the cables. Two of them showed patent the full distance to their respective units. The cables weren't the problem; the units themselves had malfunctioned. Probably trees fell on them.

If truth was the first casualty of war, communications hardware was usually right behind it, and triple redundancy was no guarantee.

The third cable showed a disconnect seven hundred meters out, in the clearing and well short of the trees, which likely meant it had been broken somehow by the storm.

All he needed to do was roll out to the broken cable and patch it. Or he could try the wireless link at a different spot. It was showing NO SIGNAL at the moment. One way or another, he was gonna have to move his ass fast, or he wasn't going to get the data he needed.

The storm wasn't done yet. According to the FCV's sensors, winds were still gusting 70 to 80 kph. Maybe he could roll and set the FCV right over where he needed to splice—hell, stay inside if he could. That would be a story to tell later. *Yeah, hurricane busted the cable, but I was able to fix it without even getting wet . . .*

The troops could stay in their igloos. Everybody would be happy.

He put in a call to HQ, got the night-watch op. "I got a broken cable here. I'm moving the FCV seven hundred meters to the northeast for repair. Let the guys in the igloos sleep. I'll call if I need help."

The fem acknowledged that.

He cranked the engines, set the AP, and engaged the forward drive, heading toward the forest.

The treads would handle any of the small debris okay, and the AP would swing the big vehicle around anything large enough to cause problems. The treads crawled slowly along, slow as a walking man's pace.

He lit the passive sensors and checked his position as he crept along the broken cable's path.

It would take a few minutes to get there.

He did a systems check while he waited. Everything else seemed to be working as it should.

One FCV looked like another though this one had been rigged to carry a four-drone platform in a stick-on module on the starboard side. There were two small drones left, and they wouldn't be going anywhere until the wind lessened. A meter-long drone wasn't any match for even a 60 kph wind; it would toss the sucker this way and that. Which it had done with the first two drones. Those had vanished within an hour of deployment, and were probably halfway to Oklahoma City by now. Or buried a meter deep in the mud.

In theory, the storm would be mostly gone by daylight, and a couple more armed birds in the air come the dawn wouldn't hurt, which was why he had brought them.

－ － － － －

He made it to the break in the cable. His connection reads changed from amber to red, flitted past green, and back to red again, depending on the signal that made it through. The wireless still wasn't working worth shit though there were a couple of spots where reception was workable. If he couldn't fix the cable, that was the other option.

Winds were down to the sixties now; he checked the passives and did a quick scan of the trees at the edge of the clearing. Nothing to see.

He couldn't pull up directly over the break; there was a section of tree as big around as he was lying on the cable, which was probably what had broken it.

Looked as if the tree had been hit by lightning, the way the wood was shredded and split.

He parked the vehicle. Ran another sensor scan. No signs of anything out there but windblown crap.

He pulled on his jacket and slapped the door release. He stepped down to the ground.

He lit the helmet lamp and started looking for the break.

It wasn't under the toppled tree, it was a meter away, and the cable had been cut, the edges sheared clean and smooth.

Shit!

He dropped flat, landing in the mud on top of the cable. He heard the shot right after he smacked down.

And guess what? The fuckers are still here!

Bullets slapped and skipped from the earth around him.

He rolled, staying prone. Time to call for help:

"This is Demonde, I have some enemy action here."

No reply.

He tried again: "Anybody awake out there? I could use a little backup."

Zip.

Great! Fucking com—!

Something on the ground dug into his right hip—

The fallen tree absorbed some of the rounds; those made heavier *chonks!* as they hit—

He scooted backward under the FCV. Not going to be safe here for long, and with no backup and no way to get into the cabin without exposing himself to fire, things were going to go to shit fast.

He pulled his sidearm, pointed it in the general direction of the incoming fire, and triggered half a magazine, just to let them know he could shoot back.

Even if he could call for help, it wouldn't get here in time. Any second now, one of the shooters would throw a grenade or decide one man with a pistol wasn't that big a problem. A captured FCV would be a nice prize.

Time to activate the gun.

The FCV had a roof-mounted extrusion machine gun with 360-degree coverage. All he had to do was telescope it up enough to depress the elevation enough and shoot the fuck out of the guys blasting at him.

He sent the command sig, ordering the gun to backtrack incoming small-arms fire and to hose those sources.

That, at least, was working: The gun rose; he could hear the hydraulics over the rain as it lifted the weapon high enough to get the right angle.

The roof gun spoke, chattering caseless 10mm into the night.

Adiós, motherfuckers!

Then somebody fired a G2G missile and blew the machine gun right off the fucking roof—

Not more than twenty or thirty meters away, he guessed. Where the fuck were they?

Shit, shit, shit!

More rounds splatted or chonked around him.

Screwed.

Wait a second, wait. The angle on the FCV, they were on his starboard side . . .

He spoke a command sequence to the FCV's tactical comp.

He fired off the rest of the magazine in his pistol to draw their attention.

The stick-on pod's doors slid open.

The drones' wings had to be manually unloaded, and the folded wings locked into place by hand or they couldn't be launched, but he didn't need them to fly . . .

The incoming fire stopped. Somebody yelled at him through the soggy night:

"Surrender, and you get to stay alive! Otherwise, we roll over you! You have ten seconds to decide!"

He lit the drones, sent the command code for the little crafts' miniguns' radar, and gave them leave to fire when they detected moving, human-sized targets.

"Hey, asshole, did your mother get those new kneepads I sent her?"

The enemy soldiers hiding in the night came up and charged—

The little drones couldn't fly, but their guns worked just fine.

He heard yelling as the drone's guns fired.

He shut them down and came up_

Don't shoot Roy, little drones—

He scrambled up into the FCV and closed the door. He plopped his wet and muddy self into the command center seat and put the FCV into reverse.

The drones had done the trick, and they still had a little ammo left, enough to keep any of the enemy still out there from any kind of run at him. He relit the drones. They'd stopped shooting, so nobody was moving around they could see.

As soon as he found a spot where the wireless connection was strong, he'd park. And he'd have to wake up the squad in their igloos and let them know they'd had company. Well. He'd tried to cut them a break and learned once again that no good deed goes unpunished.

He felt a twinge, looked down at his muddy self and noticed a darker blotch on his hip.

Blood.

He stood, noticed he had a pain just under his right iliac crest, and peeled his shirt up and pants down.

Well, shit. There were two holes there, maybe five centimeters apart. He hadn't rolled over something sharp on the ground, he'd been *shot*.

It wasn't bleeding much, and it hadn't hit anything serious, just punched a little channel through the meat below the bone. Son of a *bitch* . . .

He went to find a first-aid kit. He cleaned the wounds, dusted them with Antibiotic Clot Factor, and sprayed a bandage over it. One the patch set, he took a quick shower, and put on some clean clothes. Okay, a little harm, a small foul . . .

As he slipped the com bleed-through earpiece back in, he heard "—there, old man? Anybody home, FCV?"

He grinned. "Hello, Chocolatte, I'm here. Feeling lonely?"

"No, just figured it was past your bedtime, and I'd better call and be sure you were still awake. You didn't answer."

"Doing a little chore," he said. "How's the rain treating you?"

"Been busy. Bangs, booms, this, and that. Must be nice to be in a big ole vehicle with all the comforts of home and nothing exciting going on."

"Yep, that's me. Dull as dishwater here."

He didn't want to worry her in the middle of things; he could tell her later.

Maybe.

— — — — — —

Gunny logged off. She lay there and listened to the rain, not falling so hard now, and thought about Gramps out there in the FCV. It had become their pattern, to rag on each other, but he was not really that old, not even sixty yet.

He was decades older than she was, but technically, not even middle-aged. He probably had a few moves left.

She hadn't really thought much about herself aging until recently.

She knew it was the nature of the beast; that she was slowing down. Yeah, she was like that old gunfighter in the ancient vid; she could still catch a fly on the bar with a swipe of her hand, but once, she could have caught two of them.

There was a quick fix: A trip to Formentara's table, and the best aug available would kick her regular military-grade speed up a few notches.

Thing was, in her mind, that would be cheating.

Sure, everybody in most armies had the military issue. That was part of the requirement, and it brought you up to par; you couldn't compete without them unless you were some kind of genetic sport. But the high-end augmentation, the stuff like Jo ran, that put you into another whole class of quick and strong and all kinds of other shit.

Without that kind of work, Gunny would never be as fast as Jo. And even with it, she'd still be slower than Kay. There were limits as to how much a human body could be amped, and even staying inside them, the more augs you ran, the sooner you died. They took their toll.

Well, except if you had Formentara tuning you up now and then.

It wasn't as if she wanted to live forever, but it had

always been a point of something, pride, maybe, that Megan Sayeed had gotten to where she was mostly on her own. It was practiced skill, training, and that meant something to her. Like the climbers who scaled the big peaks without supplemental oxygen, there was a different sense of accomplishment.

She was still a young fem, but normal humans peaked in their teens or early twenties when it came to reaction time and nerve-conduction speeds, and she was past that. She wasn't going to get any faster on her own, only slower. Practice made it smooth, and smooth led to fast, but there was only so much you could do to compensate for the organic slowing.

A year from now, five? Some hotshot on the other side who was younger and faster would beat her to the draw and cook off a more accurate round before she could.

When that happened, the party would be over.

That's how she expected to go. On the battlefield, taken out by somebody better. There was always a chance of a stray shot, a bomb going off in the wrong place, a sniper so far away she couldn't see him, but mostly she figured it would come down to a younger, quicker, more accurate version of herself firing the bullet with her name on it. Not really realistic to believe that, but she'd kept that fantasy going for a while. It had a certain romantic charm. *Hey, fem, it's me, the younger version of you, come to take your place on the dance floor. Adiós, chica . . .*

So what to do?

She could walk away. She had enough money to live for a couple of years, she could get security work, could teach shooting classes, like that, and get by.

She could upgrade. Formentara could speed her up 15 or 20 percent, and that would put her into the superfast category, with superior skills that would give her another ten or twelve years better than she was now.

It was tempting.

Or she could just go on like she was and meet her nemesis whenever he or she showed up. Kinda fatalistic, but she was a soldier, had been one her whole adult life, and that was part of the trip. Play with fire, get burned; play with knives, get cut; play with guns . . . ?

She grinned. Gramps would have a field day if he knew what she was thinking. He'd be on her like fleas on an orchard rat, he knew she was even a tiny bit worried about getting old and slow, all the shit she had given him. Karma was an absolute bitch.

Good thing he couldn't read her mind.

The rain came down, and she drifted into sleep.

— — — — — —

Wink watched the MedEvac hopper as its fans kicked up water from the soaked ground; the hopper's lights caught and danced crazily over the vibrating pools as the vehicle lifted. At least the rain was not as heavy as it had been; bigger craft were able to fly.

Inside the departing unit were four troopers from another unit who'd had a really bad night when the hurricane had swept their cart into a river, and the seals had failed. His work—and Formentara's since zhe had popped by for no particular reason—was to stabilize and transship the four to the CCU at the Main Base, where General Wood's medical team treated the really serious stuff. These four had drowned, mostly, and needed high-pressure hyperoxygenation, more specialized gear than Wink had, to make sure their brains came back online as they recovered.

The sound of the hopper faded. The rain came down, the wind blew.

Now he had an empty clinic. He went back inside.

Boredom headed his way; he could *feel* it approaching . . .

Ping ping PING Ping ping PING Ping ping PING—

So much for boredom. Wink toggled his com.

"This is CFI medical, go."

"Ah, this is Field Med Orton, Fifteenth, we have two troopers down with serious blast injuries, they need evac, our transport is busy, and you are the closet. Can you help us out?"

"Stet that. How bad?"

"Telemetry uploading."

"Stand by."

Wink waved up the telemetry read:

The stats crawled. Explosive concussive effects could be all over the map, but often, somebody standing too close to a bomb when it went off looked as if they had been swatted with a giant, spiked fist. The two injured troopers were hurt pretty bad, but their vitals seemed stable, at least for the moment.

Orton was one of the FMs for the scout team next door, not part of CFI.

"Got no transport vehicles near their location," said Formentara, from behind him. "We're the closest facility," zhe said, "and our transport won't be back for forty-five minutes, if that. We'll have to go collect them in the crawler."

The doctor nodded. Only a couple of klicks, and mostly it looked like friendly territory, plus nobody was supposed to shoot at medical vehicles, which the crawler obviously was; it was plainly marked with standard Caduceus, the twin snakes twining around a winged staff, black on a bright yellow background, plus broadcasting the medical sig. Though that was kind of a running joke . . .

Corporate rules were much like the GU Army's when it came to medical vehicles and buildings—firing or bombing them was generally not allowed, as long as nobody in them was shooting at you. Not that troops always paid attention to that rule. All you needed to say was, "Hey, some asshole stuck a gun out the door and fired at me!" If there wasn't a Monitor standing right there, you could get away with it. Wink's vehicles had already taken fire several times during this war, and likely as not, their side had sent a few potshots at Dycon's medical crawlers.

Play in a war zone, why, you might get killed. Imagine that.

Still, they could zip over and back, should be no problem . . .

Wink said, "Transport is on the way. ETA your location is"—he checked the PPS—"six minutes."

"Stat that, Doc. We'll keep them alive until you get here."

- - - - - -

The medical crawler rolled along, treads churning mud, the rain, which had eased up, came back harder, sheeting over the vehicle. Winds weren't so bad, but it was breezy enough.

Wink glanced at the readouts, looked through the armored plastic into the dark night, and back again, gaze constantly shifting.

"Nervous?" Formentara sat to the left at the weapons console. Mercenaries were covered by the medical-noncombatant conventions, but the crawler was armed because sometimes you had to shoot back or get killed. Better to have it and not need it than to need it and not have it.

Wink shook his head. "Not me. It's just a walk in the park as far as I—*Fuck!*"

Bullets smacked into their windshield, ricocheted off, leaving metal-smudged dents on the stacked plastic.

"You know, they aren't supposed to do that," he said, "and yet they keep doing it. Where are the Monitors when you need them? Hey, morons, we are *medical* here!"

Formentara's hands flew over the controls as zhe initiated a suppressing fire back along the trajectory the tactical computer identified. "That will give them something about which to think," zhe said.

" 'About which to think'?"

"Grammar is important."

"Really? Grammar? How far?"

"Almost there," zhe said.

He gunned the engine, pushing their vehicle as fast as he dared on the muddy ground.

"Wink? Where the hell are you?"

"Medical evac, Colonel, and we are kind of busy here. Let me call you back."

Formentara wiggled hir fingers: More chatter erupted from their gun.

Zhe said, "They eased off, but I expect they have help coming. Negative on local air support, still too much wind and rain for the drones, and we don't have a heavy aircraft close enough."

"That's okay, we're here." Wink tapped the brake, locked the crawler to a stop.

He hauled ass back to the bay doors and opened them.

Into his com: "Orton, your ride is here. And we probably have more enemy coming, so let's move it, hey? I'm bringing gurneys."

"Affirmative, Doc. We are forty meters SSE of the crawler. I'll wave."

Wink yanked two of the slide stretchers off a table, pulling them by a thick handle. The gyroscopically stabilized gurneys rolled on fat tires, or could be skidded on almost frictionless plastic runners that would glide over pretty much any kind of terrain, and were handy when there weren't two people to carry a stretcher. He and Orton could each pull one back, or he could chain them together and haul two, if necessary.

He jumped out into the stormy night and felt his boots sink into the damp earth. Rain poured down.

The heads-up display in his helmet pinged an ID sig. Right where Orton said they were.

A walk in the park. In a hurricane. Where the park muggers are armed with full-auto carbines looking to kill you.

He grinned.

"He's in, lock it tight," Wink said.

Orton, a gaunt man who seemed made of rawhide, said, "Strapping down."

The medic finished securing the second of the two casualties and grabbed one of the handles.

Wink was about to do the same when he noticed that the soldier in the other gurney had gone a chalkier shade of pale.

Fuck . . .

"We got a new bleeder somewhere on this one," Wink said. "I need to plug it."

"Doctor, pradar says company is arriving," said Formentara's voice in his head. "I suggest you move with more deliberate speed."

"Yeah, yeah." *Got to find that hole—*

It was hard to tell in the darkness where the blood was the freshest, but it had to be on the left side, which had taken the main force of the explosion. He flared his helmet lamp to full. That would make a nice target in the rainy night . . .

He could feel time slipping away and the enemy getting closer.

Where are you, little bleeder? Come to Daddy . . .

There—!

He found the vein, managed to clamp it with a hemostat. It was meatball stuff, but it would have to do.

"Let's move!" He killed his helmet lamp. He yanked the gurney and started for the crawler.

A bullet passed through the space he'd just occupied, close enough he could hear it whistle, feel the air displacement.

Mother*fucker!*

But his adrenaline surged: *Missed me, asshole!*

More bullets whizzed past—

He yelled into the night: "Hey, dickhead, I'm a *doctor*! You aren't supposed to *shoot* at me! Don't piss me off!"

It was going to be iffy here . . .

And then he saw a blur to his right

Formentara?—what?

Zhe flashed past, firing a carbine full auto. *What in the hell—?*

Ask about it later. *Move!*

He scrabbled through the downpour, slipping and sliding. Set what was probably a record for the loaded-gurney-in-a-hurricane sprint.

Even so, Orton was ahead of him. *Second place, damn!*

The medic helped Wink slide the second gurney in, then raised his carbine to fire past the doctor into the dark—

Formentara arrived and leaped into the vehicle.

"Anytime, Doctor," zhe said. "I believe we have overstayed our welcome."

Orton slammed the doors as small-arms fire began to pepper them. None of it got past the crawler's armor—

Wink scrambled forward, Formentara already ahead of him. *That's twice I'm bringing up the rear.*

And: *Zhe moved way too fast for normal.*

He released the brake and squeezed the accelerator. The treads dug deep, and the crawler lurched forward.

Formentara raised the rotoscopic gun and ran it at 360 degrees, hosing a circular shower of jacketed death at a thousand rounds per minute, and let the pradar pick the targets.

There was rain, and then there was *rain* . . .

Nothing big enough to damage the crawler hit it, and the small-arms fire eased off as they moved away.

"Orton?"

"We're stable back here."

Wink looked at Formentara. "What the fuck was that? When did you get tuned up?"

"Recall the augmentor Gee, on Ananda, the one amping the Rel? Had not Kay been there, I would have been in considerable danger. I thought it might be useful to have some basics onboard. My autobots were sufficient for such simple installations."

Simple. For hir, that word had a different meaning than it did for others.

"You shoot real good for a noncombatant."

"You thought I was just another pretty face?"

He laughed. "Well . . . yeah."

He was as high as a kite. Been a while since he'd had a rush this good.

"Careful, Wink," zhe said. "You are very near to drooling."

"Shows, huh?"

"Yes, it shows."

"Maybe we shouldn't tell Jo," he said. "She doesn't need to know."

"Good luck with keeping her from finding out."

Yeah. But—it was still worth it.

On the noncoded override opchan, a Monitor said: "Attention, Dycon force, you are firing upon a medical transport vehicle. Cease at once."

"Oh, right, *now* they show up. More dickheads."

SIXTEEN

Cutter slowed the ATV as he paid more attention to the heads-up display. The hurricane had played hell with the gear exactly as one would expect that it might.

Mobile Base Four, just outside the woods and designated by a small red number on his display, was still not responding.

He pinged the satellite relay for an update.

Nobody at MB4 answered. Not vox, not data, zip.

It might mean nothing; a shorted circuit from the rain or interference from the trees. Or it might mean something worse.

In an engagement of this limited size and scope, it was all about getting the most advantageous position with the fewest troops. It was like a game of chess: Unlike a war of attrition, they didn't need to kill or destroy most of the opposition, just get them into positions where they couldn't win. In this case, MB4 was a valuable pawn, in the right place to cover things. If somebody rolled on them, they should have had time to call for backup.

He checked the display again. It would be a short detour on his route to the FCV, and MB4 was in CFI's territory. In theory.

He glanced at the heads-up display. What was the point in being in command if he couldn't make a command decision?

Gramps was in the FCV: He called it in: "I'm swinging out to check on MB4."

"You have people for that," Gramps said.

"I'm here, they aren't. It's our property."

"You aren't supposed to be out there. Jo will be pissed when she finds out."

"She's got other things on her plate. I'm not going to tell her. Neither are you."

"You right about that, I'm not saying shit. Be careful."

– – – – – –

As Cutter neared MB4, he turned his displays down and his sensors up, scanning the area. He rolled forward, looking for his team, then he saw the crawler and the tow gun.

No signs of life.

He did a quick scan on the sensors and saw nothing.

He did a quick query on the opchan. No response.

He rolled to a stop. Climbed out, his carbine at the ready.

He stepped carefully across the muddy ground.

The trailer with 40mm recoilless behind the crawler looked okay until he got closer.

The targeting array had been destroyed—looked like fire from small arms.

On the other side of the trailer, he found the eight troops of MB4.

The stink of death filled the wet air.

He did a quick check of the corpses; all were CFI. If any of the enemy had been killed or wounded, they weren't here now. *Fuck!*

They were mostly dead by gunfire. Two of them had no

throats left, only gaping, ragged holes where a powerful claw
had ripped voice boxes out. Lot of blood from that soaked
into the ground around those bodies.

No boot prints leaving, unless they walked in the dead's
tracks; be odd for an enemy patrol in the aftermath of a
hurricane to be that careful.

He knew what it meant. The enemy Vastalimi had been
here. Probably alone. He shot six, then took out the last two
claw-to-hand. It would have been fast and hot, and it proved
once again the worth of a Vastalimi warrior in battle.

"We have eight of ours KIA, these coordinates," he said,
"and evidence that the other side's Vastalimi did the deed."

"Aw, hell," Gramps said. "I don't suppose you can GPS
him for a drone hit?"

"Not at this time. Can they even fly yet?"

"Marginally, maybe. I'd risk one in this case. I'll get
somebody in here to collect the bodies and plug the hole."

"Yeah. I'm on my way back."

He stood, started toward his vehicle, then thought about
it. If they sent their Vastalimi here to do this, they must
have had a good reason. And if they planned to go through
the hole the Vastalimi made, they'd have to do it fast—
they'd know somebody would notice PDQ.

How long had it been? How much time left?

If the enemy punched through here, they could gain a
superior position. He'd have to move assets around and
reconfigure the lines, at the least.

Damn . . .

He ran back to the 40mm and took another look. Targeting computer was definitely dead, but—

He tabbed the main power and the drive motor hummed
to life. He grabbed the paddles and tested the barrel.
Moved fine, the touch sensors shifting the barrel okay. It
was a little sluggish—the targeting array ran an algorithm
that anticipated sensor input faster than human reflexes.
He would have to eyeball it.

The ammunition-feed mechanism was okay—he cycled a few shells and heard them snap in and out of place.

Options were get the hell out now or try to plug the gap. He thought about the men lying dead next to the trailer and the others who might be killed.

Not really a choice.

He heard the faint sounds of an engine approaching.

He slid down behind the splash shields.

"Company," he told Gramps. "Be good to get somebody here when you get around to it."

– – – – – –

Gunny woke up a few seconds before the com lit with Gramps's incoming.

"Hey, Chocolatte, got a present for you. Have a look."

"Not porn, is it?"

"Your kind, yes. Jo around?"

"Sleeping."

"Good. Keep the sound turned down. I don't want her to see this."

Gunny tapped a control and a video feed popped up on her heads-up display.

She saw a 40mm tow gun behind a crawler, a gunner in the hot seat.

As she watched, the gunner tracked the barrel of the cannon to his left and began firing.

She watched as targeting rounds stitched their way toward an incoming, lightly armored troop carrier. One of the enemy's.

She frowned. Why was the gunner missing? The gun's algorithm must be off—

Then rounds began to slap the enemy carrier *clunk-clunk-clunk!* and the EU slugs blew through the armor.

The target veered off course, but the gunner compensated, tracked it, nailing it over and over—

Like shooting fish in a barrel—

—the APC skidded to a halt on the soaked ground and rocked a little. Steam came from the ruined engine.

A few seconds passed.

No doors opened. Nobody got out.

Smoked 'em all?

She looked back over at the gunner and got it. The targeting array was wrecked. Guy had been shooting on manual.

That was more impressive. She took a closer look at the shooter.

"Hey. Is that—?"

"Yep, in the flesh. He went to check on MB4. Looks like the other side's Vastalimi paid a visit. Unit was dead when he got there."

Motherfucker. "All of them?"

"Yes. They opened a hole. He closed it. We have it beefed up again."

She knew he was good, but it was one thing to point-shoot a handgun and another thing entirely to do it with a motorized cannon.

Or, apparently not . . .

She shook her head.

"Jo's going to be pissed."

"She hasn't seen it yet—figured you'd enjoy it the most."

"Yeah. Looks like he was a little off early on, but, all things considered, not bad."

" 'Not bad'? You are a hard fem, Gunny. That was fucking great. I don't think Rags ever shot a 40mm on manual before. I couldn't have done that."

"Yeah, me, neither. The son of a bitch."

He laughed. "Don't say I never gave you anything. You gonna show it to Jo?"

"Not me. My momma didn't raise any stupid children. You do it."

"When Hell freezes over."

SEVENTEEN

The storm wasn't done, but it had slowed and begun to fall apart, and the worst was over. Cutter listened to the reports, and mostly, CFI and the other units on The Line's side had weathered things just fine. Some equipment had been damaged, a couple of people had gotten smacked by flying debris, and there were some small injuries from slipping and sliding, to go with the burns and wounds from enemy interaction. Wink had been busy, but mostly with injuries from other than CFI troops. Plus his dickhead foray into enemy territory. Sooner or later, he was going to get himself killed, skating right up to the edge the way he did.

Of course, on Cutter, it looked different. His action had been necessary and right . . .

He smiled.

A relatively quiet night, all things considered. It could have been a lot worse on any of the fronts.

He realized that it was nearing dawn, and that he hadn't eaten anything since . . . lunch yesterday? Huh.

Third shift had things under control. He ambled to the dining hall.

There were a few people on break, mostly having junk food or caffeinated beverages. They had healthier fare, for those who wanted it, but mostly, troops wanted a fix of sugar or fat once action commenced. The prevailing philosophy seemed to be, Hell, I might get killed any second now, might as well eat what I want and fuck it.

War had a way of making *carpe diem* seem valid no matter what you wanted to seize . . .

He nodded at those who looked his way, went and collected a cup of coffee and a quik-heat roll, found an empty chair and sat. He sipped at the hot coffee, which was good. That had always been part of any unit he'd been in, that he had coffee you could drink and enjoy, and not stuff better used to clean rust stains from oxidized sheet metal. The roll was sweet-potato-flour-based, not bad, but not particularly delicious. Food, and good enough for the moment.

Formentara drifted into the room. Zhe collected a piece of fruit and took a seat three or four tables over. Zhe didn't see him, or if so, didn't acknowledge him.

Zhe didn't look any the worse for her adventure with Wink. His amazement at hir actions didn't extend to Cutter entirely. He had known zhe had some augs running though not the extent. If being out in a hurricane and a firefight bothered hir, it didn't show now.

Cutter watched Formentara, his gaze mostly unfocused. He was tired; probably wouldn't hurt to get a couple of hours' rest. A good soldier could nod off falling down stairs while eating hot soup, but when you were the officer in charge, that wasn't as easy as when somebody else was responsible and giving the orders. Once a war heated up, his sleep was always spotty. Sleep, diet, bowel habits, war changed a lot of things . . .

Zhe became aware of his attention. "Colonel?"

He blinked. "What?"

"Something I can help you with?"

"Ah, no, sorry, I didn't mean to stare. I was woolgathering."

Zhe looked puzzled. Zhe stood, came over to his table. Raised an eyebrow at an empty chair.

He waved at the chair.

Zhe sat.

"Have fun out playing medical rescue with Dr. Death?"

"I did. It was invigorating. I got to test out my augmentation, and, of course, it worked just fine."

"Of course."

"What is 'woolgathering'?"

"Old Terran expression. It means a kind of mindless daydreaming."

"Wool is an animal product, the hair of ovines, is it not? How is that connected to a blank gaze? Do those kinds of animals have a thousand-meter stare?"

He grinned. "Not that I know about. As I understand it, in the prespace days, when sheep and goats were allowed to range free, they often did so among shrubs and bushes that could catch and remove bits of their hair. Enough so, apparently, that collecting the loose strands was worth doing. This was not an activity that required a great deal of mindful thought. People would wander about, plucking fur from thorns and branches, putting it into sacks, and since it didn't take much mental activity, their minds would be free for other tasks."

Zhe nodded. "I see. Moving meditation. And what were you daydreaming about?"

He shrugged. "Life, death, the universe, my place in the scheme of it all."

Zhe laughed. "Really?"

"More or less."

Actually, his thoughts were less general and more specifically about Formentara, how zhe looked as she moved.

Zhe was the brightest person he'd ever been around for more than a short time; zhe had an air of mystery about hir, and it wasn't just hir androgynous appearance, which he found attractive. He knew zhe was beyond adept at what zhe did; that there weren't a handful of aug experts in the galaxy who were as good, maybe none better. And why, he had wondered before, would somebody who could write hir own ticket, be the head of some corporation or university or just sit back and spend hir money be here, doing this? Working for him? On the face of it, it was a puzzle.

Then there was this grace-under-fire thing earlier this very night. Formentara as a fighter?

Fascinating . . .

Zhe chuckled.

His turn to raise an eyebrow query.

"You've never struck me as a . . . reflective person. More of a doer than a be-er."

"True enough. Still, when one is in a profession that deals in the possibility of sudden and maybe unexpected violent death, the questions arise now and then for examination."

"The questions being . . . ?"

"What does it all mean? Why are we here? Where are we going?"

Zhe laughed. "A warrior philosopher!"

"Not your bent, to muse on such things?"

"Oh, I used to ask myself those questions. Then one day, I realized that, as brilliant as I am, I couldn't divine the answers. That, unbelievable as it was, there had been many people *smarter* than I who had broken themselves of the rock of why-are-we-here? And, even if I happened upon The Answer, how would I know? Who would be able to verify it for me?

"Given my upbringing and experience, religion wasn't an option, the notion of Somebody-in-Charge-Who-Pays-Attention didn't work for me: Either zhe was unspeakably cruel, or unbelievably inept, no other possibility. So I let it go. Can't know the answer, no point in asking the question, is there? That way lies complete frustration. Better to concentrate one's energy on something useful."

"I suppose. I think even the remote possibility of a come-to-understand moment, wherein the scales fall from my eyes, and I can see the whole flow of the universe, the why and wheretofor, is still there. It seems to have happened to others."

Zhe shrugged. "I can do that. I can crank up the godgene, ramp it into reality for a patient so they feel that cosmic consciousness, the oneness with it all with an absolute certainty beyond question. Since I can do it? Makes it harder to believe it's anything other than an accident of neurochem; a stray cosmic ray flipping an on switch. Would that be something you'd want? A fake epiphany?"

"No."

"I didn't think so. If you got there on your own, you might buy it, but knowing it was artificially induced? Not your way. A lot of people would take the offer, but you aren't one of them, are you?"

"So we believe because we want to believe?"

"*Need*, more than *want*, I think. It's built into the operating soft- and hardware," zhe said. "Some kind of survival characteristic, maybe, a sustaining comfort when great stress arises. Our bodies are full of chemical tides that ebb and flow to balance us physically and mentally. Why not one that does it spiritually? Such yearning seems to be common among most intelligent species, certainly humans. We need something beyond what we can see and touch and smell."

He looked at hir, impressed that zhe had considered such things. He nodded again.

"Well. I will leave you to your snack and philosophy. I have augs to balance and programs to write. Good luck finding the answer."

Zhe smiled, stood, then headed for the door.

He watched hir go, intrigued.

What a truly *fascinating* person . . .

— — — — — —

Dawn came to the only hill in the area and brought at least a little light. There was still fitful rain and mostly overcast, but breaks where the sun managed to peek through.

Jo took stock of the camp. There was a lot of standing water, plenty of debris, but mostly, the storm's worst hadn't been too bad.

Parts of the old houses had collapsed: window covers blown in, doors knocked open. Portions of the roofs had been torn off and hurled hundreds of meters away. The gardens were flattened, as were ornamental shrubs and small fruit trees. Cisterns were aslant or knocked over, and a couple of the outhouse structures toppled. That would have been a nasty surprise were you sitting on the outhouse bench when it tipped over.

If the squatters who lived here decided to return, they were going to have some work ahead of them to make the place habitable again.

A couple of the igloos had damage, but none of them had been peeled from their bases. None of the crawlers or transports took anything that would interfere with operation though one of the smaller APCs suffered a cracked side window from impact with something tossed into it at speed. Nobody had been seriously injured nor gravely wounded in the firefights.

Could have been a lot worse.

She checked the time. It was early, not yet 0600. Later today, there was going to be a major push, spearheaded by Colonel Buckley's force, to take the primary wellheads. All going as planned, the Tejas forces would be in control of the objective by this afternoon or early evening, with sufficient backup to keep it for the remaining three days until the conflict's termination. Holding the ground here to make sure nobody sneaked along the nearby road was part of the plan. As was breaking out and going down that road themselves to add their muscle to the plan.

Of course, no battle plan survived first contact with the enemy . . .

There was going to be a staff meeting of the various commanders in an hour, and a report on that would be forthcoming before the push. Shaping up to be a good day.

In theory.

Jo walked the area, avoiding the deeper puddles. The air was cleaner. Nothing like a hurricane to wash away air pollution, pollen, and anything else floating around. Her troops were up and slogging about, making the camp as functional as it could be with the mud as thick as it was.

Kay appeared and moved toward her. She didn't seem to sink as deep into the mire as she should. Yeah, she was lighter, but even so.

"Jo Captain."

"Kay. Everything seems to be secure?"

"Yes. The enemy's dead and wounded are gone, no sign of activity on the hillside."

"Aircraft will be cleared, we can expect to see drones pretty soon, theirs and ours."

"Yes."

Jo nodded.

– – – – – –

Zoree Wood looked at the staff gathered in the HQ. "All right, let's share, shall we? Colonel Buckley, why don't you lead off?"

Vim Buckley was a tall, gray-haired man of fifty-five, who had been kicked out of the Blue Hats as a lieutenant for decking a superior officer. He'd gotten the rank the hard way, via field commission. His scalp was depilated and he had the Ghost Lancer sigil tattooed on his head. He was harder than a leather sack full of rocks, and as good a soldier as Cutter had ever known. If he told you something, you could take it to the bank.

Buckley said, "Op Theater North is dogged down tight. The rain and wind caused some problems, but we got those fixed. We control much of the main access road to the wells, and our troops are set for a surge when we get the word, and we won't be taking the easy road. Once we start, anybody who wakes up and tries to follow us will be stopping to pick a whole lot of nasty splinters out of their feet."

Wood nodded. "Shields?"

Del Shields had commanded the company that stood firm against five times its number during the Battle for Port Barton Samuels, on Veldt. Severely injured in that fighting, he retired a captain, and once he recovered, went into corporate military. He walked with an old-style power brace on one leg, didn't want the implants. Shields was a man who, like Buckley, if he said he'd do something, would—or die trying.

His comment was short and sweet: "Nobody is getting past our units on the Southwestern quadrant. They don't have enough troops on their side, even if the rest of you all go home."

That drew smiles all around.

"Rags?"

Cutter said, "My people control the high ground overlooking the two roads from the east into the wellheads. We have additional forces ranging the forests and making sure nobody sneaks up that way. Once Vim's troops push, we'll cover his southern flank."

Cutter leaned back and listened to the other commanders offer their comments. On paper, they had this in the bag. They had outmaneuvered the opposition strategically and tactically, and while you could never be sure until the cease-fire command, it certainly looked as if it was theirs to lose. Wood was a better general, she had picked better people, and they had done a better job of hitting their marks, before and after the shooting began. With only just over three days left until the war was over, it would take more than the other side seemed capable of doing to win.

Everybody here knew it, too; it resonated in their voices. They were all old pros, they knew which way the sun shone and the wind blew, and, for now, at least, those were at their backs, blinding and spraying grit into the faces of their enemy.

After everybody was done, Zoree said, "All right. We got this, all we have to do is keep executing as we have been doing. Don't start thinking about how you are going to spend your bonus, we don't want to jinx it, but as long as nobody screws up, we all know how this is going to end, right?"

That got a chorus of assents and grins.

— — — — — —

"How'd the meeting go?"

Cutter ambled into the office and looked at Gramps. "Fine. Nobody seems to be in any trouble, and all continuing as it is, when the whistle blows, we are platinum to the core."

"That's what I want to hear."

"Anything new I need to know?"

"Well. I talked to my contact in commercial MI, and while uplevels despise Junior, nobody has a tight enough rein on him to keep him from fucking us over if he really wants to."

"He send the shooter?"

"Nobody I talked to can say."

"Anything on the Bax?"

"Not yet."

"How's the hip?"

Gramps looked at him. "What hip?"

"The one that got *shot* while you were dicking around with the FCV next to the fucking Faraday forest."

"Oh. That. You scanned the log vids."

"My job to know what is going on in my command."

"It's fine. Just grazed me."

"You didn't feel like it merited a mention in your report?"

"Hey, I cut myself shaving last week, too. You want to know every piddly detail of my day?"

"I do indeed. You need more fiber in your diet." He paused. "Now you know how it feels, you always peeping over everybody's shoulder."

"I'll keep that in mind."

"I doubt that."

Gramps smiled.

- - - - - -

The explosion was close, loud, and the impact knocked Jo from her feet and into the air. She flew, fell, hit, managed a kind of roll, and came up into a crouch, a red haze surrounding her.

Grenade? Mortar?

Hand of God?

A quick check didn't show anything bleeding, no broken bones.

Jo scrabbled for cover and tried to call on the opchan for a sitrep from the others.

She didn't even get a carrier wave on the com. Her communication aug was off-line.

Well, shit!

She was woozy; the concussion and fall had rattled her. She also noticed that she couldn't hear much, nor could she see much. *What—?*

"Captain?"

Singh crouched next to her.

"I'm fine, but my com is out. Anybody hurt?"

Singh listened to his own com. "Not seriously, sah, but the enemy is making a serious run at us, and they seemed to have somehow gotten reinforcements and more vehicles."

"That doesn't seem likely."

"Still."

"Jo Captain?"

Jo looked up to see Kay. She had not heard nor smelled her arrival.

This was bad, that she hadn't sensed Kay. Her systems were down.

"We are outnumbered and outgunned," Kay said. "It would appear to be retreat or die. Which?"

She asked the question as if the answer didn't matter to her, and probably on a deep level, it didn't. Go. Stay. Live. Die. Whichever . . .

Jo shook her head, as if that would somehow clear away the fog. "Retreat. We were going to pull back anyhow. We have determined their weakest spots; if those haven't changed, we'll cut through one of them. Listen, my com is out and my augmentation system is damaged. Call Singh when you find out which way we need to go."

"I will."

She seemed to vanish.

Jo tried to reboot her augs, but that apparently wasn't working, either. Everything was off-line.

Fuck!

"Singh, stay with me. Put out a call, tell everybody to get ready to run, as soon as Kay finds the best route. A-1 evacuation protocols. Somebody find me an earpiece."

"Sah."

They had planned to break away to cover Colonel Buckley's advance in less than an hour; they were going to have to advance the timing on that if they were going to be of any use to him.

Or alive . . .

"Call HQ and tell them the situation," she told Singh.

"Sah."

Anything that wasn't packed and ready to go would be mined and left behind, and the fastest vehicles would lead the retreat. They had four potential routes mapped out for when they needed them, and with any luck, Kay would be calling with their pick real soon now . . .

"Sah, Kay has a route."

"Tell everybody. Where is my communicator?!"

Somebody appeared and handed the small unit to her. She slipped it into her ear and clicked it green. To Singh, she said, "Let's go."

The opchan chatter told her she was connected. Good.

She followed Singh, and when she moved, she was dizzy and nauseated. Her body seemed as if it were wrapped in a lead blanket; her senses were dull, she felt almost blind, deaf, her sense of smell dead, her sense of touch gone.

The lead crawler, its guns working, rolled down the hill, flanked by a pair of light APCs, also blasting away. Those who weren't inside a vehicle jogged alongside, firing their carbines at whatever they thought worth shooting.

"Command cart coming up behind us, sah. Get ready."

The cart slewed to a stop, throwing mud up in a ragged sheet. Jo and Singh hurried to get inside. Gunny was driving.

Once they were in, the cart resumed a controlled skid down the drenched hill.

"You okay?" Gunny asked.

"Okay enough."

The cart's longcom lit. "Jo?"

Formentara! Just knowing that made Jo feel better.

"I'm here."

"What happened?"

"Grenade, mortar, something close. I got knocked sprawling. My systems aren't running, and I can't seem to reboot anything. I'm mostly blind, deaf, smell is out, touch, proprioception, I'm physically weak."

"That shouldn't have happened," zhe said.

"Yeah, well, I don't know what to tell you about that."

"Hang in there. I'll be back."

Jo squinted through the windshield. She could see troops

moving, the vehicles, but they were fuzzy and dim images; the details she was used to were absent. It was like a hazy, dark filter over her vision.

On com, she heard:

"—clear on the left—!"

"—spike that fucker with the G2G, right there—!"

"—caboose—?"

"—they have the hill, but they are not pursuing, I say *not* pursuing! Still raining shit down though—!"

Jo said, "We have any Z-drones left?"

"We have four, Cap," somebody said.

"Can they fly?"

"Already deployed, Cap."

Muzzy, definitely. Might need the medic to check her out—

The command cart reached the flats. There were a few enemy troops still shooting there—a bullet *spanged!* from the cart's side armor—but they were falling back.

The mud was no less thick, but the cart's studded tires bit into more solid ground, and the vehicle gained speed.

"Everybody catch a ride, stat," Jo said. "CFI has left the building. Go, Gunny. Burn the tires up."

– – – – – –

"Jo?"

"Colonel."

"How are you doing?"

"We're fine. Got a few wounded, one KIA. Now on the road to cover Vim's push. The enemy will just think we are running, I don't see they'll figure it out we were leaving in a little while anyhow. Don't appear to be chasing us."

"No, how are *you* doing?"

"Can't see, hear, smell, feel, or taste worth a crap, and I'm like a baby kitten for strength; other than that and the dizziness and nausea, fine."

"Formentara . . . ?"

"Zhe's working on it, but nothing yet."

"Have your medic run some scans."

"Yeah."

— — — — — —

And here was the funny part, Jo realized after the field medic checked her. *All of her senses and reflexes and general physical fitness were straight down the middle— completely normal—*

—for an unaugmented *human being.*

It had been so long since she had started running augs—she'd gotten her first at sixteen, using money she'd saved working the opal mines. It had been one of the old CAS systems—Citius, Altius, Fortius: Faster, Higher, Stronger . . .

Not top-of-the-line, even then, just real basics, hormones, spliced virals, and connective-tissue strengtheners, but sufficient to allow her to do what she had to do to put the events during that terrible field trip to Adelaide to rest.

It wasn't until much later she realized she'd been lucky the drunken medic who had done the job hadn't killed or crippled her.

Lot of water under a lot of contested bridges since then, and many more augs. That she wasn't halfway to an early grave because the augs were perfectly balanced was entirely due to Formentara's genius.

This was the default sensor system, and Jo marveled at how puny it was. Unaugmented people didn't realize how . . . *little* they had.

She sure hoped Formentara could pull another miracle out of hir magical bag of spells . . .

"Jo."

Speak of the devil.

"Here."

"I've run the computer simulations. It took a while to get the conditions right; it shouldn't have happened, but there is a precise distance and pressure wave that will do what it did. One chance in a million. I should have picked that up before. It looks as if your hypothalamic regulator has been kicked off-line from compression shock."

"Can you fix it?"

"*Of course* I can *fix* it! But I need you on my table, I can't have some ham-handed FM dicking around in there, even with me looking over his shoulder. This is delicate stuff. I can rebuild the V&H so it won't happen again, but I have to have hands on."

"I'm kinda busy now."

"I understand. I've read your physical-exam stats, you aren't in any danger, you can walk around without any big risks, but the way I have your systems balanced, I need half an hour to do the repair and rebuild."

"I'll have my secretary make an appointment for after the war," Jo said.

"Listen, I've put a lot of work into making you the finest soldier in this half of the galaxy; don't you get yourself killed before I can put you back into shape."

"I'll try to avoid that."

"See that you do."

Zhe disconnected without another word.

Jo started to shake her head, but that made her want to puke, so she stopped that.

— — — — — —

They pulled over for a quick break ten klicks from the hill, a pee break, to stretch.

Kay ambled over to where Jo stood, squinting into the bright sunshine. Hard to believe there had been a hurricane blowing only a short time ago.

Never knew how good your polarizing optics were until they weren't working.

"Be a good time for a match," Kay said. Her voice and expression were absolutely deadpan.

Kay was making a joke. Still amazed Jo every time she did that.

Jo smiled. "Right. If you tie one hand behind your back and hobble your legs, I might have a prayer."

"Probably not," Kay said. "If you are indeed constrained to your fighting knowledge and normal human speed and strength? I would be hard-pressed to calculate your chances. Something below . . . 3 percent, perhaps. I might trip, or have a stroke, or be hit by a meteorite."

Jo laughed. It made her head hurt, but it released some tension. "Thanks. I needed to hear how pitiful I am without my bells and whistles."

"No worse than any other human. No healthy Vastalimi has ever been beaten in hand-to-claw combat by an unaugmented human."

"I heard about a martial arts master named Evets—"

"A human myth, it did not happen."

"You would say that."

Kay ignored her. "And even one with increased strength and speed and other . . . bells and whistles can only manage it rarely. At least until you changed the statistics."

"Formentara says zhe can fix it, put me back to where I was before."

"That will be good. I would hate to lose a training partner who keeps me on my toes."

"Yeah, I'd hate that, too. How does it look out there?"

"The drone they had following us was shot down by our rearguard drones though it took one of them out before that happened. They seem disinclined to pursue."

"Because they don't know where we are going."

"They wanted the hill. They have the hill. They should have no idea of our further intent. They believe they have won. They are shortsighted. This often seems to be a part of the human condition."

Jo said, "If our plan works, and it is showing every indication that it will, we have this in the can. A few more days, the horn sounds, we win."

"I am compelled to point out that there are many steps between *seeking* prey and *eating* it," Kay said.

"Yeah. I hear that."

EIGHTEEN

"Say again?"

"I'm sending Brooks out to take over your unit. You need Formentara's tender ministrations, and I've got another assignment for you."

"Which is . . . ?"

"When you get here, Jo."

Jo's CFI unit had arrived at the crossroads where they would harass anybody who suddenly realized that Colonel Buckley had stolen a march on them and was on his way to occupy the primary wellheads, getting there from a direction nobody would have reasonably expected.

In a standoff, sometimes the person who moved first got enough of a jump so they couldn't be caught. Good tacticians were like magicians. While you were busy watching one hand, they'd slap you with the other.

"I'm fine out here, Rags, I—"

He had expected her to want to stay on-station, despite her injuries. "This is not make-work, I have something you are better qualified to do than run things where you are.

Brooks is capable of holding things together there. You hired her, remember?"

"Yeah."

"Nancy will be there in approximately thirty minutes. Pack your gear."

"Stet that," she said.

Two minutes after they broke the connection, Formentara stepped into his office unannounced. "Well?"

"She'll be here in forty-five minutes," he said.

"Good."

Formentara turned around and left without another word.

Cutter grinned. Genius had a few quirks; part of the price you paid to have it around. One thing it never was? Boring . . .

- - - - - -

Jo's desire was to take a long, hot shower when she got back to the base. The crawlers had outdoor showerheads, but the noodle-pinching hardware designers had been given keep-it-cheap design orders, and had apparently achieved them. Crawler showers came with absolutely unalterable timers that gave you a maximum two minutes of piss-poor pressure before they shut off; then they made you wait two *more* minutes before they would restart. Standing there wet and soapy waiting for more slow-flow rinse water was not the most soothing experience when you were scrubbing mud and blood off yourself.

More than a few soldiers over the years must have entertained the fantasy of hunting down the people who came up with shower timers and murdering them. Or at least dipping them in a latrine trench, then restricting them to a crawler shower to wash it off . . .

There was a common workaround in the field—fill a thirty-five-liter bucket with water from an unregulated fire-hose tap and, using a spare showerhead, some tubing, and a drop-in induction heater, rig your own to get five or six minutes of uninterrupted hot water.

Usually for a short stay, there was other stuff to keep you too busy to play with rigging a shower, so mostly, you just suffered under anemic and short cycles. Enough to get somewhat clean but not at all satisfying . . .

Twenty minutes under a needle shower at the base was ever so much more refreshing.

Alas, it was not to be; Formentara was waiting when Nancy taxied the hopper to the debarkation ramp.

"Come on," zhe said. Zhe turned and walked away without looking back to see if Jo was following hir.

"Maybe I'll save you some hot water," Gunny said. "But . . . probably not." She grinned.

"I hope you slip, fall, crack your head, and drown."

Gunny laughed.

In Formentara's suite, zhe said, "Clothes off, on the table." Zhe was already waving hir hands back and forth over the reader.

"Somebody pee in your oatmeal?"

Formentara frowned. "What?"

"You seem somewhat testy."

Zhe blinked, looked at Jo, but kept loading gestures into the reader. "I put a lot of time and energy into crafting your system. You are unique. I can't have you getting blown up! All my work down the fucking drain? I expect you to take better care of yourself!"

In that moment, Jo realized that Formentara was not so much angry as . . . worried? Relieved?

"What are you smiling at?"

She dropped the smile. "Nothing. I just . . . well, yes, you're right. I should be more careful. I wasn't thinking of how it would affect you if I got killed. Selfish of me."

Formentara stopped what zhe was doing and regarded Jo. After a moment, zhe said, "All right, yes, fine, I was a little perturbed that you were hit hard enough to kick your augs off-line. I would prefer that you not die, and not just for my own ego. Is that better?"

Jo nodded. "I am touched. Thank you."

"If I might continue without interruption?"

She lay back. The question was not whether Formentara could fix things; zhe'd already said zhe could. The only question was, how long would it take?

And who knew zhe cared so much? Paying so much for Kay to go hunt? Helping Wink out? Fretting over Jo's injury? The *mahu* had hidden depths, it seemed . . .

Thirty-seven minutes for the revamp, as it turned out. And zhe was irritated that it took that long. Zhe had expected, zhe said, that it would take half an hour. A seven-minute gap was like a thousand years, in Formentara-speak . . .

"Okay, we are done. Run a systems check."

"Stet," Jo said. "Systems check shows green across."

"Reboot."

"Rebooting . . ."

"Recheck."

"Green."

"Up, move around."

Jo was on her feet in an instant, and she felt like Superwoman. It had only been a short time, a few hours, but the returns of power and energy and function were amazing. You got used to being a certain way, you took it for granted; you truly didn't appreciate how being well felt until you got sick. Then you appreciated the hell out of it.

She could hear, she could see, she could smell, taste, touch, move, all parsecs beyond what she had been able to do after the mortar round had knocked her on her ass.

She was reborn.

They ran through a full-systems diagnostic. Everything was as good as it had been, and on a couple of augs, the subroutines had been improved and were actually better.

"I—thank you," she said. "I can't begin to tell you—"

"Yeah, yeah. Go on, go play soldier again. And try not to mess up my work."

"Yessah, I will do my best."

– – – – – –

Rags and Gramps were waiting at the conference table when Jo and Gunny arrived. The colonel waved them in; they sat.

"Chocolatte. You are clean and shiny. You look like a woman who just took a fourteen-minute-and-forty-two-second shower."

"You better not have had a cam in there."

"Seen one nekkid fem, seen 'em all—no cam. But the water-flow monitors will rat you out every time."

"And you check them? Don't you have any real work to do?"

"It is real work; you never know but that an enemy will try to sap our resolve by stealing all our water. After all, isn't water why we are all here?"

Gunny shook her head. She was gonna have to up her game; he was winning too many of these little dialogues.

Rags said, "Jo, you back up to par?"

"And then some. Formentara was pissed at me for allowing myself to be damaged, but zhe dialed everything back up to full operation. I feel great."

"Good. Gramps?"

"Okay, here's the deal: We've come up with some names on the biz with the Bax. As nearly as we can tell, there are half a dozen of the aliens in this area whose movements our C-AI have backtracked and determined are likely possibilities to be involved in this."

"Based on . . . ?" Jo asked.

"Patterns of travel, occupations, plus stuff we should be able to determine but can't, what sometimes goes with cover identities that seem deep, but too tight."

Off Gunny's look, he continued, "Civilized sentients have personal histories, and they tend to be jumbled and sometimes messy. Crafted, whole-cloth IDs are sometimes a little too neat. An AI running down secondary or tertiary links won't spot any inconsistencies, but past that, they should. If they don't, if a story seems too perfect? That's a warning flash. It might mean something."

"Or not," Jo said. "Good ID crafters think about such details when they build spy backgrounds, they throw in contradictory stuff."

"But 'good' is a relative term," Gramps said. "Maybe we have a Bax sneaking around who didn't get the guy who was top of the ID-maker's class. Or maybe it was somebody who didn't think a Bax needed the same layers a human might need. In any event, we have some names, and the C-AI can only do so much. We need some hands-on investigation. It has to be quick because we are running out of war."

"What exactly are we lookin' for?"

"Who is doing what and why would be good," Rags said. "Find the correct person to ask and do it right, maybe they will tell you. Wink will have some chem formulated for the Bax for you."

"Doesn't General Wood have her own MI people for this?" Jo asked.

"She does, and they are probably adept enough, but she's not overly concerned with this intel. All things continuing as they are now, she notches this war, mission accomplished, we all pack up and move along, and who cares what the Bax are up to, it's not our problem."

"But you think it is." Not a question.

He looked at Jo. "Given our recent experiences, things haven't always been what they seemed, and not knowing the truth caused us some grief. I don't really care which set of Bax gets the water rights, if that's what is really going on. That's not our worry. But anytime somebody is sneaking around doing things that might impact us, I would rather know than not."

"How would this impact us?"

"Since I don't know who is doing what and their reasons, I can't say. Once I know, then I'll have a better lens to look at it."

Jo and Gunny exchanged looks.

Gunny said, "Ah'm just a simple fem, Ah go where Ah'm ordered to go and shoot who they tell me to shoot."

Rags said, "Go find some civilian clothes that will let you blend into the local scenery. The mission parameters are in your tactical comps. Read over the stuff, go see Wink, and make a pass back here before you take off."

Rags stood, as did Jo and Gunny. Gramps came up, but slowly, and Gunny caught a hint of something flit across his features before he replaced it with a big smile. *Hello?*

"You movin' kind of stiff there, old man. Got the rheumatiz?"

"Not me, child. Must be your vision is fogged by unbridled imagination and innate jealousy."

Rags followed them out into the hall. Gramps did not. Gunny walked a little ways, then turned to him. "Gramps okay?"

Rags looked at her. "Far as I know."

"He looked a little pained there for a second."

He shrugged. "I'm not his doctor."

No, but I know who is . . .

- - - - - -

Wink was on his way to the command conference room when he saw Gunny heading in his direction.

"Hey, I heard you were back. How was it out there. Exciting?"

"Not enough for you. Rags has got Jo and me running an errand in San Antonio, and you are supposed to have some chem for us."

"Bax giggle juice. Yes, just on my way there."

He produced a handful of little-finger-sized color-coded poppers from his tunic pocket. "The blue ones are knockouts.

Over a big vein is best, takes about five seconds to kick in. Lasts about thirty minutes. After it wears off, use the orange one, and again, IV is quicker. You can ask what you want, they will be happy to tell you. Be careful, one of the side effects is urinary incontinence and sometimes projectile vomiting."

She took the poppers. "Great. Anything Ah can bring you from town?"

"A cloak of invisibility would be nice."

"Wouldn't help, Wink, they'd track your implant."

"I can disable that."

She smiled. "Ah got to go. How's Gramps recovery coming along?"

"I can't talk about my patients, Gunny, you know that."

"Come on, it's Gramps."

"Don't worry, he's fine, small-caliber jacketed bullet punched through clean, didn't hit anything, he'll have a couple tiny scars to show for it, nothing permanent."

He saw the surprise on her face and obviously realized what had just happened.

"Well, fuck! You just ran a con on me! You didn't know any of that! Dammit, Gunny—!"

"I'm sorry, Wink. The old fart wouldn't tell me, Rags wouldn't tell me, and Ah don't like being out of the loop here."

He shook his head. "Fine. You didn't hear anything from me. I will deny it to the heat death of the universe, anybody asks.

"Copy that."

– – – – – –

When they got back to the conference room after scanning the op data, Jo could see that Gunny was agitated. She didn't say anything, but there was a tenseness to her body set.

Neither Rags nor Gramps had made it yet.

"Gunny? You okay?"

"Me? Ah'm jest fahn."

Her accent, Jo had noticed, got a little thicker when she was bothered by something.

Jo waited, not speaking.

"Did you know that Gramps got shot?" Gunny finally said.

"No, really? When?"

"Near as Ah kin tell, when he was runnin' the FCV during the hurricane."

"First I heard of it. He looks a little careful in his movements, but no indication of any major injury I noticed."

"No, it apparently wasn't much. But Ah was talkin' to him on the fuckin' com, had to be right after it happened. Ah gave him a call, he didn't answer, and now Ah know why: He was getting shot and patchin' hisself up!"

"Well, he seems okay."

"What Ah want to know is, why'n the fuck didn't he tell me?"

Jo held her tongue, but the thought was there. *Probably for exactly what is happening right now—he didn't want to upset you.*

"You going to say something to him about it?"

"Hell will fuckin' freeze over before Ah fuckin' do."

Ten seconds later Rags arrived, alone.

"Are we copacetic here?"

"Read the material, I don't see any problems. We'll go, we'll poke around, see what we can see."

"The clock is running. Maybe it won't make a difference one way or the other, and maybe it won't matter if we know now or later, but . . ." He shrugged.

"Got it. We'll make hay while the sun shines. If it ever stops raining."

NINETEEN

There actually was a lull in the rain, almost no wind, and the sun was already sucking moisture up and turning the air into a steamy miasma.

Jo and Gunny avoided puddles on the way to wait for the transport. Singh, back from the front, walked with them.

They were nearly there when they heard Gramps curse: "Die, you fucker!"

They looked to see him stomping something into the mud. They went to see what all the fuss was about.

It was a little mottled-gray snake, maybe half a meter long, head crushed flat.

Gunny squatted to look at the dead creature. "Looks like a rat snake," she said. "It's harmless, not poisonous."

Gramps said, "I don't care. I don't like snakes. I don't like poisonous snakes; I don't like nonpoisonous snakes; I don't like sticks on the ground that *look* like snakes."

"Ah think maybe somebody had a traumatic event with snakes along the way. What, you had a run-in with the serpent that bedeviled Eve back in the Garden?"

Singh raised an eyebrow.

"A Jewish/Christian story," Jo said. "The reason mankind lost direct contact with God and was banished from Paradise. A snake talked the first woman into trying fruit from the Tree of Knowledge, after God had warned them not to eat it."

"Sah, I understand this god is supposedly much more powerful than our gods. I wonder, if he created all things and was all-knowing and omnipotent, why would he put such a tree there? Would he not know in advance that Eve would succumb to the temptation?"

"The tale doesn't bear too close an inspection," Gramps said. "Believers view these stories as allegories, meta-phors, rather than as literal happenings."

Gunny jumped in quickly to amend Gramps's response: "Some of 'em," she said. "Some of 'em are literalists, and crazy as space-station roaches when the hatch opens to blow them into vac. They think the Earth is six thousand years old and that every word of the Bible is absolutely true. You can have a field day pointing out inconsistencies in those stories, doesn't bother them, just bounces right off their self-righteous armor."

Gramps said, "Hmm. Somebody have a traumatic event connected to religion along the way?"

"Fuck you." Jo felt that had a harder edge than usual to it. Gunny was angry with him.

If Gramps noticed, he didn't show it. "Always the idle threat. Anyway, in the story, the serpent, who at the time was more of a lizard, with legs and all, conned the woman into picking the forbidden fruit. For his reward, God struck off his legs and condemned him and his offspring to crawl on their bellies until the end of time. God apparently wasn't big on forgiveness much in those days."

"But they let snakes onto the Ark, didn't they?" Jo said.

Off Singh's look, she said, "Another story, end-of-the-world flood, and God had one of his own build a big boat and load two of every critter onto it to be spared."

"It must have been an exceedingly large boat."

"Not really. Somebody put the measurements up in one of the holy books, and it would have been a tight squeeze just to get all the different kinds of beetles, ants, and spiders on board, much less all the other animals."

"Metaphor," Gramps said. "Offering a moral lesson. But to your point, Chocolatte, yes, I had an unpleasant experience with snakes once, and I avoid them to this day."

"One of them bite you and die from it?"

He looked at her, catching something in her tone.

"You can't leave that hanging," Jo said. "Tell us."

"It's a long story. You'll be leaving soon."

"Our ride's ETA is half an hour away."

He shrugged.

"Once upon a time, in the dawn of history, I was in basic training. Of course, back then, we still used fire-hardened pointed sticks for weapons and wore animal skins." He glanced at Gunny, who didn't smile.

"We were in a swamp somewhere, lot of mucky green water, knobby evergreen trees growing out of it, squishy ground, where there was any. Reptiles all over, alligators or some relative thereto, mosquitoes, hot, damp, a playground for mold and mildew. Kind of like this place, but worse.

"We'd been told there were snakes but that we probably wouldn't see many, they would seek to avoid us.

"Our training mission was to capture the flag on a small island smack-dab in the middle of a shallow lake. We had to wade most of a klick through scummy water that ranged from knee to chest deep, and we had to do it in the dark.

"There were dumbot guns on the island, sensors set to fire training rounds at anything man-sized. The rounds would sting pretty good, raise a welt on exposed skin, but wouldn't really damage you, we had eye-protection goggles, like that.

"The Monitors counted you dead if one of the db rounds hit you anywhere a real bullet would likely be fatal.

"To avoid being shot as we got closer to the island, we had to duck under the water and move laterally before we came back up. The dbs were set for slow acquisition, so you'd have a few seconds before you got reacquired and had to submerge again."

"Sounds like a lot of fun," Gunny said.

"To a masochist like yourself, maybe.

"The notion was that our training grenades would shut the dumbots down once we got close enough to throw them. So we had to get within grenade range, which was around twenty or thirty."

"What kind of launchers had such short range?" Singh asked

"Launchers? We weren't using *launchers*, we were *throwing* them."

"Like rocks," Gunny said. "To go with the pointed sticks."

"My squad was still sixty meters out when we came to a little oval islet of mud and sedge grass a few meters wide, sticking up maybe a meter out of the water. Our sergeant decided that this would be enough to block the dbs' sensors if we lined up behind it. Give us a chance to take a quick break, gather ourselves for the final slog. Maybe while the dbs were shooting at some other poor suckers on another approach, we could make our push and get close enough to spike the guns.

"So the sarge ordered us to line up two wide and four deep, to use the hillock for cover. He was ahead of me, along with one other newbie; the other six trainees in our squad were behind us.

"Our supposedly waterproof coms weren't worth crap, they came and went. 'Working com' in the field? That's usually an oxymoron.

"The grunt in front of me either misheard or misunderstood the message. He got to the islet and slogged right onto it, dropped prone in the mire.

"Sarge yelled at the guy to fucking get back in the fucking water, but by then, it was too late.

"The trainee had laid himself down in a nest of breeding water snakes, dozens, scores of them, and they weren't happy about it. They latched onto him, biting whatever they could reach. He screamed, stood, tried to run, but sank hip deep into the mud.

"He was covered with snakes, beating at them with his hands, screeching like a banshee.

"The dbs locked onto him, and because he was thrashing and waving around, they peppered him and kept doing it.

"He looked like Medusa's hair.

"That image is seared into my memory. A screaming, panicked, trapped man, slapping at snakes that hung off him like fringe.

"In his struggles, he threw snakes every which way. One of them hit me in the chest, sank its fangs into me, just above the right collarbone. I grabbed it and slung it and did some serious screaming of my own.

"Bite burned like electric fire, and I lost it. I turned and ran as fast I could in the chest-deep water, but it was like running in a nightmare, so slow! The dbs raked my back with stingers, I found the marks later, but in the moment, I was beyond feeling them.

"The rest of the squad also scattered, save for our medic and the sarge, I found out later, who went to try and help the guy stuck in the ooze.

"I didn't look back.

"I remember the sound of a fanboat roaring toward us, Monitors coming to see what the fuck was going on. After that, things got hazy, and next thing I remember, I was on a muddy shore with the medic telling me I was going to be okay, the antivenom I had circulating would counteract the poison."

"What of the man on the islet?" Singh asked

Gramps shook his head. "Not enough antivenom in the world to counteract all those bites. He died stuck hip deep in the mud."

"I can see why you might not care for snakes," Singh said.

"Fun story." Jo glanced at Gunny. "I'm going to the landing pad," she said.

"And I have to report to Formentara," Singh said. "I will take my leave, sahs."

"Go ahead, Jo," Gunny said. "Ah'll see you at the pad."

After they were gone, Gramps said, "Something wrong?"

"Ah'm fahn; why do you ask?"

"You seem a little more pissed off at me than usual."

"Nothin' wrong here."

He hesitated for a moment, then decided. "Listen, Gunny, I . . ." He ran down.

"Cat got yore tongue?"

He shook his head. "During the hurricane, when you called the FCV? The reason I was late getting the call, I was in the shower."

"Nice to know you haven't completely lost your sense of personal hygiene."

"See, the thing is, I went out to fix a busted cable and in the rain and wind and shit, we had a little enemy infil, some rounds were exchanged, and I got a little nick. So I was washing away the mud and blood when you called."

"Really." It didn't sound like a question.

"Yeah, it punched a little hole through-and-through on my hip, here."

"And this happened *before* Ah called?"

"Yeah."

"And you didn't think to fuckin' *tell* me?"

He looked away, sighed, then back at her. "It was already done, the damage was minimal, and . . ."

"And what?"

"I didn't want to worry you. You had plenty going on to think about where you were."

"You didn't want to *worry* me? What makes you think Ah'd been the least fuckin' bit worried? Every morning I get up, I expect you to have keeled over and croaked during the night. I don't worry about you!"

He shrugged. "Sorry. I should have told you."

"Yeah, you should have." She paused a second, then said, "And it's a good fuckin' thing you finally did, 'cause that would have *really* pissed me off."

"What can I do to make it up to you?"

"Ah will think of something. Meanwhile, Ah got to go, my ride is here."

"Be safe, Gunny."

"Dammit, you don't need to tell me that!"

But she smiled, just a little, and he knew she wasn't really mad at him for saying it. And he felt better for having told her about the hip, too.

TWENTY

When they got to the pad, Wink was there.

"Come to wish us a bon voyage?" Jo asked.

"Nope, I'm going with you."

"Really? Why would you think that?"

"Our esteemed commander allowed me to convince him that a visit to a modern Terran city is probably not as intrinsically dangerous in and of itself as being in an active war zone; besides which, if you need to question a Bax, I might be of some assistance, my happy juice notwithstanding."

"You know I'm gonna call him."

"You don't trust me? I'm wounded."

She accessed her aug: "Rags?"

He was expecting the call; there was no preamble: "Yes, I said he could go."

"Got it."

"Don't let him get into any trouble."

Jo felt like a new woman . . .

Actually, what she felt like was her old self. Formentara had repaired and reset her system, all of her augs were functioning as they were supposed to; the well was flowing now, and she appreciated the hell out of it.

Gunny said, "Ah always feel like an impostor in civilian weeds."

"You look fine," Jo said. In truth, Gunny had a military look about her no matter how she dressed, and Jo supposed the same was true about her. Then again, they were going to San Antonio's *Cuarto Extranjero*, the alien quarter, and in an exteetown, the things that humans noticed weren't always picked up by offworlders.

Wink didn't look like he was in anybody's army; he looked like he was dangerous to any fem within range. Husbands and Significant Others instinctively moved closer to their mates when he was around, which was a good idea. Wink welcomed trouble, he gloried in it, and making a run at an attached fem with her partner standing right there wouldn't faze him. He lived to walk the razor's edge, and falling off didn't seem to bother him at all.

Jo had been in a few exteetowns. They all had their own sensibilities, depending on which alien visitors predominated. This one had wide sidewalks, so nobody worried about bumping into anybody else. The various buildings were decorated in odd colors, and sometimes door and window shapes appeared off to human eyes. Signs were often repeated in five or six languages, and tightcasts tracked passersby with open coms, to offer the spoken version of the main language inside, for those who couldn't read it.

It wasn't as if the Terran city stopped as if sheared by a blade on one corner, and exteetown began on the next one, but you couldn't help but notice when the shift became apparent. Here, you were strolling down the walk of a

NorAm human city, and a couple of hundred meters past that, you were in a place that catered to people who didn't look or act like you.

"And welcome to exteetown, people. Careful what you say, and if you smile crooked when you say it," Wink said.

"You be sure and take your own advice, Doctor Death."

"Hey, my heart is pure, don't worry about me."

"Right."

What a lot of humans apparently didn't understand was that other intelligent aliens didn't always get along with each other, that lumping them together in a district like so many odds and ends was an ignorant thing to do. Rel didn't socialize with Vastalimi, given that Kay's people thought of Rel as prey. Bax and Zinna had a long-standing antipathy for each other, going back five hundred years. While offworlders weren't required to stay in the exteetowns once they cleared customs and, sometimes, medical isolation, many of them did. Being an alien among humans was not always comfortable or safe. There was still a lot of xenophobia on the human homeworld. Better the ghetto, some thought, than being surrounded entirely by savages. When it came to civilization, humans were not the top of the heap. Not even close.

Even a few friends to watch your back was better than none when among the humans.

Most of the offworlders in San Antonio's exteetown were either Rel or Emov. There were a few others, among them, a handful of Bax. No Vastalimi on record at the moment, and any Zinna onworld were apparently somewhere other than San Antonio, too.

Kay would have come along, but her presence would have been too notable. When a Vastalimi entered a room with Rel or Emov, those aliens would, as soon as they could manage it, leave. Along with some of the more skittish humans.

Blending in was not in the cards if you were a Vastalimi on Earth. People would stop and stare.

Few people wanted to relax and sip a drink next to

somebody who, given the right circumstance, would happily kill and eat them. Such was illegal, of course, simply not allowed on civilized worlds, but the predator/prey relationship was hardwired in, and if you were prey, you didn't feel comfortable under the predator's gaze.

Rel and Emov came from herd cultures, they were vegetarians, and while Bax were omnivores, they had seemingly civilized themselves beyond what Vastalimi considered predator behavior . . .

The plan was to locate the targets, talk to them, and determine, if they could, which needed further interrogation.

"I am a little late to the party," Wink said, "so tell me how we are going to do this again?"

Jo nodded at the storefront just ahead. Neo-neon signs outlined the entrance and spelled out words in a bright rainbow of *Chau*, the Bax's main trade language. "That's a Bax hangout."

Wink said, "The writing looks like it was done by a pair of agitated spiders dancing on a hot skillet with paint on their feet." He pulled his belt reader, pointed it at the building, and thumb-waved a command.

The unit made the translation. He squinted at it in the bright sunshine.

" 'House of Beroh'? What does that mean?"

"Look it up, you'll remember it longer," Gunny said.

"Why would I want to remember it at all? I haven't dealt with a Bax since I was a resident."

"Yeah, but they are about to be in your immediate future."

He shrugged.

Jo went on: "Beroh is a gambling game the Bax love. Kind of like a cross between poker, roulette, and craps, with a dash of chess thrown in."

"That sounds like fun," Wink said. "I put myself through medical school playing poker. Maybe I'll sit in a few hands."

"As I understand it, the rules and combinations are . . . complex. There are, according to the b.g. I read, a thousand ways to lose and one way to win. Serious players have to do complicated mathematics in their heads while rolling eight-sided dice, tallying cards, and watching a wheel with eight differently colored balls drop into slots that are even or odd, including negative numbers. The combination of cards, dice, and balls gives a choice of pieces and the order of moves on the game board, which looks kind of like three-dee chess, but on circular boards four times as big. The player who controls the central sixteen squares for two moves is the winner of that round."

"Hmm," Wink said. "Might be tricky."

"It gets better. The chess part is different with each deal, with handicaps given, based on who lost which pieces the previous round. How much you win is based on how many players there are and how much they bet along the way. You could bet a hundred to win one, or vice versa."

Wink said, "Or, maybe I'll just watch until I get the hang of it."

"Probably a good idea."

"Won't we stand out?"

Gunny: "You had thirty minutes on the ride here, Doc, didn't you read *any*thing?"

He smiled at Gunny. "I have to save my dendrites for the important stuff, Megan. You can do my light-fighting for me, can't you?"

"Sheeit."

Jo said, "Apparently there are more than a few human gamblers who want to try the game. The Bax are always happy to take their money. As far as I can tell from the b.g. material, there are only a handful of human Beroh adepts, and they are fairly far along the autistic spectrum."

"I'll definitely stick to poker. Let's go see."

They made their way through the garishly outlined door, and Jo noticed the scanner and the two guards watching it as they cleared the entrance.

NO FIREARMS ALLOWED, a big sign just inside the door said.

Jo knew that, so they weren't carrying any. That was a good idea in a place where somebody might come in rich and walk out poor. Unhappy people with guns could be a problem for management. Most casinos of any kind Jo had been in didn't allow the patrons to come in armed with projectile weapons.

In a room full of unarmed people, Jo's augs and fighting skills gave her an advantage.

Wink had his knife, and apparently the Bax weren't worried about that since nobody stopped and told him to check it.

Interesting.

They weren't planning on doing anything in here that needed killing hardware; though Gunny allowed as how she felt naked without something tucked into a pocket, she also had a small knife in her boot. She wasn't as good with a blade as Wink was, but she was likely better than most anybody else in the place save Jo.

It would have been fun to watch the reactions if Kay had come along.

Inside, Jo took stock, looking for the usual strategic and tactical stuff—where the exits and entrances were, the patrolling guards, the layout. The room was essentially a big square, with several pods that included the dealers, players, and equipment. There was a bar and food-service area at the far end, and fresher doors down another wall.

The lighting was dim and diffused, not what you might expect, given the bright signs outside, but the background noises were what you'd expect in a similar human casino. Balls clattered into slots, dice tumbled on soft surfaces, people talked, laughed, drank, or sat quietly and concentrated on their play.

Holoprojections flashed numbers over the pods, both Arabic and *Chauian*, and now and then, a cheer would go up when a number flashed and blinked a brilliant purple.

We have a winner!

People everywhere loved to see somebody beat the house. It meant they had a chance to win, too. The house knew this and trumpeted winners; since the odds were in their favor, the more people who played, the more they could win.

There were maybe eighty Bax at the game tables, half that many humans, and a few Rel.

Bax musk was thick, like fresh ginger, with something that smelled kind of like wood smoke underlying that, not at all an unpleasant scent.

There was an area set aside for nonplayers, who could sit or stand and watch the games on monitors or directly, depending. There were fifty people there, again mostly Bax, humans, and a couple of Rel.

Jo made her way to the observation area, Wink and Gunny trailing.

The Bax at the entrance to the area smiled, showing some impressive canines. "Six *erill* each, fem. Currently, the exchange rate rounds that to three New Dollars apiece."

Not much of an accent, his speech, but there was a throaty undertone that gave his words a kind of melodic lilt.

Jo nodded, waved one hand at Wink and Gunny. "Three of us," she said. She tapped the number into her belt comp.

The Bax looked at his meter. "Thank you and enjoy your visit to the House of Beroh."

Something about his attitude seemed to add an unspoken phrase: *you foolish gawking humans . . .*

As they moved past him, Jo took stock of the Bax taking the watch fees.

He was a head shorter than she was but broader through the shoulders and thicker through the chest. His fur was almost henna-colored, short and smooth-looking. His arms were as big around as hers and the muscles lean, his hands four-fingered, actually two thumbs and two fingers in opposition, and his head and face did look like a wolf, albeit the muzzle was shorter and the prick-ears smaller and tighter. He had eyes the color of amber, with a darker brown center, and the irises were larger than a human's, no white showing around them.

There were variations in height and build and fur coloring, some lighter, some darker, but the Bax in here looked much more like each other than did a similar group of humans.

The three of them found an empty table and sat. "Let's not forget fugue," Jo said.

Wink said, "That's for my benefit, isn't it?"

"If the boot fits . . ."

What Jo meant was simple: There might be ears or eyes or both tracking them, and better they were circumspect in anything they said.

They had six names, and four of them were identified as serious Beroh players. Since this was the only establishment in exteetown that specifically catered to such players, chances were one of them might be here. No guarantees, of course, but it was what they had.

They also had images of the six in their tactical computers, and Jo's optics, with which she could examine every Bax she could see and compare their stats to those on file. Facial-recognition software wasn't perfect, but it was close enough for their purposes.

If they spotted any of their quarry, they would set up on them and wait for them to leave.

After that, they'd see what happened.

TWENTY-ONE

Formentara, on hir way to collect some new gear, heard music. It was some kind of electronic instrument, and whoever was playing it seemed quite adept. It sounded familiar, but zhe couldn't quite place it. Zhe listened for a moment, trying to identify the piece, and finally got it: Montenegro's "Prelude" to *The Symphony Galaxia.*

Zhe listened, enjoying the performance.

Zhe had never been much of a fan of pop music, but the classical stuff had a certain mathematical majesty zhe liked. Not hir art, but certainly zhe could appreciate expertise in other fields.

The piece drew to a close, and curious, she headed that way.

Gramps sat in an empty conference room, an odd-looking instrument balanced on his lap. It seemed to be little more than a fretboard. As wide as a man's hand, maybe 115 cm long, ten strings, to judge from the tuning keys at the top end. There was a crosspiece at the base balanced on his legs, and it jutted up past his head at a slight angle to his left.

"Very nice," zhe said. "What is the instrument?"

"Chapman Stick," he said. "Played by tapping the strings."

He tapped out a melody to demonstrate. "You can do the lead or chords with either or both hands."

"I didn't know you played."

"I usually do it in my quarters with earphones."

"You do it well."

He shrugged. "Not compared to people who are really good, but I enjoy it. I try to get in an hour a day when I can. I should be doing at least twice that."

"How long have you been at it?"

"Thirty-three years."

She did the math. *Hour a day, call it fifty weeks a year, thirty-three years . . .*

"You have your ten thousand hours, right?"

He smiled. "Yep."

That was the old Anders Ericsson Postulate: To become an expert at something, you needed about ten thousand hours of mindful practice at it. In reality, it didn't always work that way, you had to allow for genetics—all the practice in the world wouldn't make you taller, say—and other factors, like natural bent and desire, could shorten the time necessary, but it was a good starting point for many activities.

"Why continue to practice so much? I mean, you have it down by now, yes?"

"There was famous musician a hundred years back, a master of this." He hefted the instrument. "This guy was interviewed when he was ninety-four; he was still practicing five or six hours a day. The interviewer said, 'You are one of the most accomplished players to ever hold the stick, you have been doing it for more than sixty years. Why do you feel the need to practice so much?'

"And he said, 'Well, I think I'm finally starting to get the hang of it.' "

Zhe laughed.

"You are really good at what you do," he said. "And apparently more adept at violence than I knew."

"Word gets around."

"Yep. Does that decrease in any way your desire to keep doing what you love?"

"Point taken." Zhe paused. "If you didn't work as a soldier, if you had more free time, would you play it more? To the point of doing it professionally?"

He thought about it for a couple of seconds. "I don't know. On the one hand, it would be interesting to see how far I could go; on the other hand, doing it as a job might change how much I look forward to doing it. Now, I do it because I want to, not because I have to." He paused. "I knew a guy once who was a commercial artist. He came up with a design that became very popular and made him rich. One day he looked up and realized he wasn't having as much fun doing art as he once had, so he quit. Went off to brush up his chops on the piano, got pretty good at it, and became a musician. He never made nearly as much money doing that, but he loved it, and he had enough in the bank, so he didn't have to worry if the gigs paid much.

"For me, it's a moot point. I haven't put by enough to retire yet, and I love soldiering, too. *Comme ci, comme ça.*"

Zhe nodded. "Well, sometimes those choices present themselves. Good to have considered it, in case it ever does."

"Sure. When my ship comes in, I might just become a traveling bard and sing and play about the exciting lives of corporate army folk."

"Stranger things have happened," zhe said.

- - - - - -

Fugue:

"I'm glad we came, this is really interesting," Jo said. *Got one!*

Wink and Gunny glanced at her.

"You remember that fellow on that planet not long ago who took a dislike to our furry friend?" Jo said. She was speaking of Ganesh, the Rajah's security head. He was a largish fellow, and xenophobic to the core. He had taken it upon himself to express such to Kay. That had not been a good idea.

They both nodded.

"If he had a slightly smaller brother, what do you think he would look like?"

The tallest Bax in the building stood security at one of the pods toward the south wall. His fur was a bit darker than most, and Ganesh's hair had been dark.

That clue should be enough to mark him for Wink and Gunny.

"Ugly, I would imagine. Why bring that up now?" Wink asked, to keep the fugue going.

"Oh, no reason, just an idle thought. It's not really him I was recalling, but the guy who he usually parked himself behind."

That was a tad obvious, but even so, anybody listening to their conversation wouldn't have any context to make it work. Wink and Gunny did.

Look at the Bax sitting in front *of that big guard over there.*

Gunny said, "Huh, yeah, I remember him. He came from a big family, right?" *That's one. Any others?*

"Huh. I thought he was an only child." *Nope, just the one.*

Wink said, "My, look at the time. As much as I'm enjoying this, probably we should think about heading back to the hotel. It's getting late." *One is better than none, let's collect this guy.*

"You're right. A little while more, we don't want to miss seeing the night's big winner."

As soon as he leaves, we follow him.

Anyone who might have listened to this conversation should not be able to make heads or tails of it; no way they could interpret it to mean the three of them were going to tail and maybe kidnap a Bax now in one of the pods gambling. They might think the three humans were passing strange, given a trialogue that seemed so disjointed, but there was nothing actionable there. They spoke of something that happened somewhere to somebody but without any names to any of those things. Completely meaningless.

Crazy, those humans. Who knew what they were up to at any given time?

— — — — — —

"Soon" was a relative term, but the Bax in question, whose ID offered his name as Titkos Napló, ran out of money or desire about an hour later. He stood, stretched, and by the time he started for the door, Jo, Wink, and Gunny were already moving. Gunny moved faster, managed to get ahead of the Bax, with Jo and Wink falling in behind.

If the Bax security wondered about one human hurrying to get out the door before her companions, they didn't show any evidence of it.

Wink peeled off and headed for the rental cart, parked nearby. Two reasons for that: If the target elected to ride, they could stay with him; plus, the lockbox in the cart's luggage compartment had in it three small pistols. When you were about to get active, weapons were a good idea.

He reached the cart, removed the bag with the handguns in it, and climbed into the driver's seat. He waved the electric motors to life and engaged the drive. It was a four-seater, and no different from thousands of others on the road.

"Looks like he's going to catch a cab up ahead," Jo said over their com.

"Ah'm slapping a bug on it in case Doc can't get his slow ass over here in time to keep visual contact."

"I got the cart," Wink said. "I'll be there in thirty seconds."

"So you say," Gunny said.

He saw Jo on the sidewalk ahead, pretending to look into a shop featuring items of interest to Emov. Twenty meters ahead of her, Gunny walked in Wink's direction.

Behind her, a two-person autocab pulled out from the curb.

"Come on, Wink, you slow as molasses in a blast freezer!"

"Keep your pants on, I'm right here."

Jo got in first, moved into the back, as Gunny arrived and slid in next to Wink.

"Go," Gunny said.

"You want to drive?"

"Ah would, but you'd probably break your leg trying to move over to swap seats."

He shook his head. "No wonder Gramps gives you so much shit."

Jo smiled. "Doctor, if you wouldn't mind? The cab is moving."

"I got him. Day I can't follow a speed-governed auto-cab, I will give up my license to drive."

— — — — — —

The cab stopped a short distance later, in front of a plain-vanilla multiplex three stories tall. It was late enough that there weren't a lot of pedestrians on the walks.

"Not a walker," Wink said. "Less than a kilometer. That a species trait or personal?"

"You ever consider actually *reading* a b.g.?"

"Dear Gunny, why would I when there are so many people willing to tell me what it says and feel smug in the doing of it? Need to know and duplication of effort and all."

Wink pulled over before the Bax alighted. Gunny and Jo got out quickly and started moving.

"Let's go, Gunny," Jo said. "We don't want to let him get inside."

"You need my help?"

"Just move the cart up and be ready to roll once we collect M. Titkos Napló."

"I live to serve."

Jo and Gunny alighted and moved across the street, angling to cut off the Bax, who was taking a more direct, but slow path to the front of the plex.

Jo called out: "Citizen Bax! A word?"

Napló turned. "Yes?"

"My comrade has never met a member of your race, would you be so kind as to allow us to take a holograph with you?"

The Bax smiled his wolfish smile. "Why, I would be honored."

Gunny moved over to stand next to the Bax. Jo backed up a step and pointed a small camera at the two of them. "And . . . your father is a rhinoceros . . ."

Napló looked puzzled, as well he should, and Gunny hit him over the right jugular vein with a blue popper.

Pssht!

Napló snarled, showing impressive canine teeth, and took a swipe at Gunny, who had already danced backward.

"Hey, over here!" Jo said. "Look what I have."

He spun to face her as she pulled her pistol, holding it down by her leg. "Don't move," Jo said.

Napló blinked, swayed, and would have collapsed, but Jo got there in time to catch him. She tucked the pistol back out of sight.

Gunny didn't offer to help; she knew Jo could carry him on her own.

A couple of passersby on the walk glanced their way.

"Our companion overdid it at the pub," Gunny said. "Can't hold their liquor very well."

Gunny pulled the seat back, and Jo shoved the unconscious Bax into the cart.

"Good evening, fems," Wink said. "Your companion appears to have overdone it at the pub."

"Just drive," Jo said.

TWENTY-TWO

It was late, or early, depending on how you viewed it, and traffic was light. There wasn't anybody following them, as far as Wink could tell. He made a series of random turns, watched his rearview cams, no sign of a tail.

Of course, that only spoke to direct visual surveillance, and in this day of implants and augmentation, because you couldn't see somebody, it didn't mean they weren't there, tracking you via LOS or radio or even a satellite twenty thousand kilometers up. Somebody could have an on-demand transmitter that would be inert until a specific frequency painted it, so you couldn't detect it with a scanner until it was too late; the device could be tiny, made from organo-plast components, and running off biological juice, hidden inside a bone, so it would take a vigilant search to pick up on a standard ARI or MRI scan.

They didn't have an ARI or MRI machine on them . . .

Napló, snoozing there in the back, might simply be a plain-vanilla Bax citizen, innocent as a newborn kitten and as far from being wired as somebody could be.

Much more likely, he was what Gramps's AI had pegged him as: a probable spy. If so, he wouldn't be complaining to the local authorities about being kidnapped, which was good for them. And also as such, somebody keeping tabs on him was not unlikely.

They needed to know and deal with it if the latter was true. And while they could run a wide-frequency jammer to block any signal an implant in the Bax might be narrow-casting, that would block their own implants. Plus, if somebody showed up, that would make the case for M. Napló here being more than he seemed to the casual gaze. Knowledge was power.

Which was why Wink was out there. He was the medic, he should stay with the Bax, make sure he stayed under, monitor him and all, but it was paint-by-numbers medicine, and anybody with CFI's basic training could do it, no problem. Jo was the ex–psyops officer; she was a better interrogator than Wink or Gunny. Anybody could circle back and see if they had been followed.

Gunny would have rather gone outside, but when they flashed fingers to see, she called "Even," and the count came up three.

"Ah dunno how you do it, but Ah'm sure you are cheatin' somehow."

"You fems constantly wound me," he said. "It's just pure luck you always pick the wrong number of fingers."

"How many fingers am Ah holdin' up now?"

"Nobody likes a sore loser, Gunny."

"And nobody likes an obnoxious winner, either."

He smiled.

They carried the still-out-cold Napló into the rented cube, making it look as if he was at least partially upright on his own. Inside, Wink moved quickly through the unit, which was bare of furniture, save for a single couch. He moved to the rear entrance. He stopped there and changed clothes. He pulled a skinmask from his pocket and smoothed it onto his face, covering it, as well as his ears. Wasn't perfect, but it would make it hard to identify him if somebody did a check of the cameras in local buildings. Somebody would see him if they did, but they probably wouldn't be able to ID him—he wore a cheap coverall and slippers, nothing to stand out. Just another no-collar worker.

He walked through the yard, nothing more than a dry patch of dirt with a few scraggly bushes in it, to the high plastic-link-fence-enclosed back of the unit. He opened the gate with the code-of-the-day, which came with the rental, and locked it behind him.

The fence was three meters tall and topped with burr-coil. Anybody who wanted to get past it would need the gate code, since climbing through burr-coil was a bad experience even in armor, and the plastic fence links completed a circuit that would raise an alarm if cut.

Not that either would stop serious intent, but the fence would let those inside know about it.

He circled around the block and back to the street where he could see their rented cart.

Gramps had been careful when he'd chosen the area. It was in a district that bridged residential and light industrial, had virtually no foot traffic, and offered lots of nooks and crannies in which somebody could remain largely unnoticed. Plus, in this part of the world, people didn't seem to do a lot of walking. No pedestrians out in the darkness.

He found a doorway he'd scouted earlier, an empty miniwarehouse a couple of hundred meters north of their unit. He moved into the hard shade.

"I'm in place," he said.

"Copy that," Jo said. "He's waking up."

"Hit him with the orange anytime."

— — — — — —

"Who the *bassza* are you? What do you want?!"

Gunny tapped the orange popper against Napló's neck.

"Bassze meg te seggfej! Te Kurvas!"

"Ah really don't speak their language, but didn't he just offer some kind of sexual congress at the same time he insulted our reproductive organs?"

Many soldiers might not be able to order dinner or ask where the fresher was in a foreign language, but a lot of them could call you nasty names in your own tongue. If it pissed somebody off, that could be turned to your advantage. Pissed-off opponents made mistakes.

"Well, I wouldn't like us either, in his place," Jo said.

The stream of what was certainly Baxian curses ran on for another few seconds, then just petered out. Napló's eyes widened, his pupils dilated.

"I feel . . . ill . . ."

"Hang in there, you'll be fine," Jo said. "So, you are a spy, right?"

He stared at her. "Spy. Yes."

Gunny shook her head. "Well, that was too easy."

Napló retched, heaved, and puked in Gunny's direction, spewing vomitus in a surprisingly long spray.

Gunny scrambled backward and avoided most, but not all, of it—

"Fuck!"

She swiped at her shirt.

"I feel better now," Napló said. "Who are you?"

"We're friends," Jo said. "Might want to see if you can find a wet wipe," she said to Gunny.

"Ah'm gonna kick Wink's ass for this."

"Why? He warned us."

"He cheated so he could go outside, Ah know he did, just not how."

"So, M. Napló, could you help me out here?"

"You are my friend?"

"Yes."

"Of course I will help you. That is what friends do, is it not?"

Wink saw the cart round the corner and move slowly past the rented cube. There were two people inside, and it wasn't until they pulled to the curb past Wink that he got a good look at them.

One human, one Bax.

The cart stopped.

"We have company," he subvocalized. "One smooth, one hairy. Still in their vehicle. Odd coincidence, or our friend is sending out a pulse. How's it coming in there?"

"M. Napló is singing arias like an opera star."

"Anything useful?"

"This and that."

"He ask you to get naked yet?"

"Fuck you," Jo said.

Wink chuckled. On Ananda, that guy they hit with happy juice had been really into the idea of Jo's taking off her clothes, and Wink had fanned that desire a little. She didn't think it was nearly as funny as he had. Of course, that guy had been human, and who knew what Bax found sexy?

"They've parked, and they are watching the building."

"Ah'll go cover the door. And you owe me a new shirt, Wink."

"Me? Why?"

"Our friend here puked on me."

"How is that *my* fault? I *told* you he might!"

"You shoulda been in here getting alien vomit all over you."

"Fem up, Gunny. If I had a demi noodle for every patient that has puked on me, I could buy you a dozen new shirts."

"Just the one will be enough."

He grinned. Never a dull moment.

The Bax alighted first. He was lighter in color, taller than Napló, and more muscular.

The human was right behind him. He looked like a

mixed martial artist who'd overstayed his time in the ring a few bouts too many. The surgery to correct his cauliflower ears didn't seem quite right, and his nose looked to have been broken enough times so it likely made that surgeon's job equally challenging.

Couple of thugs, obviously tracking Napló, and here to . . . rescue him?

Both of them carried good-sized handguns in badly concealed holsters. The Bax had in hand a dark blue package the size of a rounded brick, and when he got to the door, he squatted and began to fiddle with the thing. The doorway lighting was dim, and at first, Wink thought it might be the tracking device, but as he watched, he had a different realization.

"Gunny, I think they are setting up a bomb on the stoop. It looks big enough to do more than open the door. Maybe they aren't here for a rescue but a deletion."

"Stet."

"Give me eight seconds," Wink said. He was already moving, and drawing his knife. He had a gun, but no point in making noise. "The Bax is squatting by the door, the human behind him. I got the human."

"Copy. In eight . . . seven . . . six . . ."

Wink ran.

The Bax continued to do something to the package, and the human, who should have been looking around to see if anybody was observing them, didn't. He watched his partner.

Made Wink do a quick scan as he ran, just in case they had backup.

Nobody else around—

". . . two . . . and the door is opening *now*—!"

Which the door did, and fast.

Gunny stood here, pistol in hand. "Freeze!" she said.

The Bax dropped the package and clawed for his sidearm. The human reached for his weapon.

Morons! You can't beat a drawn *gun! And sure as hell not* Gunny's—*!*

Wink arrived as Gunny stitched the Bax with three quick shots in the chest, so fast—*pap-pap-pap!*—they sounded almost like one shot. She didn't even swing her pistol over to cover the human since she knew Wink was there—

Wink thrust his knife—

Base of the skull, slid in and out like a needle through a wet sponge—

The human went boneless and collapsed.

Wink looked at the downed pair, then frowned. How many times had he taken out somebody doing this very technique? Knife to the high spine?

Three times. On Ananda, then on Vast, and now, here.

It was a fine technique, but not such a good thing that he had used it again. Unthinking, autocontrol, step-and-stick, and while you wanted your body to be able to move without the slowness of conscious thought once you got rolling, you didn't want to get into a pattern that let the reptile run things. Reptiles liked to stay with whatever worked before. They didn't parse the situation in fine detail; it was a broad stroke kind of process. *Did it last time, it will do now . . .*

Hey, no sweat, we are platinum here!

That it had gone three for three was all well and good, but habits got people killed, and while he didn't mind dancing with Death, he didn't want to step stupid and let Her get him too easily . . .

"A problem?"

He looked at Gunny. "Not yet. But it could be if I let it."

She shrugged. "Then don't let it."

She leaned over and put a round into the head of the paralyzed thug.

Enemies who would have blown them all up? The response needed to balance the attack. Fuck with the best, die like the rest . . .

He smiled. Ever pragmatic, Gunny.

He wiped the blood from his knife on the dead man's sleeve, resheathed it. No point in looking too far down the road that he might have taken . . .

"Well. Let's get these bodies inside," she said. "Don't want the neighbors or the trash-pickup din getting excited."

TWENTY-THREE

Cutter leaned back in his chair. "And . . . ?"

Jo, Gunny, and Wink also sat at the conference table; Gramps stood by the door, leaning against the wall.

Jo said, "Good news, bad news. So our boy Napló is indeed a spy, in the employ of some jawbreaking Baxian sub-rosa agency called the, um . . ." She blinked, apparently accessing her memory: *"Külföldi Ugynökség."*

"I can give you something for that sore throat," Wink said.

She ignored him. "There are two other operatives working for them in this area though he is the most senior and in charge of the team."

"Isn't that nice?" Rags said.

"We thought so, but if he knows more than they do, it isn't much. Napló was most forthcoming in his responses, but there are big gaps in his knowledge. He pretty much doesn't know why the two factions of Bax have squared up over this though he did offer a few choice words on the opposition, who, he said, have sexual congress with their grandmothers and who thrive on a diet of reptile feces."

Cutter shook his head. *Something was going on here, something they needed to know.*

"We learned that he has a contact working for our opposition's army, but all of their communication has been by coded message, and he doesn't know who the contact is. We do have the information on how to make that link. Maybe Gramps can fake being our guy and hook us up."

"Not a lot of information," Cutter allowed.

"At least a lead we didn't have."

"What about the dead muscle?"

"We left them in the cube with Napló. Once he comes around, let him worry about it. I expect he won't want the local authorities involved, so he'll get rid of the bodies and keep his mouth shut. The bomb the muscle had would have taken half the building down. Saying anything about what happened would only make him look untrustworthy to his people, who apparently would have killed him without a second thought, so he wouldn't want to seem a liability. I don't see that he blabs.

"In less than three days, we'll be done, and he doesn't even know who we are or represent anyhow. It's a big planet. He isn't going to run into us in the next sixty-some hours unless he steps into a restricted war zone."

Cutter nodded. "Okay." To Gramps, he said, "See what you can find out. The clock is still running. There's something here, I can feel it."

"Got it. I'll go play with Jo's data, see what I can do."

Gunny said, "How's the war going otherwise. We miss anything?"

"Nope. Vim has the wellheads, we are in position to hold off the worst the enemy can throw at us. We're still up more than a few pieces. Ours to lose."

"Well, that's good." Wink said.

- - - - - -

Gramps ran the protocols on the information the captured spy had provided. It was fairly straightforward, codes and rerouting and no names. Once he had the feel for how Napló wrote, he composed a message:

I have new and critical intel and need to offer it directly— it is too dangerous to risk transmission.

It wasn't two minutes later that the coded reply came back:

I can't meet you now, circumstances don't allow leaving the WZ. Send it, we will accept the risk.

Gramps had the best military-grade cracker and snoops dancing all around the exchange, but they weren't giving him anything. Well, there was something to be said for doing it the old-fashioned way.

My superiors forbid it. This wins the war, imperative you have details.

There was a longer pause.

I can't meet you. I will send a courier. Provide a location and time.

Gramps grinned. *Gotcha, asshole!*

"Rags? You there?"

"I am."

"Our spy's contact wants to send a courier to collect the information that will win the war for them."

"By all means, let's pass that along."

- - - - - -

The designated meeting was to be at a commercial vehicle-recharging station on the southwestern outskirts of San Antonio. It was on a stretch of road with little else around. Scrub growth, vacant lots, a cafe half a klick away. Had a baked-earth smell. Not much civilization, it could have been on a sparsely settled semitropical planet anywhere, broiling in the hot sun.

Jo, Gunny, and Wink were there three hours before the appointed time.

The station had been leased by Wood's quartermaster for the duration, and those people who normally worked it had been sent home.

Gunny became the charge attendant who made sure the inducers were set and locked; Jo ran the payment kiosk; Wink rubbed lube into his hands and wore a stained coverall in the guise of a mechanic working the repair bay.

An hour before the courier was to show up, a cart with somebody trying to look as if they weren't paying attention arrived. The driver alighted and asked that his vehicle be charged.

Gunny obliged.

The driver stretched, walked to the fresher, came back, and paid his tab. He drove off.

Gunny said, "His batteries were almost topped off when he got here, he coulda run another five hundred klicks, easy."

On the opchan, Jo replied, "Scout, checking us out. They are watching, Rags."

"Copy. We're sending in the dummy, forty minutes."

- - - - - -

Right on schedule, a cart arrived and pulled up next to the station and parked.

Visible in the cart was what appeared to be a Bax in the driver's seat.

At least anybody watching would think so since the dummy was made of medical-grade silicone with fake hair that should fool anybody peeping through a distant scope. They weren't going to get that good a look at it: A few seconds after it arrived, the cart's windows opaqued. The motor continued to run, and the cart's air coolers kicked up to high.

The cart was being remotely piloted by somebody back at the base; easy enough to do.

"Bait's in place," Jo said.

A few carts and trucks came and went. Gunny worked the electrics, Jo took their money. Nobody remarked on the personnel changes if they noticed.

Thirty minutes later, the cart they'd seen scouting arrived and parked next to the one holding their fake Bax. The driver, same one as before, alighted and tapped on the window. He couldn't see inside.

Gunny walked over. "You looking for the furry? He's in the station."

The man looked at her.

"He said somebody was coming and Ah should send you in when you got here."

Gunny turned and walked away, as if she could care a rat's ass what the guy did.

He hesitated a moment. Jo could almost hear his thoughts: *Did the Bax get out, and we missed it? Crap . . .*

He headed for the door.

The shades on the building's windows had been angled to reflect most of the hot afternoon sun away, and you couldn't see much past them from the outside.

Jo came out of the fresher as the courier entered. She looked at him. "You the man meeting the Bax? He's in the office. Down that hall."

The courier nodded. He moved through the hall and stepped into the office.

Wink, behind the door, hit him with the soporific popper, covered his mouth with one hand, and before the guy could do much, Jo was there to help hold him down. She peeled off the com stuck behind his left ear and pinched it hard enough to crush it.

It was overkill—they had a WF jammer going the second the guy stepped into the building. It didn't matter that theirs wouldn't work; they didn't need them now.

The courier struggled for a few seconds, then his eyes glazed over and rolled back to show white.

Jo picked him up, slung him over her shoulder, and took him to the garage. There was a large cart parked in one of the three bays, and she dumped him into the back.

Gunny came into the garage from outside, shut the other bay door, pulled off her coverall, and slid into the cart's control seat.

Wink shed his oily coverall and got into the back with the unconscious man, and Jo entered the front and sat on the passenger side. They opaqued the cart's windows, save for the front windshield, opened the bay door, and backed the cart out. Gunny wheeled it out of the parking lot and drove away.

They left the jammer running, just in case.

"How long, you think?" Wink asked.

Jo said, "Maybe ten minutes before anybody gets worried they can't see anybody, another five minutes before they go check, and then they have to think about what happened and what to do about it. We'll be back to the base before they get their shit together and realize it was us."

"You think this guy has anything to give us?"

"Won't know until we ask him; whatever he has is ours," Wink said. "My magic potions will not be denied."

- - - - - -

Kay caught the residual scent as she moved through the forest bordering their position. Not fresh, but not too old; maybe two hours past, Grey had been here.

Come to check on them.

To check on her . . .

He wasn't here now, but she drifted through the woods, sniffing and looking. Plenty of sign to view.

The scent was thickest just ahead. She examined the spot. He had lain prone; there was a faint imprint of his body on the dry needles. A good place to observe the camp.

Had he known she was here? She was convinced it was so. He could have seen her, and once the rain and breezes had stopped, caught her scent easily enough since this spot was downwind of the camp.

What was his intent? Maybe he could have assassinated her from concealment, and certainly that would have been a smart move. An enemy Vastalimi would be a target of choice. If she had the chance, she would kill him once the war began.

Really? If he popped up right now, would you shoot him out of hand?

Certainly. Well. Probably.

She grinned to herself.

She had seen the video of the killed troops at MB4, and she could see it had been a Vastalimi's work. She agreed with Cutter Colonel; likely Grey had taken them all out. With his superior speed, he could have shot several, then elected to slay the last couple with claws rather than a gun. She could understand that need to challenge one's self; any Vastalimi worth the name would understand that. Going against an armed opponent who could kill you as far as he could see you with naught but your own claws? That was a better test of one's prowess than shooting him.

He was adept. That was pleasing even though they were on opposite sides of a conflict. Yes, he was an enemy, but he was also an attractive male, with qualities that gave him some depth. Even on Vast, with others around, such qualities were not always easily found. It would be a shame to have to kill him though she would have to if she had the chance.

Duty was supposed to triumph desire.

Even if it would be a terrible waste . . .

TWENTY-FOUR

In the colonel's office:

"And . . . ?" Rags asked

"Dhama," Jo said.

"As in the man who offered you and Gunny seven million noodle to help throw the war?"

"That's him. That's pretty much all we got out of the courier, but it seems like it might be a good idea for us to have another little chat with M. Dhama."

"You think you can call him up and arrange a meeting?"

"Probably not. He is in the middle of an action, and I suspect that when his courier doesn't show back up with the secret knowledge that gives his side victory, he might become a tad suspicious if we contact him for any reason. Even a blind pig finds an acorn now and then."

"The finish line is in sight, and probably we could let this go," Rags said, "but . . ."

". . . something isn't right about all this," she finished.

"That's what it feels like. I don't see them pulling out

any magical tricks to beat us, we have this, and failing a massive attack of the stupids, we should win it going away."

"And yet."

"Yes. And yet. What do we know about where Dhama might be?"

"We have a general idea. And maybe Kay and I could, you know, ask somebody who had more specifics. Then drop round and see what Dhama had to say about it."

"Okay. Have a look. I don't want you killed doing it since it probably won't matter anyhow, but if it is doable, let me know."

"Absolutely."

They waited until dark, and it was just the two of them. They separated as they entered the forest and checked with each other via the com. When they could make a connection, which sometimes didn't happen. There were a lot of trees down, and they blocked straight-line transmission when they were in the way.

Kay said. "I'm almost there."

Jo replied.

"You are breaking up," Kay said. "I got only part of that."

Jo checked her internal PPS and adjusted her course a hair to port. Six hundred meters, though the forest was thick enough so that was way past visible even in full daylight, which was hours gone.

The ground had not dried out, all the rain that had fallen. Downed trees here and there slowed movement as well as breaking up the com's sig.

She dodged the trees, keeping up as steady a pace as she could, her augmented vision making the run almost as manageable as if the sun were up.

The sentry turned to look at her, and while she couldn't see his face, she imagined he was frowning. No ping on his helmet transponder, so she wasn't one of his, but neither was she IDing as enemy. Until he saw her, he wouldn't have known she was there.

It made him hesitate a heartbeat as he lifted his carbine. *Who . . . ?*

Jo shot his right thigh. The little amped-up AP pistol round punched a neat hole through his armor, the muscle and bone on the way in, and the muscle and armor on the way out. He fumbled the carbine, went down, and Jo was on him before he could recover. She kicked his carbine away and pointed her sidearm at him. "Easy does it. Sudden moves will be fatal."

He froze.

"The wound is a through-and-through, probably broke the bone, but it's an AP hole, so you probably won't bleed out even if the armor doesn't plug it. I ask, you answer. If you don't want to play, tell me now, and I'll find somebody else, but . . ." She waved her pistol.

The sentry was an SoF veteran; she watched him weigh his response. "Ask."

"I'm looking for Major Dhama."

The suit's smart armor whirred and whined a little as it sealed itself and the bullet holes in the man's leg. The sentry frowned around his pain. "Dhama? He's a no-dick lackwit, I can't understand why anybody in their right mind hired him. Talks the talk, looks the part, but he can't find his ass with both hands."

"Tell me where he is, you collect a WiA bonus. I'll take your boomware and helmet, so no recording, and nobody knows we had words."

"I could send you to the wrong place."

"And I could come back and express my displeasure."

"Not if I sent you into a trap."

"Or, I could light you up now and go find somebody less devious. Tell you what, I'll give you something: Dhama is not what he appears to be, he's got his own agenda, and both your side and ours will be better off without him."

"Maybe."

"We have others looking for him. We will compare notes as soon as we all get a location, and if they line up, you are golden; if not, I come back and smoke you. One way or another, we *will* find him. Only question is, will you be dead or alive when we do?"

"How do you know I didn't yell when I saw you?"

"You didn't. Your com's not working."

"You think?"

"Try it."

He did, but she knew her short-range jammer was killing his signal. Hers, too. She'd never be standing here having this conversation otherwise.

After a couple of seconds, he knew it.

"Well, fuck-oh-dear," he said. He considered it for a second. "Okay. He's at the Mobile FB Op Center. I don't know exactly where it is at the moment, somewhere in the woods, and the fucking trees screw up transmissions."

She nodded. That made sense. A heavily armored crawler, at least a squad of troops, he'd feel safe enough there, but not too far away from the action. "Pop the helmet, toss it and your sidearm over here."

He complied.

"Nice doing business with you. Have a good rehab. If you need work down the line, look us up; always room for a smart soldier in CFI."

"I just rolled over and gave somebody up."

"And in this case, you did everybody a favor. You live to fight another day, which is smart. No use for another dead dumb-ass."

She ran a hundred meters into the dark forest and tossed the arms and helmet into a bush. Maybe they'd find it, but the helmet's cam was thoroughly dead, and chances were, it would be all over when and if they did find it.

She killed her jammer.

"Got a location," Jo said into her coded opchan. It was a crackly connection. Under the trees, it sorta worked. Getting the sig out? Not gonna happen. This forest was something else when it came to radio waves.

"As do I," Kay said.

"Let me guess. FB Ops?"

"Yes. There are only a couple of places it can reasonably be."

"Yes. I'll check the north, you the south. If you don't see it, come find me."

"Stet."

Jo started an easy lope. Couple klicks, shouldn't be a problem. They'd figure out how to pry Dhama loose when they got there, then they'd have a little discussion with the bastard . . .

- - - - - -

Kay got to the right location a minute before Jo Captain. There was much activity ahead, but the combination of metal-bearing trees and the dampers she and Jo Captain wore should be enough to fuzz any sig recognition from the opposition; given that her com couldn't parse the enemy's ID sigs, that would seem to be the case.

Kay began marking targets she could see and smell and hear.

Jo arrived.

"What do we have?"

"The Mobile FB Op is three hundred meters to the northwest, camp lights bleeding all over the night. There are seventeen soldiers on the ground around it. They are not moving around much."

Jo nodded. "It's still mostly a mire out here. So, you want to distract or fetch?"

"Distract. I am faster than you over this ground."

Jo consulted her onboard timer. "Four minutes. Mark."

"Mark." Kay's sense of time was innately better than most humans, but she had a clock on board.

Kay slipped off into the soggy night.

Kay circled the crawler and its troops. She had a dozen small grenades, frags, flashbangs, strobes, and an EMP spewer.

She approached the mobile base, dropped to her belly in the mud, and crawled the last few meters.

The nearest guards were no more than twenty meters away.

Five seconds. Four seconds. Three . . .

First the EMP. It wouldn't do much against heavily shielded electronics, but it would douse the camp's lights and maybe affect some suit elements.

She threw the spewer, triggered two of the pulsars, and threw them, one, two. The strobes, weighted to fall diodes up, would begin flashing as they fell and keep doing so until the batteries died, twenty seconds or so. Anybody wearing augmented night vision would be hobbled as the automatic shield cut in and stayed on to protect the wearer's eyes. They'd have to remove the goggles.

While the first two grenades were still arcing upward, she triggered two flashbangs and tossed those.

The camp lights went out—

About the time the first flasher ignited, she added two of the frags.

Blasting light, loud noise, and shrapnel erupted in the darkness.

Temporarily blinded soldiers screamed, began firing wildly at nothing, and dived for cover.

Kay came up to one knee, unslung her carbine, and fired two quick five-round bursts at the crawler. The rounds wouldn't penetrate the thing's armor, but they would get their attention and keep those inside there.

She rolled, crawled quickly a dozen meters away, and fired another full-auto burst.

She kept moving. If they managed to figure out where she had been and returned fire, she wasn't going to be there anymore.

— — — — — —

Jo came in fast, her inbuilt polarized optical filters set to mostly zero out the strobes' shifting spectrum. That was doable if you had the frequencies. Made for funny lighting, but enough to see. She had her carbine up, and she fired at the scrambling troops, tapping several hard enough to put them down.

The unit was in major disarray, shooting at trees and each other. They had not been expecting an attack, but the surprise wasn't going to last long.

Jo reached the crawler, which was—no surprise— buttoned up. She didn't have the codes to open the hatch, and they probably weren't going to let her in if she knocked, but she did have a twenty-centimeter length of oxycord. She arranged it in a ragged circle around the hatch's latch, thumbed the trigger, and ran a quick three meters, dropping, turning away, and closing her eyes as she shut her optical aug completely off.

Three seconds later, the oxycord lit, and anybody facing that way when it ignited was going to be blinded if their eyes were open; even with the lids closed, it would sear an image onto a viewer's retina. Oxycord burned with a star center's heat and created enough light in the process to turn night into day for the few seconds it lasted.

Even three meters away, she felt the heat on her back and saw red behind her closed eyes.

It went dark. Jo restarted her opticals and turned around.

The edges of the hole glowed orange with residual heat.

Jo moved fast, peeled the door open by grabbing it well

away from the ragged hole, and tossed a flashbang into the crawler.

Again she turned away, and the light and noise spilled past her and out into the forest.

There was a lot of yelling going on, inside the crawler and out, and she dropped to her belly and dragged herself through the opening.

Somebody fired her way, but the rounds were aimed at chest level, half a meter above her. She saw the unarmored trooper, shot him several times, and kept crawling.

Men and women were holding their ears or rubbing at their eyes. Some of them were trying to get into armor. Some of them were frozen in shock.

She didn't see Dhama, so she shot everybody she could spot.

She scuttled through the mobile command center, knocking down targets.

Things got quieter.

She came to a closed locker.

Somebody was inside; she could hear the rapid heartbeat.

The door wasn't armored.

"Weapons down, come out, or I put a couple AP through the door. Three seconds. One . . . two . . ."

"Don't shoot! I surrender!"

The door opened, and Dhama stuck his head out.

She turned the hypojet ring on her right middle finger around, thumbed the trigger cover off, and slapped him on the neck.

There was a *psst!* of compressed gas as the injector punched trank through his skin and into the underlying vein.

Better living through chemistry . . .

He screamed. After a second, his eyes rolled back, and he fell.

She dropped the carbine and dragged him to the hatch. Along the way, she used her sidearm to shoot two people still moving.

Outside, she paused long enough to toss a couple of fragmentation grenades to clear a path, then hoisted Dhama over her shoulder in a fireman's carry and hurried into the night. He was heavy, but with her augmented strength, not so much she couldn't move.

Two soldiers shouldn't be able to pull off a raid this way, but part of why they could was because nobody expected to be attacked by two soldiers. And part of it was because one of them was heavily augmented and the other was a Vastalimi.

Four hundred meters away, Kay joined her. "Should I carry him?"

Jo smiled. "I'll let you know if I get tired. Let's go."

TWENTY-FIVE

The interrogation room at the base was nothing but an empty cube, no windows, no furniture except a single chair bolted to the floor, and the door was electronic, no knobs or latches accessible from inside.

"Let's just head this off, save ourselves the threats, the bribes, like that," Jo said.

Dhama seated in, but not strapped to, the chair, ignored that. He started with bluster: "You are breaking all kinds of laws! I will have you all buried under the jail!"

Nobody paid any attention to that. He waited a moment, then moved on to money . . .

"My people will pay ransom—"

"You aren't real bright, are you?" Jo said. "We turned down seven million noodle the first time we met. If we wanted money, wouldn't it have been a lot easier to collect it then?"

He glared at her. "Then what?"

"Information."

"I'm not required to give you any. Rules of Industrial War say that—"

Jo laughed. She looked at Kay. "The man is quoting RIW at us."

Kay moved in a hair closer.

Dhama flinched at her move.

"What do you want to know?"

"All about who hired you and why."

He looked away from Kay at Jo. "I can't tell you that."

"You do know, right?"

He shook his head. "Sorry. We can't go down that road."

Kay whickered. He snapped his gaze away from Jo to look at Kay.

"Wink? You out there?"

Wink came through the door. He held a popper in his hand.

"What are you doing?"

"In about five seconds, I'm going to hit you with a lovely cocktail, whose recipe I got from an old doc I used to know in Terran Intelligence."

Dhama stared at him.

"What's in it, you ask? Why, attend: a couple of tranquilizers, a barbiturate or two, some lionfish extract, a dab of psychedelic toad secretion . . . some other things I have lying around. It's what ole Doc Auel liked to call zombie juice. Five minutes after you get it, you will tell us anything we want to know in as much detail as you can remember, and if you wake up in eight hours or so, you'll have a terrific headache."

"*If* I wake up?"

"Oh, yeah, there's a nasty side effect I should mention. Now and then somebody particularly sensitive to zombie juice doesn't wake up. They don't die, at least not right away, but they enter a kind of trance, akin to a coma, and are pretty much nonresponsive from then on. We don't know, for sure, because sometimes people do die down the line. I seem to recall the record for the coma is . . . thirty-odd years? Something like that.

"Hold him still, hey? I don't want to be spewing this stuff all over the place—"

"That's *illegal*!"

"So sue me."

"Wait—! Don't! I'll tell you what you want to know!"

"You sure?"

"Yes!"

"Shit," Wink said. "That was fifty, right?"

"You wish. It was a hundred," Jo said.

"But he looks so steely-eyed and brave."

"You should know better than to take my bets by now."

Wink nodded. "I should. But the first win is going to be so sweet!"

"Good luck with that." She turned back to Dhama.

He licked his lips, which looked particularly dry.

"First up. Who are you working for? Who hired you?"

"General John Allen."

That caught them flat-footed.

"What? Why?"

"I'm supposed to make sure my side *loses*."

Jo said, "What the fuck are you talking about?"

"You are supposed to win, asshole. Because *you* are working for General Allen, too."

Nobody had anything to say at all. They just stared.

TWENTY-SIX

Kay patrolled the perimeter of the base. Halfway through her sweep, she scented the approaching men. She stopped, waited until she could see them.

She recognized the troops; they were GU Army Special Ops, ten of them, in light armor. They had their weapons aimed, and they moved well.

It would be an odd coincidence if they just happened to be approaching the base where she was.

Coming for me. Why? How did they know where I would be?

That indicated a depth of surveillance that meant serious intent. Sat overfly? High-altitude drone, looking for a Vastalimi sig?

If she took off at full speed right now, she might be able to avoid being hit if they began firing, but the odds of success were not good.

She should have run the moment she caught their scents, but being around humans for years had made her more curious. *What did they want?*

Somebody in operations would have already spotted them on sensors or their own overfly; they weren't wearing stealth gear. Help would already be coming.

They kept coming, slow but steadily. They were well within range but had not started shooting, and that would have been the smart thing had they intended to kill her; in fact, a drone strike would have been better still.

She could wait for them to get closer and attack, but her victory was unlikely.

She reasoned they weren't intending to kill her yet.

She waited. The nearest soldier drew to about ten meters, then stopped.

"Don't move," he said.

"Had I wished to do that, I would already be gone," she said. "You would not have seen me."

He waved one hand, and the others formed a half circle.

"We have orders to arrest you," he said. "There are another dozen troops blocking your possible escape."

Not true about the troops, she thought.

"On what charge?"

"Need-to-know, and I don't. We were told to bring you in alive if possible, but that if you made it necessary, we are empowered to use deadly force."

She triggered her com. The carrier sig was live. Odd that it would be. "Let me see if I understand it correctly: You are a Galactic Union Army unit sent to arrest me on a charge you don't know but are allowed to use deadly force if I resist?"

"That's it. And we *do* know all about Vastalimi, so if you twitch funny, we will chop you down."

"My people will want to check the legality of your order."

"I am First Lieutenant Huss, and I am here under the direction of General John Allen."

In her ear, Jo's vox said, "Oh, shit! Don't give them a reason to open up. We are almost there. Forty-five seconds."

Kay didn't allow the conversation with Jo to move her

gaze away from the soldier's face. "If you are lawfully empowered to collect me, I will accompany you."

"On your knees, hands behind your back."

"No."

"No?"

"I have said that I will go with you, and if I do, I won't try to escape. I will not allow myself to be bound like an animal so that you might feel safer."

"I could shoot you right here."

"You could. This conversation is being relayed to and recorded by my comrades in CFI. Did you assume that an *alien* wouldn't be outfitted with a working communicator?"

A frown flitted over his face. "Fuck. Radio, you didn't jam her transmissions?" he said.

"Sorry, Loot. Nobody told me I needed to worry about that, and you wanted our opchans working."

"It's *your* fucking *job!*"

"Too late now," she said.

"I still have leave to kill you if you resist."

"I am not resisting, I have said I would go with you. If your orders are legal."

"I'm here pointing my weapon at you, you don't need to worry about that part."

"Shoot me, and perhaps you and your men will be legally covered. That will not stop my friends when they come for you."

"You think that is going to scare me? I'm Special Ops." He smiled.

- - - - - -

"Maybe this will do the trick," Jo said from behind the GU soldiers.

That startled Huss. He turned to look. No doubt wondering how she had sneaked up behind them.

He saw fifteen others in combat gear arriving behind Jo, carbines leveled to cover him and his troops.

The GU unit looked uneasy. Their guns started to come up . . .

Huss waved them down. "Nobody moves!"

Jo said, "Good idea. Right now, Lieutenant, my unit's best shooter has a bead on that bare spot between your helmet and your collar armor—not that your armor would stop the round anyhow. You shoot her, my sniper shoots you, and the rest of your troops will have to dance pretty good to avoid being cut to fucking pieces. I wouldn't want to swap boots."

"You'd be guilty of murdering soldiers in the performance of their duties."

"No. If you shoot a single round, I would be defending myself and my troops against an unprovoked assault by armed troops in a civilian venue. Truth-scan would verify my testimony." There wasn't any bluff in her tone.

Huss considered that. "The GU Army will fall on you like the wrath of God."

"Surely it will. But you won't be here to see it, and neither will your unit. Your call."

There was a moment of silence. Then, "What do you want?"

"I want to see legal authorization for you to arrest my soldier. A Vastalimi's word is better than ours, and if your warrant is legal and she says she'll go along, she will. Anybody who attempts to bind her will surely die trying."

"I have the warrant on my reader."

"Show me."

She approached him, held up her own reader. He waved his device at hers. There came transmission/reception *beeps*.

"Hold." She opened the file and scanned it. It didn't take long.

Everybody stood really still.

Generals in the GU had a certain amount of power, a broad military fiat, and that included dictates regarding civilians in a war zone, humans as well as alien species; but

this was Earth, there wasn't any war going on but the corporate one CFI was involved in, and as nearly as she could
tell, nobody had declared martial law.

Junior had no legal cause to detain Kay. This was bullshit.

To be sure, she zipped a copy of the warrant to Gramps
to run through the legal AI.

On her com, he said, "Stall him for a minute. I'll get an
injunction."

"Stet that." To Huss, she said, "On the face of it, your
warrant is invalid," she said.

"You a lawyer, Captain?"

"I know the applicable military statutes about arresting
civilians. If General Allen has a problem with *Kluth*fem,
he needs to make his case through civilian authorities."

"I have my orders, fem, and a warrant issued by my
commanding general. You can sort all the rest of it out after
I deliver my prisoner."

"She's not your prisoner until I say she is. There is nothing to sort out."

He waited a couple of seconds, then: "I can have an
armored assault company here with cannons blazing in
five minutes. I can make it rain fire and brimstone and turn
this place into a burned-out crater. In the long run, fem, the
Galactic Union Army is *never* outgunned."

"That I know; however, in the long run, Lieutenant, all
of us are dead. Some of us will get there before others.
Twitch, and see who goes first."

From her com: "Jo. Legal says the warrant is bogus. It's
some of Junior's shit. We have a civilian cease-and-desist
order on the way."

"Lieutenant, my AI says your warrant is smoke and mir-
rors, and I have a C&D in transit. Now here is how I see it.
You hold off for two minutes and I present you with the
C&D, which according to the Rules of Engagement regard-
ing civilians in this venue, you are legally bound to observe.
You go back to General Allen, tell him you had no choice

but to step off because we had more guns *and* the law on our side. He might piss and bitch, but he won't give you any real shit because this whole thing is illegal, and he knows it. He won't make an issue of it.

"He knows, I know, and you, being an officer and supposedly familiar with the Army's ROE, should know it. If you didn't before, you do now."

He thought about that.

"Step away, or somebody gets to spend quality time cleaning up blood and bodies."

"I'm a soldier. That's part of the job."

"I'm a soldier, too, and I have you by the short hairs. Give me a reason, and I'll tear them out by the roots and feed them to you. That's how it is. You can walk away on your own, or you can be carried away. *That* is *your* choice. You won't be here to see what comes later."

There was a long pause, and the longer it went, the less likely it was that the soldier would initiate a firefight.

"Show me the C&D," he said.

Jo smiled.

— — — — — —

"Junior is in serious harassment mode," Gramps said. "You think he knows we know he's up to something? Going for a preemptive strike?"

Cutter leaned back in his chair. "Maybe."

"You gonna call him on it?"

"I don't see any point. We might be able to scream loud enough to get the mostly deaf UCMJ's investigators to look our way, but we don't have anything other than he overstepped his authority, and, so what? He gets a wrist slap. If we had given up Kay, we might have a case for false detention, but it didn't happen, and again, it's a so-what?

"We got a guy on ice who says Junior is in bed with the Bax and dicking around behind the scenes in a corporate war, but that's not going to be enough to stir the pot. We need to know why, and we need proof."

"Probably got some poor major or captain lined up to take the fall on the warrant and the Bax thing anyhow," Gramps said.

"Tell me about that."

Gramps shook his head. "Still, we might have to do something about him eventually."

"I have an idea."

"Why don't I like the sound of that?"

Cutter shrugged. "There's an element of personal risk involved. If I'm right, it's not a problem."

"And if you are wrong?"

He shrugged again. "Cue up *Pachelbel's Canon*, and break out your dress blacks."

Gramps shook his head. "Got to be another way."

"We'll see. First we have to get there. I'm working on it. We just have to remember we're fighting on two fronts and make sure our backs are covered."

"Fucking Junior."

"Yep."

Gramps blinked into a long stare. "Speak of the devil."

Cutter looked at him.

"Incoming on one."

Cutter waved at his com control, put it on speaker.

"That you, Cutter?"

"What do you want, Junior?"

"You get to keep your tame alien monster, but you need to understand that I am monitoring your moves. Any illegal activity on your part will be brought to the attention of the local *civilian* authorities, who have leave to deal with such in a heartbeat. You might want to consider backing off this little corporate dustup and going back to catching shoplifters at TotalMart, leave the soldiering to those qualified to do it."

Gramps pointed at his ear and waggled his finger, the sign for "being recorded."

Cutter nodded. Of course; both of them would be doing that.

"Is that a threat, General Allen?"

Junior laughed. "Of course not, merely a warning that criminal activities from a man drummed out of the service for the wholesale slaughter of innocent civilians will not be tolerated. The GU Army never forgets, you know."

"CFI does not engage in criminality. Watch all you want, we have nothing to hide."

They were both talking for the recorders, and both of them knew it.

"We'll see."

Junior shut off the com at his end.

"What was that about? He didn't really think you were going to lose it and start screaming, admit to something he could use?"

"He might be that stupid, but, no. He was just jabbing so we didn't forget he was there."

"He's worried that you will somehow bring Morandan onto his plate again."

"Maybe, but I think it's about whatever he and Bax are up to. He doesn't want us poking around in it. It can't just be about the water."

"Yeah, that always seemed kind of strange to me."

"Exactly. But the war is almost done. Whatever it is, we don't have much time left to find it."

"I'll see if I can stir up the AI," Gramps said.

TWENTY-SEVEN

Gramps was waiting when the last of them filtered in. He said, "Our C-AI has been crunching everything that links 'Bax' and 'water.' It took a while because it's a big secret and traditionally has been worth-your-life guarded, restricted to the priesthood.

"And surprise, surprise, it *is* about the water. It's holy."

"Holy water?" That from Gunny.

"Apparently. It turns out this ancient Terran water has some kind of mineral combination that's passing rare. Something in Bax biochemistry gets activated when they drink it. For humans, you could drink ten liters, bathe in it, wash your underwear in it, and nothing would happen except you'd have to pee and you'd get wrinkled and have clean crotch cover. For Bax, it's a euphoric chem that somehow puts them in touch, they believe, with their god. Their priests have been using the homegrown version for centuries."

"Direct com to God? I can understand how that might be valuable." That from Wink.

"It gets iffy here, but this is what the AI speculates: The

natural stuff on the Bax homeworld started to run dry, and the artificial solution they came up with didn't have quite the same kick. So they started searching for a new source and somehow stumbled across it here.

"It's Stradivari's crawfish."

Gunny looked at Gramps. "Say what? Crawfish?"

He smiled at her.

"Oh, sheeit, Ah know that look! Forget Ah said that. Don't tell me. Let's just move on."

"Stradivari was a master violin maker on Earth in the late 1600s. His instruments that survive are highly valued, prized for their unique tones. All of them are worth millions, some *tens* of millions."

"Ten million for a *fiddle*? Wait, Ah don't care. Don't say it, just shut up. Get to the point!"

He kept on as if she hadn't spoken: "There was, for years, some question as to why his in particular were so esteemed, and the assumption was that it wasn't the wood, nor the construction, but the varnish he used.

"Varnish is—"

"Ah know what fuckin' varnish is!"

"You young people have no patience.

"One of the more interesting theories speculated that in the varnish were ground-up bits of a crawfish native to the rivers where the maker worked.

"The local crawfish went extinct, and so subsequent makers didn't have it available, thus they didn't have the same dulcet tones when played."

"Why is it every time Ah ask a simple question, you babble like a stoned sociology professor giving a lecture? You could talk the leg off a cast-iron statue."

And then, because she couldn't help herself, she asked, "It is true? About the crawfish?"

"Great story, but, no. Scientists have done analyses on several of the Strads, and there's no evidence of animal proteins in his finishes. The difference was that he was a better craftsman than his contemporaries. He picked better woods and put them together better. "

"So why are you tellin' us all this crap?"

"I'm getting there. Stradavari's instruments were good, they held up well, and people came to believe they were superior, so that's what they heard when one was played. The Bax scientists' concoction of god juice is probably chemically identical to the natural waters on their world, but they don't really believe it, so . . ."

"Psychology," Jo said. "Got to love it."

"Says the woman who came from PsyOps," Rags said.

"What about Junior?" Gramps said.

"Junior seems to be in bed with both sides."

"Why?"

"That's the part we don't know."

"So what good is knowing this stuff about the water?"

Kay said, "Both sides want it enough to sponsor an expensive war and to offer large bribes. General Allen has found a way to benefit. There must be a link."

Rags said, "And if what Dhama said is so, if we are in possession of the wells, come the final whistle, it looks like Junior walks away rich. And somehow, I don't think that's the worst of it. This thing reeks of intrigue, there's something else going on."

"What?"

"I don't know."

"How are we going to find out?"

"I'm working on it," Gramps said.

It wasn't more than an hour after that when Gramps showed up in Cutter's office. This time, it was just the two of them.

"Something?"

"Oh, hell, yeah. The rest of the story about the Bax versus the Bax and the thrilling adventure of the Holy Water of Tejas."

Cutter nodded.

"You aren't going to like it."

"I already don't like it a whole bunch, I don't see how it could be worse. Tell me."

So Gramps did.

When he was done, Cutter said, "Well, *shit*. It *is* worse."

"Yeah."

"We are screwed either way."

"Well, one side, they use lubricant, but, yeah, I'd call it a no-win situation. I don't see a solution."

Cutter thought about it for a few seconds. "I do."

"Really?"

"Yep. But nobody is going to like it. Something I came up with a while back when I was lacking better ways to spend my time. Not how I would have used it, but the principle is the same."

Gramps raised an eyebrow.

Cutter told him.

"Christus! You have a sick mind! You think you can get that by General Wood?"

"I don't know. The fem I used to know, back in the day? Maybe. But she was a lieutenant on the way up, not a general running a small war. She might not see it the same now as she did then. Only one way to find out."

– – – – – –

Wood was not at all happy to hear what Cutter had to say. After a string of choice curses, she stared at him.

"You're sure about this?"

Cutter said, "Pretty much, yeah."

Wood sighed. "Well, *shit*."

"Yeah, that's what I said, too."

She didn't say anything for a moment.

He knew what she was thinking, or at least what he'd be thinking in her boots. Balancing what she had and what she wanted against what she now knew.

"No other way?"

"I looked, I don't see it. It's all circumstantial. We couldn't step in front of a judge and make the case, especially not a military tribunal, we're not a parsec close to the standard of proof. He walks. At the least."

"Shit."

"It's your call, Zoree."

"My call, yeah, right!"

"I'm sorry—"

"Fuck you. You know I can't pretend I didn't hear this."

"Yeah, I couldn't, either."

"Shit, shit, *shit*!"

"It's not just about Junior—"

"I know, it's the fucking Bax and their fucked-up business! Why is it people like us have to be the galaxy's conscience?"

"If you can see a problem, and you have the ability to fix it, it becomes your responsibility. It's always been that way."

For a long time, she didn't say anything. Then, "Nobody can know but us. If heads roll, they should be ours."

"Yeah."

"That will make it a bitch."

"It's a bitch no matter what."

"You think you can pull it off?"

He shrugged. "Maybe. Lot can go wrong, but if we don't, Junior walks away clean and almost certainly with his pockets full; the Bax could have a major sociological screwup, could work itself into a civil war. The cure will taste bad, but it probably won't kill us."

"Probably."

"I'm sorry," he said. "I know it sucks."

"You didn't create it, you just pointed it out. If I thought shooting the messenger would fix it, you'd already be bleeding out."

"I'll make it up to you."

"How?"

"I dunno. Maybe my rich uncle will die, and you can have a chunk. Go buy that star-fruit orchard."

"You have a rich uncle?"

He chuckled.

"Yeah, that's what I thought. All right. Let's hear this plan of yours." She shook her head. "You know, being a general isn't as much fun as I hoped it would be."

– – – – – –

Cutter called his people in and laid it out. When he was done, nobody said anything for a few seconds. They looked stunned.

"If anybody else has a better suggestion, I'm open to it."

Nobody spoke to that, either.

Then Jo said, "It's just this side of insane; maybe the other side, but if that's how it has to be, then that's how it has to be.

"If it were easy, anybody could do it."

That got a quiet chorus of agreement from the others.

He wasn't really surprised. They were smart, they were loyal, and they were, as much as anybody he knew, honorable, whatever that meant these days. It was a bad situation, he had looked at it from every angle he could, and while there wasn't any path he liked, this one was the least harmful one he could see.

"We have four hours until the final horn blows," he said, "and a shitload of stuff to get done. Let's get moving."

TWENTY-EIGHT

One hundred and ninety-six minutes . . .

If they were going to bag it, the time was now.

"I'm still not sure about this," Gramps said.

"You and me both. It's a terrible idea—except all the others I can come up with are worse. As I said before, I am open to better notions."

Cutter locked at the others.

Jo shrugged.

Kay did her version of the same gesture.

Wink said, "I've been getting stale, I'm up for it."

Gunny said, "Who wants to live forever?"

Formentara added hir shrug. "I'm good."

Cutter nodded. "Okay. Understand, people are going to be pissed at us if we screw it up."

"If we screw this up, we probably are all going to be dead," Jo said. "I don't expect that we'll worry a lot about how pissed off they are."

"Point taken. All right, here's how I have the scenario running . . ."

He started talking, and they all listened intently.

This is really nuts, his inner editor said. *Why don't you just jump off a bridge or pull the tab on a grenade and drop it at your feet? Be faster . . .*

– – – – – –

CFI's advantage was that most troops in a war didn't have the full picture, and in this case, the commanding general who did could alter and tweak things to make them fuzzier to her own people. Without that, they'd play hell getting it done.

The commander of *this* unit knew where his people and equipment were, but not necessarily where the command of *that* unit had all her resources; nor was there the need to know. When your responsibilities were narrow, that's where you focused; unless you were given different orders, that was what you did.

The real trick here, at the end of it all, was to convince the Tejas commanders that they were doing the job they were supposed to do, so none of them would believe otherwise. Like a good close-up magician, if you could misdirect watchers at exactly the right moment, they wouldn't know what you had done; they would think they had seen something else.

"You think Vim will go for this?"

"I would. So would you."

Jo nodded. "Yeah, but . . ."

"What we have to hope is that Vim is as good a soldier as we think he is."

– – – – – –

Every soldier and piece of rolling or flying hardware on the field of battle could theoretically be observed via overflights, except those under the tree canopies, so that's where Gunny and Wink met to assemble the scooter. The parts had been trucked into the woods inside various transports, and the key element to the plan had been keeping it secret.

The scooter was small, computer-controlled, and had markings that would identify it as belonging to Dycon if anybody was able to examine it closely.

Which, Cutter hoped, wouldn't happen. It wouldn't be transmitting, but its receiver had Dycon bounce-back codes, and if some crackerjack communications op managed to get that far, The Line would certainly think it was the opposition's vehicle.

Vim's people had to do it; it couldn't be handed to them. In a war, you trusted your allies, but only so far. You depended on the people who had been with you the longest, who had demonstrated the ability to cover your ass. That's how Cutter did it.

He hoped that was how Vim thought, too.

— — — — —

Gunny and Wink bolted and clicked the pieces together, and they wore thinskin gloves to do it. The thing wasn't supposed to survive, and when it went nova, it wasn't supposed to leave any big pieces, but you never knew, so no DNA left on it if they could help it.

It took about fifteen minutes, and when they were done, they had a heavily armored, squat, two-wheeled box just over a meter-and-a-half tall, not quite that wide, kept stable with rapidly twirling gyroscopes, and preprogrammed to approach-and-evade. It would resist small-arms fire, small rockets, and regular grenades; anything big enough to knock it out would theoretically need somebody calling it in.

Which, theoretically, wasn't going to happen. If . . .

If, if, if . . .

The target was the main wellhead where Vim's troops were ensconced.

They had to see it coming. They had to think they knew what it was, and the window of time and space where that needed to occur was small. If they didn't, the operation failed.

There was a list of suppositions that needed to be made, and if those didn't take place, the mission would fail.

Rags had told them if he were in Vim's boots, he would make certain assumptions, and if Vim didn't, it failed.

If somebody cranked off an antitank round they weren't supposed to use, it would fail.

If the sucker got stuck in a rut, the motor crapped out, it was going to be a failure.

If, if, if, and *failure-failure-failure . . .*

Nothing about any of this was going out on any communications medium. If anybody thought to backtrack the recordings six months down the line and look for connections, nobody in CFI wanted there to be any. Not even a hint.

The base recorders had been shut down whenever they talked about it there, and that had been in fugue and code anyhow.

"Okay, we're good," Gunny said. "Let's crank it up."

She triggered the starter, and the wheeled robot whirred to life. It ran a self-check, then started rolling.

"*Adiós*, little din," she said. "Okay, I need to go places and shoot people."

"And I guess I need to go back to medical and fix the ones you hit with friendly fire," Wink said.

"Piss on you."

"I didn't cheat, Gunny, you're just a bad gambler."

They grinned at each other.

Seventy-seven minutes . . .

TWENTY-NINE

Tracer rounds burned a path over her head as Kay flipped over the low adobe wall for cover. She landed, felt something give under her foot—

Jebati!

She froze.

"Jo, I have a problem here."

"Go ahead."

"I'm standing on an AP mine trigger."

"On my way. Don't, uh . . . move."

Kay whickered.

She looked down. Rules for the engagement set the devices to go inert and biodegrade within specified time limits, so they wouldn't be a danger to someone a few weeks down the line, but it didn't help her now.

She crouched, working to hold still.

Too hard. Relax.

A bead of sweat rolled down her back. Even she wasn't faster than this machine.

A large buzzing insect flew by and landed on her leg. She watched it crawling around, searching for something, doing whatever bugs did when they landed. In the moment, the colors of its body seemed vibrant and full of life. Would it be a surprise to the bug if the mine went off? Did it have enough brain to care?

Ahead, one of the enemy popped over the top of the wall.

She didn't move, but she figured she could raise her weapon and, if he looked this way, shoot without blowing herself up. She brought her carbine up . . .

There was a crack from behind her and the trooper on the wall fell back, shot through the head. She didn't need to look to know:

Jo Captain had arrived.

Jo moved to where Kay was, her own carbine held ready.

"You aren't supposed to step on those, didn't you get the memo?"

A fusillade of small-arms fire zipped overhead; more than a few of the bullets smacked harmlessly into the wall. Could have been worse; the mine could have been on the other side, where the guns were talking.

"I must have misplaced it. I'll get to it as soon as I can."

Jo bent down, removed a canister from her belt. Inside, under pressure, was liquid nitrogen, carried for just such occasions.

"Let's see can we cool things off a little . . ."

The grenade flew toward Gunny as if it were in slow motion, a high, lazy arc.

All the years of training told her where it was going to land: *Too fucking close!*

Without thought, her gun appeared in her hand, and she fired—

- - - - - -

"You're gonna have to move, Wink," came Gramps's voice. "You're about to become the front."

As if to punctuate his words, there was an explosion outside, and the walls of the crawler rattled.

"Monitors! Where the fuck are you? Dammit!

"Get us rolling," Wink said to the driver. "And I'm in the middle of surgery here, don't hit any bumps—"

- - - - - -

"Go north!" came Gramps's voice. "North!"

"Tell it to the driver, I'm busy—"

- - - - - -

Cutter stared at the readouts, watching red and green triangles, squares, and circles intersect and change colors as his side met the enemy.

He listened to various channels and snippets of conversation, key phrases tied to the different shapes on the screen:

"South side of Well Two, suppressing fire—"

"Inbound armor coming from the west—"

"I need air support! Got two drones pinning us in the creek bed south of Well Three—"

Cutter punched buttons, redirecting troops and machines. This part still had to be done even though time was running out—

Sixty-eight minutes . . .

- - - - - -

Gunny's pistol slugs hammered the grenade, *one-two-three-four*, enough to deflect it. It fell short and to one side, exploded—

—bits of shrapnel blew her way, but not much, and none of it hurt her though something bounced off her shoulder armor.

Where is the shooter—?

There—a blurry outline—a shiftsuit. She toggled her magazine switch to AP, fired twice—

Gotcha!

– – – – – –

"I can slow it down, but the inbuilt heater will compensate pretty quick—we'll have maybe three-quarters of a second."

"Ready," Kay said.

Jo sprayed the liquid nitrogen. Kay felt cold splash up to bathe her foot.

"Three . . . two . . . one—*go!*"

Kay sprang over the wall—

Jo landed beside her. The wall stopped the blast.

They exchanged glances.

Kay nodded.

Jo nodded back.

No time for more.

Both fems brought their carbines up and began firing—

– – – – – –

Sixty-three minutes . . .

Formentara looked over at Cutter. "Here it comes," zhe said.

He knew, he was listening, but he nodded.

They had Vim's opchan:

"—scooter approaching, coordinates—"

"—the fuck did it come from? Where's the hole in the line—?"

"—Blue Squad, can you get a cam on that—?"

"—how the fuck did it get through—?"

"—Drone Operations, you got anything in the air close enough to intercept—?"

"—sir, but it will be right on your doorstep by the time I can shoot—"

Cutter listened, knowing what he knew, as Vim's troops

tried to deal with something that didn't look particularly
threatening but might well be.

How had the enemy found a spot to sneak this through?
Well, it was easier if you were sneaking through your own
lines and you knew where that was possible.

*The fog of war. The uncertainty that came with bullets
and bombs and enemies charging or retreating, You could
never be sure exactly what was happening on the battlefield, no matter how many eyes and ears you had watching
and listening. Never.*

"—it's not on our list, Colonel—"

Vim's voice: "Okay, somebody needs to punch a hole in
it, where is the recoilless thirty?"

Cutter said, "Okay. Now."

Formentara didn't speak, just waved hir hands over the
board. "Sent."

*Okay. Let's hope Vim's people are as good as he wishes
they are.*

Come on . . . come on . . .

"—R-30mm is lined up. Should I send a round and
knock it down?"

Come on . . . Come on . . .

It seemed like hours passed in the next couple of seconds.

"Hold up, hold up! Don't shoot! This is Forward Sensors, Colonel, we have a radiation trail out there!"

"What kind of radiation trail?"

"Sir, it's transuranic . . . it's plutonium's sig. Some Lith-
ium 6, maybe . . ."

"Say again, FS."

"Sir, we have a weapons-grade-fissionable-material
reading at these coordinates." He rattled off a series of
numbers.

"Is it that scooter?"

There was a long pause.

"Sensors? Don't dick around here!"

"Sir, I-I can't be sure. The sig and the scooter are in

approximately the same location. Nothing else there. Got to be."

"*Shit!*"

Cutter could appreciate Vim's predicament. There weren't any nukes allowed in this engagement, *absolutely not*!

Tactical nuclear bombs had been used only a few times legally in corporate dustups, and those on mostly empty moons in the middle of nowhere. The idea that there was one on Earth? Rolling toward his position?

Inconceivable!

But: If it *was* a little nuke in that rolling box? Holy *fuck*!

"Colonel, I have a bead on it, I can spike it—"

"—Negative, negative, Thirty, do *not* fire! Nobody shoots nothin'!"

Cutter nodded to himself. Same thing he would have said. A standard box nuke, you could blast it, because it wasn't going to go off unless the trigger clicked. Yeah, you'd spread radioactive material all over the place and you'd have to clean that up, but punching a hole in a nuke wouldn't light it. Unless . . .

. . . unless the scooter was rigged with an impact switch. There were all kinds of timers fast enough to detonate the bomb between the time the AP round touched the armor and it punched through.

If the box was rigged that way, and you hit it hard?

Boom . . .

"Somebody call the Monitors, right fucking now! How far?"

"Seven hundred meters from the main wellhead."

"Fuck, fuck, *fuck*!"

Cutter felt for Vim. In this situation, there wasn't any good response.

"Out, now! Everybody, retreat, fall back to Beta Staging, now, right fucking *now*!"

It's what he wanted, but Cutter had mixed feelings about it. Colonel Buckley had no choice. He had to assume the worst, that the bomb was there, that it was protected, that if it got close enough to the wellhead—and it might already be—it would detonate. Even a low-yield pocket nuke at ground level in this scenario would wipe out the wellheads and anybody in the open for a few blocks in any direction.

Troops under your command would die in a war, but to lose them all this way? That was futile, and no commander worth his own piss would allow that.

Of course, there wasn't any nuke, it was fake, the signature picked up by the sensors a clever implant Formentara had built, and that sig would disappear in a few minutes, no way to trace it to its source. Everybody would assume UMex and Dycon had come up with the ruse, but nobody would blame Vim because anybody with command experience and a couple of working brain cells would make the same choice. As long as there wasn't any actual nuke on the field, there wasn't a lot the Monitors could do about it afterward.

We thought it was a nuke!

And you were wrong. No rule against outsmarting you. Too bad.

It was a house of cards, but Vim couldn't risk his command. Cutter would have pulled his people out, given the same choice.

"Get to the choke point," Cutter said. "Now all we have to do is keep Dycon away for a while."

Forty-seven minutes . . .

THIRTY

The fake bomb was the easy part. Now, with less than a short company, Cutter had to hold off at least twice that many Dycon troops. Normally, they would get support, but given the bomb scenario, nobody would be in a hurry to move into the potential blast zone, at least nobody on their side.

For the plan to work, General Wood's monitoring crew had to know what Colonel Buckley's troops had done, and why, so she couldn't send her people in.

Dycon, not having a clue about the nuke they supposedly sent, would see Vim's troops pulling out faster than a teenaged sailor on shore leave. After a few minutes of wondering what the fuck was going on, they'd realize they could walk in and capture the objective, and they'd hurry to do that. Even if they suspected a trap, how could they pass it up? All they needed to do was be in physical control of the wellheads when the horn sounded, and they'd win.

The trick was to attack Dycon before they were through wondering what was going on.

"Colonel Cutter, this is General Wood. Where are you going?"

She knew full well, but this was for the record, and it had to stand up to what would likely be intense scrutiny.

"Colonel Buckley has lost his fucking mind! He's retreated from his position, the wellheads are unguarded! CFI is going to cut off Dycon's advance at the crossroads just north of here."

"Negative. You need to stay away from the area surrounding the wellheads."

"Say what?"

"Colonel, we have intel that indicates Dycon has a robotic nuclear device on the field. We don't know the yield of the weapon, we need the area cleared for a minimum of two kilometers."

"A nuke? That can't be! The Monitors will crucify them! They'd all spend the rest of their lives in court!"

"Undoubtedly, but if the device ignites, we don't want our people there. Back off."

"If it's a DC, outside a half kilometer is safe."

"And what if it's bigger than a DC? You can't do it, Rags. You need to stand down."

"It smells wrong, Zoree. It's got to be a fake."

"Maybe. Probably. We can't take the chance."

"Even if it is a tactical nuke, as long as we stay outside a klick, we're probably good. We head them off that far out; otherwise, they just waltz in and take it!"

"Too risky."

"What are the Monitors doing about it?"

"They are investigating."

"By the time they figure out what's going on, we will have lost the fucking war. Sorting it out later might take forever."

"I'm sorry, nobody wants to win more than I do, but that is the situation."

He let that lie.

"Rags? You there?"

"My com is acting up," he said. "Say again?"

"Don't do it!"

"General Wood? I can't read you. Must be the damned trees. We are almost in position and well outside tactical-nuclear-blast radius. General Wood?"

"Dammit, Colonel, do *not*—"

That should be enough for the record.

He shut off his link.

"Okay, people, let's get set. Company is coming, and we need to make sure they don't get past us."

Forty minutes . . .

— — — — —

Kay caught a glimpse of Grey as the enemy troops approached, in vehicles and on foot. He was running fast, he was too far away, and then he was lost in the dust before she could get her sights lined up on him. At this juncture, in a frontal assault, she'd have plenty of other targets. No finesse in this situation, it was going to come down to who shot better, who was steadier, who was willing to hold or give ground.

— — — — —

Jo stood by the medical crawler with Wink, watching the dust as the opposing army approached. "Stay inside the crawler," she said.

"Sure," Wink said. "Absolutely. Biggest target on the field, first thing the assholes shoot at, every time."

"A live doctor is useful," she said. "A dead one, not so much. Although in your case it might be six to one, half a dozen to the other. And don't say, 'You wound me.'"

He grinned. "Well, you do, you know. Be safe, Jo."

"I'll try."

Twenty-six minutes . . .

THIRTY-ONE

Parked in the Command Cart with Rags, Jo looked through the windshield at the Dycon line ahead. She knew what their CO must be thinking: *What the fuck?* First, the unit that had the wellheads secured and locked into a sure win just up and fucking left! And now, another company was rolling toward them at speed! Why? Why didn't they just take over the wellheads? They could hold off a larger force for the twenty minutes before the whistle sounded—

What the fuck?

Rags, on the opchan:

"Okay, people, everybody park and throw what you got, TOA. War is going to be called in eighteen minutes, no point in us saving ammo. Light it and flight it."

If the officers in the field wondered what the hell he was doing, nobody brought it up. Jo would have asked if she hadn't known what she knew.

The first streamers following their rockets appeared, and the booms of RCLRs began, joined by the machine guns and assorted grenade launchers and mortars.

If it didn't catch the opposition totally by surprise, it certainly gave them something to think about.

They returned fire, and the battle began.

— — — — — —

"—two APCs coming from the south, mortars, you see 'em—?"

"—copy, L1, we have them, keep your head down—"

"—body spike that grenadier, he's walking 'em right at us—"

"—man down, man down, can I get a medic these coordinates—?"

Jo said, "There's a gap in our coverage, seven hundred meters west, we have enemy boots approaching. Kay?"

"Here."

"Let's go."

Nine minutes.

— — — — — —

"—somebody lay some grenades on top of that APC—"

"—got two men down here, I need a medic—"

"—you think, asshole? Eat this—!"

— — — — — —

Jo looked at the overview, listened to the chatter. Dycon was attacking, and CFI was getting hammered, but they were holding.

For now. Another seven minutes to go, and it was iffy; the numbers didn't favor them.

Shit.

No help for it now, they were committed—

"Jo, we got help coming, hang on!"

"What?"

"A company of Vim's troops, from Dycon's rear."

"Christus, with an atomic bomb about to go off?"

"Volunteers," Rags said. "And Colonel Buckley is leading them."

Jo laughed. "Got more balls than brains. But we won't be able to get back to the wellheads in time."

"Even so, nice to know they won't let you get shot to pieces out there. Maybe we can't win, but maybe we won't lose, either."

"I'm gonna buy the man the biggest steak in Tejas," she said. "Ow!"

"Jo?"

"Some asshole *shot* me! Hold on a second . . ."

She examined the wound. Through her lat, just under the left arm.

"Jo?"

"Still here. It's a through-and-through, didn't hit anything serious.

"No problem," she said, "minor." She allowed her neurochem to flood some painkiller dorph into her system.

"And I'll make sure Vim has something good to wash his steak down," Rags said.

– – – – – –

Two minutes.
One minute.

– – – – – –

The Monitors sent the signal, and it blew across every open channel in range, the traditional ten-second countdown:

"ATTENTION COMBATANTS: HOSTILITIES MUST CEASE IN TEN SECONDS . . . NINE . . . EIGHT . . ."

Jo, her wound already itching under the pressure-stik bandage, worked her com: "Almost done. Nobody on either side is at the wellheads."

Rags said, "We didn't lose."

"But we didn't win, either."

"... THREE ... TWO ..."

Almost a kilometer behind Jo, the fake-nuke robot exploded. It was simple-chemical, but sufficient to scatter the thing over a couple of hundred meters. Didn't do any damage where it was when it went up, save for a shallow crater in the ground under it.

The horn sounded: *Ooogah!*

The Tejano Conflict was over. Neither side got the water they wanted.

THIRTY-TWO

Junior's rage was palpable even though he tried to keep his voice low and even; he couldn't keep it from seeping through:

"You need to pay me a visit, Cutter, and I don't mean tomorrow or after lunch, I mean right *now*."

"Sure, Junior. I'll be around directly."

He waved the com off, glanced at the time sig. "I'm surprised he waited this long."

Gunny stood there. Gunny had a burned patch on her shoulder armor but didn't look otherwise damaged from the grenade fragment that had bounced off her.

"Gunny?"

"Of course Ah can do it, but Ah'm not sure Ah should."

Cutter nodded. "I understand, but you need to trust me on this, Gunny."

She looked at him. "What if you are wrong?"

"Then we'll find out, won't we?"

Gunny shook her head. "I never liked *Pachelbel's Canon*. I don't want to have to listen to it at your fucking funeral."

"Me, neither."

- - - - - -

In Junior's office, he was on his feet, waiting.

"Come in, Cutter. I'd ask you to have a seat, but you won't have very long to get tired standing."

The door closed behind Cutter.

Junior raised his sidearm and pointed it at Cutter. From four meters, it would be hard to miss.

Cutter kept his hands spread wide, away from his own weapon.

"Take your pistol out, two fingers, and put in on the floor."

Cutter did so, moving slowly and carefully.

"Shove it over here with your foot."

Cutter obeyed.

Junior came around from behind his desk and bent to collect Cutter's gun. He glanced at the condition-read, nodded. He pointed it at Cutter, moved back behind his desk, and opened a drawer. He put his pistol into the drawer and closed it.

"What's the matter, Cutter? No cries of outrage, no 'What are you doing, Junior?'"

Cutter shook his head.

"You know, my father never said so, but I know he thought you were a better soldier than I was. When you were cashiered out? He knew you'd been set up to take the fall, and I'm sure he knew it was my doing, but he never spoke to that, either."

Cutter remained silent.

"You fucked me on this war. You worked it so it ended in a draw, and that cost me a shitload of money. You were supposed to win."

"You wanted us to win, why did you send an assassin after me?"

"You're a fucking moron, you know that? I didn't think for a second that clown had a chance of killing you! That was just to keep you looking the wrong way."

Cutter thought about that. "What about the bribe Dhama offered?"

"Not a chance in hell your people would have taken it. You are all too fucking *honorable* for shit like that. And if they had? They would have been put to work doing something that didn't matter anyhow. It was just more misdirection."

Cutter didn't speak to that.

"I never liked you, Cutter, but this war was your side's to give away! Wood should have kicked their asses seven ways to Sunday! Why the hell did you throw it?"

"Justice. Balance."

"What the fuck are you talking about?"

"We looked at the bottom line. We won, you got rich. We lost, you got rich. Nobody wanted that. Nobody likes you, Junior."

"You fucker!"

"Just part of it. We figured out what the two factions wanted. One side is religious, they want the water for their ceremonies. The other side is secular, they think religion is a shackle. If they had won, they would have poisoned the water or blown up the wells.

"I'm not much on religion, but nobody makes the Bax drink the holy tonic if they don't want it; the secularists would have denied that possibility. One offered a choice, the other didn't. So we decided the best thing was to put it in abeyance. If the religious group wants the water, they can cut a deal with the government, which will take over the wells. They had any brains, they'd have done that in the first place; they were trying to get it for the price of a little war, and they didn't. So nobody gets to screw with Earth's resources on our watch."

"You fucking assholes! *I* wanted the religious side to win! They have more money, so it would have been a bigger payout, but that would have given you your fucking *justice*!"

"But if they'd lost, you would have still done okay. The only way you'd have come up empty would have been if the Monitors zeroed it out or it ended in a draw."

"Which you saw to."

"Life is hard."

Junior came back around the desk, still covering Cutter with his own weapon.

"And for some, life gets cut short. Here's how it is going to go. I am going to shoot you. Then my staff will hear signs of a struggle. The door is locked, so they'll have to override the program to get in. By the time they do, they'll find you dead on the floor and me a bit winded. You came to kill me, but you got careless. We wrestled for your weapon—mine was in the drawer and I couldn't get to it—and during the struggle, the gun went off."

"You'll have to be closer than you are to make that scenario work, Junior."

"Go ahead, take what little joy you can calling me that; your clock is running out. Oh, and my office recording system is on the fritz. Been acting up all week, the tech came, fixed it, but it's something in the hardware. And there's a jammer on my secretary's desk stopping any UA transmissions from in here, so if you came wired, too bad. The only person who can offer up what happened here is me, you being dead and all."

Cutter shook his head. "Got it all worked out, haven't you? What about what my people and Zoree Wood know?"

"Knowledge isn't proof. Besides, you won't care, being dead and all. Not going to beg me to spare you?"

Cutter shrugged. "Would it do any good?"

"No. But I'd love to see it. My father thought you were a superior soldier, but I was always better at sub-rosa tactics. I outmaneuvered you on Morandan, and I did it here."

"Except for the war and the money."

"But I'll be around to figure out another way to get more. You won't be. My father would be upset to see you go down this way."

"Is that what this is about? Your wanting to prove something to your father?"

Junior gave him a mirthless grin. "Maybe a little. He'd be distressed that you were so easy to set up and take down, his shiny samurai. He thought you were quite the strategy-and-tactics guy.

"Thing was, the samurai were brave and loyal and fierce fighters, but the ninja had their place. Straight up, maybe you'd win, but you don't get the choice."

"I've already paid for your screwup on Morandan."

"There are people who know you got a raw deal. They'll understand how you would want to see me dead. You got to the place where you couldn't stand it anymore, came to take me out, but too bad for you, I beat you. A classic tragedy."

"So you murder me to keep covering your ass for the death of all those civilians."

"That and you screwing me out of all that loot. This time, the bullet you take will be real and fatal."

Junior took a step forward. Still outside Cutter's hand-to-hand range.

"Come on, Cutter. Come at me. That's your only chance."

"Yeah. You're right."

He jumped—

The muzzle was only centimeters away from his heart when Junior pulled the trigger—

The loudest sound in the world is *click!* when you are expecting *bang!*

But if you know that *click!* is coming? It gives you an advantage.

Cutter grabbed the surprised Junior and brought his knee up—

—Junior's responses finally came to life, and he turned, brought his own knee up to block—

—Cutter swung his right fist in a tight uppercut, driven by his hips, and slammed Junior under the chin, a solid blow. Junior's head snapped back and he fell, stunned. He hit the floor hard. He lost his grip on Cutter's pistol. He tried to come up, but Cutter drove the heel of his boot into Junior's forehead. Junior's crown smacked the floor, and even though the carpet was plush, it wasn't enough padding to keep him completely conscious. His eyes lost focus.

Just like that, done.

Cutter bent and retrieved his pistol. He ejected the doctored magazine and dummy round in the chamber, caught the fakes, then replaced the magazine with a fully functional one and chambered a live round. *Good job, Gunny.*

He could have set it up differently. Could have arranged it so he shot Junior. He had thought about that. It wouldn't balance the scales, but it would have been personally satisfying.

But, no. Better to let the Army do that, in its own way. Avoid the paperwork.

"Your secretary is out to lunch, and his jammer got shut off when I got here. Have a look."

He reached into his tunic and removed the tiny VP mikecam disguised as the top button on the tunic. The feed had gone a couple of places; there had been people listening and recording on the transmitter's band.

Too much for the Army to ignore, especially here on the homeworld. They'd have to do *something*.

Junior was fucked, and he had done it to himself.

He angled the mikecam to get a shot of Junior on the floor. "Because the samurai were honorable didn't mean they were stupid.

"Junior."

He turned and headed for the door.

— — — — — —

"How did you know for sure?" Jo asked.

She leaned on the wall next to Gunny.

Rags said, "There were two possibilities as I saw them. He was worried that I had some evidence that might point a finger at him. He was pissed we'd cost him the Bax's money. So, I went to his office full of remorse and committed suicide, or I went to assassinate him and he outfought me and took me out instead. Either way, he needed my weapon to make the scenario work. I was betting on the fight—his ego made that more likely. A heroic encounter with a bitter old enemy who came to gun him down in cold blood? An unarmed man at gunpoint who prevails? That's a much better story than suicide. He couldn't resist polishing it that way."

"You think the GU Army will court-martial him?"

"I'd guess they'd rather not air this dirty laundry. This business with the Bax would do it, but it's been a long time since Morandan, and other heads would have to roll if that came up. Some of the folks involved back then have risen in the ranks and doubtlessly have influential friends. That part would get messy, and Junior's lawyer would know it and wave it at them. Bad PR for the military all the way around, so why go there? Better to let sleeping dogs alone."

Jo said, "Junior is going to have a sudden fatal medical condition or an accident."

"It's been done before."

Gunny shook her head. "They do it that way, you don't get exonerated. No reinstatement."

He shrugged. "It doesn't matter anymore. People will know the truth. And I'm happy with where I wound up. It doesn't bring back all those civilians, but I will always remember the look on his face when he pulled the trigger, and the gun didn't fire."

Gramps stuck his head into the office. "Hey. Formentara wants to talk to us. Says it's not that important, but we might find it interesting."

- - - - - -

They were gathered around the table, waiting for hir to speak: Rags, Jo, Gunny, Gramps, Kay, and Wink.

Formentara smiled, and it was a blend of happy and wicked. "The program I've been back-burnering is a one-size-fits-all male/female multiorgasmic aug. Install, light it up, and you can screw your brains out and climax as many times as you can stand before you pass out."

"Christus," Gramps said, "you'll make a fucking fortune!"

Gunny looked at him. "That's a really bad pun."

"But true," Jo said. "Congratulations, Formentara!"

"Thank you. I've sold the aug to Galactic Pharmaceuticals. Sixty million advance against 5 percent of gross royalties."

"Whoa!" Gunny said. "That's a shitload of noodle!"

"Not to GP—they'll make that all back in the first thirty days if the aug is as good as I think it is, and, of course, it is."

Jo laughed. "I knew you were well-off. I had no idea how well-off."

Formentara's smile grew larger. "You still don't. If I converted all the money I have into big-denomination t-note bills and started shoveling 'em into a furnace? I couldn't burn it fast enough to get ahead of the royalties that come in every year. I might have mentioned that I'm good at what I do."

"So now you'll be superrich," Wink said.

"Already am that."

"Really? Just how wealthy are you?" Jo asked.

"I don't keep close track, I have people who do that. Three or four billion?"

"Mother*fucker*!" Wink said. "No shit?"

Gramps shook his head. "Buddha's nuts! I've been making jokes for years about how rich you are, but I didn't have a clue. Why are you *here*?"

Zhe shrugged. "Here, there, it doesn't matter. It's about the work. I can do it anywhere. And I am accepted here;

none of you has ever looked at me crooked because I am *mahu*. Not once."

Zhe nodded to herself. "That means something to me, you don't know how much. I'm giving you a token of my appreciation."

Gramps looked at hir. "What are you saying?"

"You are my family. During this war, I could have lost any or all of you to a stray bullet, just like that.

"When Jo got hurt, it . . . disturbed me. They are your lives, you can live them as you want, but I thought you should have a choice. So the money from the new aug? It gets divided equally among those of you sitting around this table, advance and royalties.

"If you want to keep soldiering, you can. But you don't have to, and you don't have to risk the stray bullet."

The stunned silence was so deep, Jo could hear their heartbeats. *Ten million New Dollars each? Plus royalties on what would likely become the best-selling aug ever? Holy shit! They'd be filthy rich!*

Formentara laughed. It went on for a while, and zhe had to wipe hir eyes when zhe was done. "I wish you could see your faces in this moment," zhe said. "I really do.

THIRTY-THREE

As the group left the conference room, Formentara stopped Jo. "I have a new aug for you."

Jo looked at hir. "I thought you said I'd reached my limit."

"Well, yes, that was true, but I have been noodling with an idea. It's a one-off."

"Really? When can I get it?"

Formentara laughed. "Don't you even want to know what it does?"

"I trust you."

"Yeah, that's the problem."

Jo frowned. "Why is that a problem?"

"There are three, maybe four people I know of who can keep as many augs as you have balanced."

Jo nodded. She knew that. Normally, every major system augmentation you had installed cut years off your life, the balance of natural and artificial hormones, nucleo- and myotides, the biodegradation, everything combined to cause wear and tear. If you were running fifteen or twenty augs, you could effectively be superhuman, but not for long. Jo had known that from the beginning and elected to go that route anyhow. It wasn't until Formentara told Jo zhe could keep her balanced that she had any notion of living past fifty or sixty.

"So, you have enough money to find one of those people and pay them if I get run over by a pubtrans bus or something, but let's face it, the best of them won't be as good as I am."

Jo laughed. Formentara could say that with a straight face because it was true, and zhe had never been one to offer false modesty.

"And with everybody rich, I don't know what will happen to the Cutters. I'm thinking maybe we might all go our own ways. If you and I are halfway across the galaxy from each other, it might make tune-ups a problem. So I came up with the new aug. It's a regulator. It will monitor and record your systems. Plug yourself into a docbox anywhere and run it, it will balance you. Not as good as I can, we're talking art more than craft, but better than almost anybody else."

Jo blinked. She managed to get "Uh . . . ?" out, then ran out of speech.

Formentara grinned. "Didn't see that one coming, did you?"

Jo found her voice: "No. I didn't."

"Thought about marketing it, but that's not a good idea. Aug hogs would push the limits of what a human is way past where you are, lot of folks would install a score of programs, and I can see how that could get nasty. Not everybody needs to be able to run like the wind or kick serious ass."

"Playing God, Formentara?"

Zhe shrugged. "I've been doing that all along. If you have the tools and the knowledge of how to use them, you get that option."

"Thank you," Jo said.

Zhe nodded. "All in a day's work, sweets."

Grey waited by the kiosk as Kay approached. Troops moved around them, moving this way and that. Nobody drew close, though.

"Still alive, I see," he said.

"As are you, I notice."

"Does this please you?"

She said, "It does not displease me."

He smiled.

"It was an odd engagement," he said.

"Yes. I would never have predicted this outcome at the onset. There were reasons; perhaps we could speak of them later."

"I would be happy to do that."

She paused. "You seemed to have done your job well. We saw evidence of it."

"One does what one is contracted to do as best one can."

"Of course." She paused, then, "I would have you meet my friend Jo Captain."

"I would be delighted to do so."

Kay said, "Jo?"

"On my way."

She arrived less than a minute later. "Jo Captain, this is *Grey*masc."

Jo nodded. "We saw examples of your work; you seem passing adept."

The Vastalimi nodded. "Thank you. It is my pleasure to meet you. A friend of Kay is by default my friend."

Jo grinned a little.

They exchanged a few more words.

He had a dry, quick wit, certainly a point in his favor. He seemed at ease talking to Jo. Kay liked males who were quick. And strong. And not hard on the eyes.

Jo said, "I have to get back, much documentation to be done before we decamp. Could I have a word privately, Kay?"

Kay looked at Grey. He gave her an openhanded shrug. "I will wait for your return."

Jo moved away, and Kay followed her.

"Well?" Kay said.

"He's smart, funny, and while I'm no real judge, good-looking for a male. Stands well. And he adores you."

"You can tell that last part?"

"Oh, yeah. His attention is focused. Radiates from him. My approval isn't necessary, but he looks like a keeper to me."

Kay smiled. "Good to have my own view confirmed."

- - - - - -

Grey waited for her, smiling as she approached.

"And so now to matters of some importance?"

She considered him. "To what do you refer exactly?"

"The war is done. I speak of us."

"Us?"

"Yes, fem, us."

"You have a proposal?"

"I do. I would have us contract and be mates."

That should have surprised her, but it did not. She had known he was going to say that before he formed the words— she could taste it, smell it, feel it.

It was quite the thrill. She felt it all over her body.

Still, she needed to offer the logical argument. "We hardly know each other."

"But we do know each other, cherished fem. I have been looking for you since I ran *Seoba* in the Great Grassland as a *dijete* cub. I simply didn't realize who you were until we met. You are the one; there can be no other."

She was inordinately pleased. "Really?"

"Thirty seconds into our first conversation, I knew it. No doubt. It will be something to tell our offspring. Did you not feel the attraction?"

She had. She still did. She looked at him. "I spoke earlier of a history on the Homeworld. I should tell you of it."

"It doesn't matter."

"It might, should we ever wish to go back to Vast."

"We established that neither of us wish to be on Vast, else we wouldn't be *here*. Whatever you were, whatever you did, anything that passed before? None of that is important, only *now* matters. If you will have me."

"There is another complication."

"You toy with me as a *div maka* does its prey."

She grinned. "Perhaps a little. Still, I need to tell you. I find myself unexpectedly wealthy."

"So? Little money or a lot, who cares? It doesn't matter. Will you have me?"

She nodded. "I will."

He looked relieved. "Good."

"Were you truly worried I would not?"

"What mere male can fathom the mind of a fem?"

She whickered. "A good attitude. Perhaps we could find a private place and do a little . . . grooming?"

"Oh, I would very much like that!"

He moved forward; she stepped to meet him. He offered his face to lick. She did.

It tasted like pure joy.

THIRTY-FOUR

The general was packing personal gear when Cutter arrived.

"Hey, Zoree?"

She stopped and looked at him. "What? More bad news? I've already had two potential clients cancel on me. Even if it isn't your fault, I don't much like you right now. Why are you smiling?"

"Remember my rich uncle?"

"The one you don't have?"

"Yeah, him. Turns out I kinda do have one, sort of."

"What are you talking about?"

"Go find that star-fruit orchard you wanted."

She looked at him. "What?"

"Price it, give me the number, I'll transfer the noodle, with enough extra to build a nice house, buy a shitload of puppies, and send the grandkids to summer camp. Make your wife happy if you retire in one piece."

"Are you having a psychotic break from your guilt here?"

"Nope. I'm sharing the wealth.

"Did I ever tell you about our resident genius Formentara?"

— — — — — —

Jo was talking to Wink.

"How is the lat?"

"Hardly notice it. My enhancements are busily healing it."

"Yeah, and my medicine."

"That, too. Oh, look, here she is."

Kay appeared, and while her manner told Jo she didn't really need to ask, she asked anyhow. "So . . . ? How did it go?"

Kay smiled. "We are going to contract as mates."

"Outstanding!"

"I am pleased, yes."

"Congratulations from me, too," Wink said. "We survived another war, there are new liaisons, and, now, all that money . . ."

Jo shook her head. "It is pretty amazing."

"It is a lot of money," Kay said.

"I hear a 'but' in there," Wink said.

She looked at him. "How many beds can one sleep in? How many homes does one require? I have sufficient for my needs. And now a mate. What is more important than that?"

"Fem has a point," Jo said.

"Yeah, but you can smooth a lot of paths with that kind of noodle. Make the walk a lot easier."

"And which of us has ever chosen the smooth and easy path? You?"

Wink laughed. "There is that. Still, it's good to have a choice. What does your Grey think about this?"

Kay shrugged. "It doesn't matter to him. All he desires is me."

Jo said. "There's the mate I want."

"I will share him with you if you like."

Jo chuckled. "No, that's not necessary though I appreciate the thought. I just mean in general."

"Life is unpredictable," Kay said. "It can end at any moment, and it twists and turns in unexpected directions. Had I not raised the issue of the poisoned elder on my world, had I stayed there and partnered with Jak, my path would have been much different. We would have never met and become family as we have. Nor would I have met Grey. Standing here, I would not change anything that brought me here.

"It will be good to be able to do what we wish, Grey and I, but what we want is to be together. Where does not matter, and the how of it? We will address it as it comes."

Wink snorted. "I hate being the least philosophically evolved in the room."

"As is usually the case," Jo said. "You need to find a good fem and work on that."

"You offering?"

"Maybe. Now that I am among the idle rich, I might need a new boy toy."

"Hey, I'm as idle and rich as you are. You won't have to pay me."

They both grinned.

– – – – – –

People bustled around, packing, breaking things down, getting ready to move.

In his office, Cutter smiled at Formentara. "Drink?"

Zhe shook hir head. "Might as well sip paint thinner."

He laughed. "This is maybe the best bourbon for a thousand klicks in any direction unless there are some serious collectors hiding here."

"So, high-class paint thinner. I can afford to lose a few brain cells, but, no. Never developed a taste for it."

He waited a few seconds. "I have a question for you."

"Really?" Zhe raised hir eyebrows. "You want me to fund a new army for you?"

"No. Your gift is already beyond generous. I am speaking on a . . . more personal level." He paused, sipped at his bourbon. Hesitated, then said, "If you don't mind my asking, what are your, um . . . sexual preferences?"

Zhe blinked at him. "Really? You've never wondered about such things before."

"Not aloud, no, but I have wondered."

"And this is because . . . ?"

"Because . . . look, I'm not good at this, forgive me, not much practice, but . . . because it has, um . . . become relevant."

Zhe smiled. "Why, Colonel Cutter. Are you making a run at me?"

He blew out a sigh. "Yeah, actually, I am."

"Well, I'll be damned."

There was a long—and for Cutter—uncomfortable moment.

"Innie or outie, I'm good either way," zhe said. "And while I am pretty choosy about my partners, you have been at the top of my would-do list for a long time."

"Really?"

Zhe laughed. "You have no idea how attractive you are, Colonel."

"Call me 'Rags,'" he said. "Maybe you could show me . . . ?"

Zhe laughed.

THIRTY-FIVE

"You know what the good part about all this is?"

Gramps looked at her. "What?"

"Even all the biz with the Bax, it was straightforward. We thought Junior was the bad guy once we found out about him and the aliens, and it turned out he was. Not like it was on Ananda, and on Vast, where we never had a clue who was doing what until the end. Maybe we are gettin' smarter."

"I suppose that's possible," he said.

There was a pregnant pause.

"So," Gramps said.

"So," Gunny echoed.

"You're a rich woman now. Got any plans?"

"Not really. Ah never expected to find myself in this situation. Always figured Ah'd die in a battle somewhere. Here Ah'm a multimillionaire for less than an hour, haven't had time to think about it."

"Me, too," he said. After a moment, he said, "I can open that pub."

"You could open a chain of pubs, buy the brewery, build

your own town, and be the mayor. You don't have to work anymore."

"True, but I can't see myself as one of the idle rich."

"Me, neither."

"Formentara just made our choices legion."

"Zhe did that."

He shook his head.

"Problem?"

"Maybe. I'm thinking the important question is not so much what I'll do with all that money and time." He paused again. Looked at her, waiting.

"Uh-huh?"

He took a deep breath. "I'm thinking it's the company I want to keep while I'm doing whatever I'm doing that matters."

She raised an eyebrow. "Uh-huh?"

"Butter wouldn't melt in your mouth, would it? You aren't going to make this easy for me, are you?"

She smiled. "Why start now? Where would the fun be in that?"

He grinned back at her. He took another deep breath. "Okay, let's just throw it out there. Um. I—oh, hell, Megan. I love you."

"Ah know that."

"And . . . ?"

"Yeah, well, all right. Me, too."

He smiled. "You wanted me to say it first."

"Why not? You've done everything else first, old as you are."

He held out a hand. "Want to come over here?"

"Oh, Ah expect Ah'll want to come in all kinds of places." She caught his hand in hers.

When they hugged, he couldn't remember its ever feeling so good with anybody.

"Maybe you can spend some of your money on rejuve

treatments," she said. "Although you might not have enough to pay that tab."

"Sheeit, Chocolatte, you won't be able to keep up with me as it is."

"Talk is cheap. Don't tell me, show me."

So he did . . .

— — — — — —

"Damn, old man, where did you learn how to do that?"

"Centuries of practice. Want to do it again?"

"Now you are just bragging."

"Well, I'm not up to everything, but there are ways, then there are ways."

She laughed. "If you promise not to keel over with a heart attack."

"I won't if you won't."

Both of them laughed.

FROM *NEW YORK TIMES* BESTSELLING AUTHOR

STEVE PERRY

THE VASTALIMI GAMBIT

CUTTER'S WARS

Hundreds of alien Vastalimi are dying mysteriously. It falls to Cutter Force Initiative members Kay and Doc Wink to discern whether the plague is a work of nature or a bioengineered virus purposefully unleashed...

PRAISE FOR *THE RAMAL EXTRACTION*

"Pulse-racing action on the tip of the spear in a cutting-edge future. You gotta read this book."
—Mike Shepherd, author of *Kris Longknife: Tenacious*

"A cutting-edge, militaristic sci-fi novel."
—*Fresh Fiction*

themanwhonevermissed.blogspot.com
facebook.com/AceRocBooks
facebook.com/DestinationElsewhere
penguin.com

M1547T0814

FROM
STEVE PERRY

THE RAMAL EXTRACTION

CUTTER'S WARS

At the close of the twenty-fourth century, a series of revolutions has caused the galaxy to descend into chaos. With the Galactic Union Army stretched thin, mercenary units have arisen for those who have the need—and the means—to hire them...

Captained by Colonel R. A. "Rags" Cutter, Cutter Force Initiative is one of the best of those units. A specialized team consisting of both aliens and humans, the Cutters offer services ranging from fight training and protection to extraction and assassination—as long as the target deserves it and the employer makes good on payday.

When they're hired to find and rescue the soon-to-be-married daughter of the Rajah Ramal of New Mumbai, the Cutters soon realize that their in-and-out extraction job is about to get a lot more interesting—and a lot more lethal...

"A master of military science fiction."
—William C. Dietz, author of *Andromeda's Choice*

themanwhonevermissed.blogspot.com
facebook.com/AceRocBooks
facebook.com/DestinationElsewhere
penguin.com

M1360T0813

Want to connect with fellow science fiction and fantasy fans?

For news on all your favorite Ace and Roc authors, sneak peeks into the newest releases, book giveaways, and much more—

"Like" Ace and Roc Books on Facebook!

facebook.com/AceRocBooks

M988JV1011

Step into another world with

DESTINATION ELSEWHERE

A new community dedicated to the best Science Fiction and Fantasy.

Visit /DestinationElsewhere

M1160G0712